The Days of Elijah

Book Three: Angel of the Abyss

Mark Goodwin

Technical information in the book is included to convey realism. The author shall not have liability or responsibility to any person or entity with respect to any loss or damage caused, or allegedly caused, directly or indirectly by the information contained in this book.

All of the characters, places, and incidents are products of the author's imagination or are used fictitiously. Any resemblance to actual people, places, or events is entirely coincidental.

ISBN: 1546882251
ISBN-13: 978-1546882251

DEDICATION

To Jesus, my Messiah.

Abide in me, and I in you. As the branch cannot bear fruit of itself, except it abide in the vine; no more can ye, except ye abide in me. I am the vine, ye are the branches: He that abideth in me, and I in him, the same bringeth forth much fruit: for without me ye can do nothing. If a man abide not in me, he is cast forth as a branch, and is withered; and men gather them, and cast them into the fire, and they are burned.

John 15:4-6

ACKNOWLEDGMENTS

Special thanks to my beautiful wife and faithful companion. Thank you for your love, encouragement, and support.

I would like to thank my fantastic editing team, Catherine Goodwin, Ken and Jen Elswick, Jeff Markland, Frank Shackleford, Kris Van Wagenen, Sherrill Hesler, Paul Davison, and Claudine Allison.

CHAPTER 1

Therefore shall the land mourn, and every one that dwelleth therein shall languish, with the beasts of the field, and with the fowls of heaven; yea, the fishes of the sea also shall be taken away.

Hosea 4:3

February-Near Woodstock, Virginia.

Everett Carroll stared blankly at the barren moonscape surrounding the cave entrance. Nothing remained but rocks, mud, and a few charred remnants of tree stumps, which had not been totally destroyed in the fire. The new growth, which sprung up after the all-consuming blaze, was now brown and withered. Very little plant life had the tolerance to withstand the prodigious amounts of arsenic released into the surface water and top soil by Wormwood's debris field. No animal life survived.

Not only did the landscape look like an uninhabited planet, it was also as silent as a grave. No birds sang, no squirrels barked, and no chipmunks scurried about the leaves on the forest floor. Bleak. Miserable. The morning felt like wearing a pair of wet socks at the beginning of a soggy day.

Two months had passed since the Earth had smashed through the comet's poisonous debris field. Five weeks had gone by since Moses and Elijah set out for their journey to Jerusalem.

Courtney Carroll emerged from the cave followed by Sox, the cat.

Everett turned toward her. "Don't let him out! We have no idea how much arsenic is still in the soil. He'll get it on his feet, then when he washes, it will get in his system."

Courtney quickly scooped up the animal and held him in her arms like a baby. "He just wants some fresh air like the rest of us."

Everett forced a smile. "I know. I didn't mean to be so abrasive. Cabin fever is getting to me."

A gust of cold air sent chills through Everett's body, and he turned his face away from the wind.

"You mean cave fever. We've had cabin fever. This is way worse." Courtney shielded the cat from the breeze. "Complete desolation."

"Yeah, even the cave seems inviting compared to this." He stared down the path which led to the creek. "I wish it would snow. A blanket of clean white powder would go a long way in making everything look better. Nothing is more depressing than this muddy, scorched terrain."

"You miss Elijah, don't you?"

"Yeah. I miss his guidance, but it's more than that. I felt like we had a purpose when he was here. Now, I feel like we're just waiting for the end. Like serving a prison sentence."

"Me, too. It's like we're waiting to die."

Everett wished he hadn't said anything. He was supposed to be the spiritual leader, the one who keeps everyone's spirits up by offering an encouraging word. Courtney, Kevin, and Sarah were all counting on him to keep things together. Now he'd failed. Courtney's hope was slipping away. And so was his.

He dug down deep for a small sliver of inspiration. "We have to remember that we won't be here much longer. Glory is right around the corner." The words sounded flat, empty, insincere.

Courtney glanced over at him, still holding the cat close. "You don't have to fake it, Everett. It's okay to feel a little down. It's the Apocalypse. It's supposed to be bad."

"Hmm." He couldn't do that either. If he allowed himself the least amount of self-pity, he'd be on a slippery slope that would end in utter desperation.

"I'm going back inside. I've seen enough of this." Courtney turned toward the cave, ducked down and sent Sox in ahead of herself.

Everett continued to stare at the bleak nothingness. He watched as the bitter wind swept up ash and dust, swirling it into a dismal cloud, and obscuring the desolate landscape behind.

Inside the dust cloud, Everett noticed ghost-like figures, almost human in their form. The mysterious apparition sent chills up his spine, adding to the wintery bitterness, which was already making him shiver. He waited for the whirling mass of filth and grime to subside, and for the shadowy form to dissipate. It did not; rather the phantoms drew closer and became more lifelike. Without turning away from the two approaching wraiths, Everett stepped back toward the mouth of the cave and picked up his HK rifle.

The figures drew closer and it was apparent to Everett that this was not just an illusion. "Am I having a vision?" He squinted at what appeared to be two men dressed in long, hooded cloaks. Their faces were wrapped, and they shielded themselves from the frigid elements.

"Who would be out in this? Who could have even survived?" Everett held his rifle at a low-ready position as he peered harder at the two uninvited visitors. He ducked down and yelled into the cave. "Kevin, we've got company. I could use a little help out here!"

Seconds later, Kevin emerged from the cave, AR-15 in hand. "I was starting to think we were the last people alive around here."

Everett continued to watch.

Finally, one of the men removed his hood and called out while he was still some distance down the trail. "Hello!"

Everett tilted his head slightly. "Did that sound

like Elijah?"

Kevin's forehead puckered. "Yeah, it did."

Everett lowered his rifle, but only slightly. "Elijah, is that you?"

"Yes, yes. It is I."

Everett let his weapon hang from the sling and began walking toward the two men to greet them. Kevin followed close behind.

Moses pulled the hood off his head. "Can we go inside? We've been in this blustering wind for days."

"Of course. Are you okay? What happened? I thought you were going to Jerusalem." Everett was dumbfounded.

"We hit something of a snag." Elijah sounded discouraged.

Kevin walked next to Elijah. "What happened?"

Moses scowled. "New Atlantis lies in complete ruins. The Global Republic is breaking camp, and is taking everything to Israel. We went to the airport in hopes that Jehovah would open a door for us, which would allow us passage to Jerusalem. It seems that the guards restricting travel for those without the mark are the only form of government left."

"We were very nearly captured," Elijah added.

"Where's your truck?" Everett asked.

"We ran out of fuel near Centerville. We had to walk the rest of the way," Elijah answered.

"You must be exhausted." Everett stood to the side, letting Moses and Elijah enter the cave ahead of him.

"And famished," Moses commented as he

ducked low to enter the cave.

"We'll get you something to eat." Everett put his hand on the old prophet's back as they entered the cave.

"Elijah!" Courtney exclaimed.

"Hello, hello, child." Elijah embraced her, giving her a kiss on each cheek.

Sarah greeted him next. "It's so good to see you, but I'm afraid it means your mission isn't going well."

Moses put one finger in the air. "All is progressing according to His will. We cannot know why things do not work out as we suppose they will. It is only for us to accept the circumstances as they come and trust that He is still in control. If the Holy Scriptures say we must prophesy for 1260 days, then we will indeed prophesy."

Everett retrieved two canteens full of water and offered one to each of the men. "What brought you back here?"

"We had nowhere else to go." Elijah took the canteen and drank deeply. "At least here, we have shelter, food, water, and good company."

"You're always welcome." Courtney smiled.

Sarah brought MREs for the two men. "Eat all you want, but you might want to save some room. We're making chili mac tonight. I've perfected the recipe using the long-term storage food ingredients."

"Chili mac?" Moses' bushy eyebrows knitted together showing his curiosity.

"Yeah, I use TVP, tomato sauce, canned red beans, and macaroni."

"What is TVP?" Moses sounded suspicious.

Sarah seemed to fight back a grin. "Textured vegetable protein. Mixed in a recipe like my chili mac, it tastes like ground beef."

"Almost like ground beef." Kevin winked.

"To be honest, I've forgotten what real ground beef tastes like." Sarah turned to begin gathering the ingredients for dinner.

Kevin sighed. "I haven't."

"Let's hear about your trip." Everett anxiously changed the subject. He'd slaughtered Elijah's two pet goats shortly after the prophets left weeks earlier. Elijah had given him expressed permission to do so, but that was when he thought he'd never be back. All this talk of meat and the obvious absence of the two animals had to be painful for the old man. Everett took the canteens from the men. "I'll refill these for you."

Elijah reclined on one of the sleeping bags, which Courtney had laid out for the two visitors. "When we left here, we went straight away to Dulles International, certain that God would provide passage for us. The airport itself was in shambles from the impact with Wormwood's debris field. Only two of the runways were operational. Both were damaged. The underground people mover that carries passengers from one concourse to the other was completely shut down, so the airport is using above-ground trams to ferry travelers from station to station.

"I saw this as an opportunity. We found a damaged section of fence along the perimeter and used it to get inside without a security screen. We walked up to the Air France terminal and asked one of the baggage handlers where the flight to Tel Aviv might be. He most graciously pointed us in the right direction. We proceeded to the plane, which just so happened to be boarding, and got in line.

"When we reached the door, a woman wanted to scan our Mark implants. I held out my hand hoping that Jehovah would work a miracle with the machine, but . . ."

"Wow!" Courtney explained. "That took a lot of faith."

"No!" Moses held up his index finger. "If God had told us to do such a thing, it would have been faith. Jumping into this reckless action and making assumptions about how God should act took an abundance of foolishness."

Elijah scolded him in retaliation for the harsh comment. "You should have voiced your opposition to the plan *before* the attendant called security, and we had to flee for our very lives."

Moses crossed his arms and turned away from Elijah. "Hmmf." The old prophet did not refute his part in going along with the scheme, but neither did he seem ready to accept responsibility.

Elijah continued his debrief. "Anyway, we made our way to the coast and looked for ships that might carry us to the Holy City. Obviously, we proceeded with an abundance of caution. We traveled from port to port, praying, fasting, waiting, and trying to talk to anyone who might help. We spent three weeks looking but found no opportunities."

Moses finished one MRE and tore into a second one. "We had no money, and no provision, so Elijah proposed that we come back here until the Lord will show us the way."

Everett sat with his index finger on his lower lip. The finger showed his pensive state, but it may also have acted to keep his lower jaw from hanging wide open in absolute shock that God had not opened a door for the two men to get to their destination. Both had been brought back from the other side of the veil; from the realm of the spirit to the land of flesh, blood, and decrepit mortality. The mission had been specifically prophesied of 2,000 years ago. The entire chapter of Revelation 11 was dedicated to the two men sitting in the cave with Everett and the rest of his compadres. And here they sat, in a cold hard cavern, perfectly sidelined, thoroughly dissuaded, and 6,000 miles away from their objective. If God would not act on their behalf, they might as well be on the opposite side of the universe.

The group continued to listen to the specifics of Elijah and Moses' travels while Sarah made supper. The two prophets were still able to eat healthy portions despite having eaten two entire MREs each.

After dinner, Elijah insisted that they sing several worship songs to feed their disheartened spirits. By the second song, everyone was participating; even Kevin, who rarely sang. Afterward, they turned off their flashlights, one by one, and the cave took on its distinctive, complete, and absolute darkness. Encouraged by the time of praise and worship, Everett slept better that he had in months.

The next morning, Everett was awoken by Moses and Elijah. They were filling their canteens and placing some provisions into daypacks. Kevin was speaking quietly with the prophets.

Everett got out of his sleeping bag, slipped on his boots, and made his way over to the three men. "Where are you two going?"

"The mountain. We must seek the face of the Lord." Moses fastened the flap on his pack.

"We're on a mountain." Everett zipped up his sweatshirt.

"*Another* mountain," Elijah said.

"Would you like some company? I'd be happy to come along for security." Everett took the cup of coffee that Kevin offered to him.

"No. God will be our rock and our shield." Moses' response was delivered very matter-of-factly.

"We shall return when we have heard from God." Elijah hoisted his daypack on his shoulder and led the way out of the cave.

Everett's eyebrows showed his concern. "Have a good trip."

Kevin waved. "Take care."

Once the two men were out of the cavern, Everett turned to Kevin. "I think I should tail them, from a distance."

Kevin nodded. "Yeah. It's not safe for them to be out there unarmed. But if you're going, you better pack warm. If you build a fire, they'll spot you. And there's no telling how long you'll be out on the trail. It could be days or weeks."

Everett grabbed a large backpack and began filling it. "I'm not staying weeks. I'll provide over watch for up to three days. After that, they're on their own."

Courtney was up and had her blanket wrapped around her. "Not exactly on their own."

A pang of guilt hit Everett. "Yeah, you're right. But you know what I mean." After everything he'd been through, he knew none of them were on their own. They'd have all been dead ten times over if they were.

"But you're going to tail them anyway?" Courtney raised a brow.

"God doesn't expect us to be morons. We're responsible for being good stewards of the common sense he gave us." Everett tucked several magazines in his pack on top of the wool blanket and MREs.

"Well, they'll be insulted that you followed them after they asked you not to." Courtney took a seat on the upside-down bucket next to the rocket stove where Kevin was making coffee.

"Better insulted than dead." Everett gave her a quick peck on the cheek. "I'll be back by sunset Saturday. I'm not staying out in the cold more than two nights."

"You take care of yourself, Everett." Her eyes showed her concern.

"I will. Don't you worry." He made his way to the mouth of the cave.

Kevin offered him a smile as he left. "We'll be praying for you."

"Thanks." Everett waved, ducked low, and exited the cave.

He stood up and took a deep breath of the fresh air. The wind had died down, so it was no longer stirring up the dust and debris. The temperature was near freezing, but the lack of wind and warming rays of the sun made it feel much warmer. "Let's hope it stays like this." Everett slowly started down the trail which led to the creek. He didn't see the two prophets, but he felt certain this was the way they'd gone. Once he spotted the men in the distance he slowed his pace.

They won't go east toward Woodstock. Even though no one is left, Elijah will still think of it as a population center. He won't follow Trout Run because that's the valley. And the two of them are still tired, so they'll be looking for something close by. They'll head to that peak along the ridge, off to the west. But it's wide open; no foliage whatsoever. I'll have to stay back and use the stumps for cover.

Everett maintained his distance as the prophets made their way down the mountain, across the narrow valley below, then back up the adjacent ridge.

He took cover behind a seven-foot-tall, burned-out tree stump and retrieved his spotting scope. "Yep. That's exactly where they're heading." He surveyed the surrounding topography. "If any threats come from the West Virginia side of the mountain, I won't be able to see it until it's right on top of them. But if I go to the other side, I won't see what's coming from this direction." Everett continued to study the area through his scope until he identified a good location from which he could watch over the two men.

"There's a small knoll with some big stumps for cover. I guess that's where I'll be for the next couple of days." He stowed his scope and continued along his journey.

CHAPTER 2

In the year that king Uzziah died I saw also the Lord sitting upon a throne, high and lifted up, and his train filled the temple. Above it stood the seraphims: each one had six wings; with twain he covered his face, and with twain he covered his feet, and with twain he did fly. And one cried unto another, and said, Holy, holy, holy, is the Lord of hosts: the whole earth is full of his glory. And the posts of the door moved at the voice of him that cried, and the house was filled with smoke. Then said I, Woe is me! for I am undone; because I am a man of unclean lips, and I dwell in the midst of a people of unclean lips: for mine eyes have seen the King, the Lord of hosts.

Isaiah 6:1-5

Friday morning, Everett awoke at first light. He couldn't remember going to sleep. He could only recall his desperate shivering, which lasted until the wee hours of the night. He was still very cold. Hating every second of this frigid existence, he felt like a tropical bird, maybe a parrot or a toucan that had been accidentally locked in a meat cooler, exposed, painfully gelid, counting each sorrowful second as it passed.

The thick, gray wool blanket covered him, with only a small camping mat insulating him from the cold ground beneath. No natural materials like leaves or branches remained after the fires and Wormwood. He had nothing which could be used as additional insulation nor medium for constructing a shelter. Everett greatly wanted to chip away some of the dead, charred wood from the stump at his head for a fire. He longed to heat his water, to put something inside his stomach that might warm him up. But he couldn't. He'd be noticed for sure.

Everett rolled to the side and pulled out his spotting scope. He peered up the slope and watched as Elijah and Moses kindled a fire using bits of the remaining stumps around them. "It's like they know I'm here, and they're mocking me."

He rolled back behind cover and took an aged granola bar from his pack. He opened the package and poured the crumbly contents into his mouth. He washed it down with water that was much too cold, then returned to his lookout position.

Everett watched as the two prophets had breakfast, coffee, and then took out their Bibles. The two read silently as he looked on from a distance.

The sun slowly rose and began to warm the air. Everett felt more comfortable. The temptation to nod off crept in; his eyes grew heavy. Like a voice from outside, his weary mind called. *You could rest for a few minutes. After all, you barely slept last night. They'll be fine.*

"No." He vocalized his objection. "I came here to keep watch over them, and that's what I'm going to do!"

The morning progressed and the two prophets stood up suddenly. "They must have heard something!" Everett traded his spotting instrument for the scope affixed to his rifle. He watched carefully, waiting for something, or someone to come over the ridge.

A sudden glare began to burn his eyes as if he were looking into the sun. He turned to the side and blinked several times, giving his eyes a rest. "Sunlight must be hitting the lens of the scope." He looked over the rifle with his naked vision. The glare persisted, even with no scope, no glass to catch the rogue beam of daylight. Everett put his arm up to shield his face from the ultrabright luminescence. "It's a person, inside the light." He knew inside that this image was not a threat to the two prophets, so he did not draw his weapon.

The bright-shining figure's glow softened, and Everett retrieved his spotting scope. His heart quickened. The man who appeared to them wore a bright-white robe, whiter than anything Everett had ever seen in his life. The man glistened like water in a flowing brook struck by dawn's first rays. He spoke with Elijah and Moses as the two prophets listened intently.

"It must be an angel!" Everett focused the scope on the man's hands. They were pierced. Everett's hands shook as his eyes welled up with tears. The scope dropped from his quaking fingers. His dry lips mouthed a single word. "Messiah!"

The man in white looked toward Everett with compassion and love. Everett felt the strength leave his body and he lost consciousness.

Everett was aroused by someone shaking him. "Wake up, boy. Stand up. Stand on your feet."

It was the voice of Moses. He was speaking brashly, and his face shined.

Everett became aware of his surroundings and quickly realized that what he witnessed was not a vision. It was real. He glanced up at Elijah whose face also had a gentle glow. He was smiling tenderly at Everett.

Everett looked up the slope where Elijah and Moses had been when he blacked out. He turned back to Elijah. "Where is . . ."

Elijah chuckled and offered Everett his hand. "He'll be back."

Everett stood up and collected his belongings. He felt confused, dizzy, a little light-headed, but in a good way. He slung his pack over his shoulder and picked up his rifle.

"Do not speak of this to the others." Moses began walking back toward the cave.

Everett nodded and followed the two men.

Once back, Everett entered the cavern behind the prophets. He dropped his pack near the opening and sat down.

"Hey, you're back!" Courtney kissed him.

His delayed response betrayed his preoccupation. "I missed you."

"Are you okay?" she quizzed.

He forced himself to snap back to the here and now. "Oh, yeah. I didn't sleep much last night. It's got my head sort of foggy."

Kevin greeted the returning team. "So, did you get an answer?"

Moses positioned a bucket near the rocket stove. "Yes."

Sarah looked at him as if she were waiting for him to finish. "And?"

Elijah placed his hand on Sarah's back as he took a seat next to Moses. "You are to assist us in getting out of the country."

Her eyes showed her lack of clarity. "Me? Personally?"

"All of you." Moses' face was stiff as if he'd been inconvenienced. He pointed at Everett. "I think it is because of this one, if you're looking for someone to blame."

Embarrassed, Everett felt like he'd been caught stealing a mint from the purse of the preacher's wife. He pleaded his case with Moses. "What? No. I didn't mean any harm by following you. I didn't intend to spy on you. I was just looking out for you. Elijah is an old friend. We've been through a lot together."

Elijah laughed. "No. That is not what he means. Moses is saying that he believes God has a certain role for you to fulfill concerning these final hours of Earth's history."

"Oh. Okay." Everett let out a sigh of relief. He was not being scolded like a school boy for having surreptitiously tagged along. "What does God want us to do?"

Moses laid out the requirements in a very economical fashion. "You must take down Dragon so Elijah and I may travel to the Holy Land without the Mark."

Everett's renewed sense of purpose quickly faded in the face of the impossible task. "Take down Dragon? We can't take down Dragon. The system is self-aware. Artificial intelligence. It defends itself. Besides that, the Utah Data Center is the single most heavily-armed military installation on the planet. We can't do it."

Moses put both hands in the air. "Listen, I don't know anything about artificial intelligence, or military data centers, or all these things, okay? I wasn't planning to be around here for so long. I have no intention of learning all these computer things now. So, please don't talk to me about this." He pointed at Everett and lowered one eyebrow. "But one thing I know. If God says you can do it, you can. Don't tell me what is impossible. I saw water turn to blood, sticks turned to snakes; I saw frogs and locusts cover the earth, I walked through the sea on dry land." He paused but kept his finger pointed at Everett and his eyebrow cocked. "And I suspect you have seen the hand of God for yourself. So, do not tell me you can't. And I might warn you against telling Jehovah that you can't as well. Forty years I wandered because I was yoked to faithless unbelievers. I will not suffer it again."

Now Everett had been put in his place. He nodded humbly and dared not to look Moses in the eye. "We'll figure it out."

"Good. Now let's eat." Moses slapped his hands on top of his thighs as if it were to issue a command for manna to fall from heaven.

Everett helped Courtney prepare lunch. She winked at him. "You got taken to the woodshed. Yikes! I'm sorry I didn't stick up for you, but I didn't know what to say."

Everett huffed. "No. Moses is right. I shouldn't be so disbelieving. After everything I've seen, I don't have an excuse."

She spoke softly so no one else would overhear their conversation. "So, do you have any ideas?"

"Not one." He pressed his lips together.

"John Jones left those schematics of the Utah Data Center in his safe."

"It's a smattering of hand drawn figures in an old notebook. It's little more than sketched-out boxes with barely-legible labels. You're getting pretty liberal with your use of the word *schematics.*"

"I just thought maybe we could get some ideas." She dropped her head like a scolded pup.

He took her hand and smiled. "It's a good plan.

We'll dig the notebook out after dinner."

Once lunch was finished, Sarah and Kevin insisted on cleaning up. Everett and Courtney climbed the ladder into the long tunnel portion of the cave used as a storage area. They began looking through the various bins until they found the collection of John Jones' belongings.

Everett finally located the old, spiral-bound booklet. He thumbed through the pages.

"Did you find it?" She shined her light in his direction.

"Yeah." The notebook was filled with notes and flow-of-consciousness thoughts. Many of the pages were a sort of diary. "I feel like I'm violating his privacy."

"He wouldn't mind. Just flip through to the diagrams." Courtney looked over his shoulder.

Everett turned to the back. "Data Center."

"What does that say?" Courtney pointed to some chicken-scratched notes.

"1.7 million gallons water per day."

"What's 1.7 million gallons of water per day?"

Everett shrugged. "That's probably what it takes to keep the server stacks cool."

Everett turned the page. "Look, there's a scale at the bottom of the page. Here's the Data Center and here's the pump station, all the way down by Lake Utah."

"So according to Jones' scale, that's what, four miles?"

Everett nodded. "Yeah. No water, no Dragon."

She stared at the hand-drawn map. "I'm sure the

water supply of the global order's motherboard is going to be guarded."

"But not like the Data Center itself." A smile slowly began to creep across Everett's mouth. "Come on. Let's go tell the others!"

Everett led the way down the ladder and took the notebook to Elijah. "This is a loose diagram of the Utah Data Center where the seven quantum computers that make up Dragon are housed."

Kevin and Sarah looked on from either side of Elijah.

Kevin pointed to the area on the map next to the Data Center. "Jones wrote National Guard base. This map was drawn pre-Global Republic. The GR base is probably much larger now."

"I don't doubt it," Everett said. "But we're not focusing on the Data Center or the military base." His finger glided across the page to the notes. "According to this, Dragon needs 1.7 million gallons of water a day to keep the server stacks cool. The pump station that supplies the water is four miles south on the bank of Lake Utah."

Sarah crossed her arms. "That pump house is critical infrastructure. It's going to be heavily guarded."

Everett rebutted, "We don't know that. Think about how vulnerable the sea ports and critical infrastructure were in America prior to the collapse. I think you're overestimating the GR's competence."

Sarah shook her head. "Cassie Parker, the woman in our group who saw all of this coming, said those vulnerabilities were intentional. Her theory was that by leaving the borders porous, ports susceptible to attack, and infrastructure unguarded, the globalists were inviting additional chaos from which to build the new order."

Everett lifted his eyebrows. "She was at least half-right. You can't refute the facts. But, human laziness and complacency have always been around. Courtney and I worked in the intelligence community for years, and we saw it all the time.

"The pump house probably has some security, but I'm guessing we could go in, hit them hard, destroy the water pumps, and get out before the main base knows they're under attack."

Kevin stroked his beard. "I'm not so sure about that. The Data Center will have aerial drone surveillance 24/7. Those drones could be redirected and over us in seconds."

Elijah said, "Perhaps a diversionary force could hit the Data Center head-on while a smaller contingency attacked the water pumps."

Everett nodded and looked at Kevin. "That might work. What do you think?"

Kevin chortled. "We're four people. We don't even have enough to attack the water pumps, much less split up into two elements."

"We could ask Tommy." Courtney stuck her hands in her pockets.

Sarah sighed. "The team that goes directly at the Data Center is going to take heavy losses. It would be a suicide mission."

Everett's voice sounded grim. "We've got another three and a half years on a planet that is growing more hostile by the day. I'm in no hurry to die, but I can't say I'm looking forward to what's coming either. If it's a suicide mission, so be it. It's something that has to be done."

Kevin's face looked serious as he glanced up at Everett. "You're right. I'm in."

"Kevin's not going anywhere without me," Sarah stated.

Courtney put one hand around Everett's waist. "You're not going to heaven and leaving me on this God-forsaken globe. No discussions, no arguments; I'm going also."

Everett didn't like that. He certainly didn't want to leave her behind, but he couldn't stand the thought of watching her get killed in the operation. A corner of his mouth lifted. "Then it's settled. I'll set up the radio and try to reach Tommy later this evening."

CHAPTER 3

Blessed is the man that walketh not in the counsel of the ungodly, nor standeth in the way of sinners, nor sitteth in the seat of the scornful. But his delight is in the law of the Lord; and in his law doth he meditate day and night. And he shall be like a tree planted by the rivers of water, that bringeth forth his fruit in his season; his leaf also shall not wither; and whatsoever he doeth shall prosper. The ungodly are not so: but are like the chaff which the wind driveth away. Therefore the ungodly shall not stand in the judgment, nor sinners in the congregation of the righteous. For the Lord knoweth the way of the righteous: but the way of the ungodly shall perish.

Psalm 1

Everett helped Courtney up for the first step onto the hill of mud, rock, and tree roots blocking the road.

"I hope the ATV is still where we left it." He followed behind her, using his hands to steady himself as he climbed.

"If it is, I hope it starts." Courtney reached a point where the landslide plateaued and stood up straight.

Everett joined her, also standing erect. "The snow sure is pretty."

"Any other day, I'd agree with you. But this trip is challenging enough without the added peril of slippery trails and icy roads."

He pointed ahead. "I think that's the ATV."

Courtney's eyes followed his finger. "I think you're right."

The two of them made their way to the white hump, which they suspected to be their vehicle. Everett began scooping the snow away with his gloves. Courtney joined him. They eventually dug down to the blue tarp covering the machine and removed it.

Everett said a silent prayer as he started the engine. The ATV stalled out after the first try but began humming steadily after the second start. He got on and revved the engine. "You need a ride, young lady?"

She got on the rear of the vehicle and held on to

his pack. "Yeah, but I have to be home before the street lights come on."

He laughed. "That might be a good long while."

The two of them made their way cautiously across the field of snow, slowly picking a path through the obstacles jetting up from the pure white covering. The debris, which had been left by the massive earthquake, subsequent landslide, and asteroid assault was much easier to navigate when it wasn't covered in snow.

They reached the other side of the landslide and continued on the snow-covered mountain road. Everett smiled as he looked out at the beautiful white scenery. He knew the marred countryside beneath was still grimy, gray, scorched, dead, and filthy. But for now, it was a sight to behold.

They continued slowly for three miles. Everett slowed to a stop when he saw an oncoming vehicle. "Who else would be crazy enough to be out on the roads today?"

Courtney raised her rifle and looked through the scope. "The Global Republic, that's who. Come on, let's get out of here. Maybe they didn't see us yet."

Everett yelped, "Hang on!" He gunned the engine and spun the ATV around. Everett raced to get out of view of the GR vehicle. "Did you see what kind of vehicle it was?"

"MRAP. A Typhoon I think. A newer model. Not one of the old Russian ones."

Everett gritted his teeth. "Great. A passenger van. We definitely don't want to tangle with that."

"Maybe we can get back to the landslide and lose them on foot."

"If they haven't seen us, and they're not pursuing, we might be able to, but if they're on to us, we'll never outrun that thing on an ATV. Did we lose them?" He waited for her response.

Finally, she said, "Nope. They're gaining on us. We've been made."

Everett sighed and pushed the ATV as hard as it would go.

"They're getting closer. I can see the face of the driver." Courtney's voice sounded frantic. "Can you go off-road? That MRAP can't drive through the tree stumps."

Everett looked toward the side of the road and down the mountain. "No way. We'd roll to our deaths."

"What about uphill? We just need to put some distance between us and them so they can't catch up to us on foot."

He glanced at the other side. It too was steep, but perhaps he could pull it off. "Maybe."

Everett found a navigable path and turned off. The engine whined as the ATV began storming up the steep incline. He zigzagged to decrease the effect of the sharp embankment as he maneuvered through the burnt tree stumps. "Hang on tight!" Everett gunned the engine to get over a sheer mound. The front wheels left the snow-covered ground below, and the vehicle pitched up perpendicular. Everett leaned forward, but Courtney was holding on to his pack. For a brief moment, the ATV was motionless, then it tipped backward, and the two of them fell off to the side. Everett grabbed his wife and rolled out of the way before the vehicle tumbled on top of them. The ATV flipped onto its back, then rolled sideways until it came to a stop against an incinerated tree trunk less than twenty-five feet from where Everett and Courtney fell.

"Are you okay?" He looked her over.

"Yeah, are you?"

He ran his hands across his legs and arms. "I think so."

A voice called through the loudspeaker attached to the MRAP with a thick New Zealand accent. "We can very easily resolve this issue. As of right now, you've committed no crime other than evading a constable of the Republic. It's a minor offense that I'm willing to overlook if you'll come on back down here."

"What do you want?" Everett lay prone in the snow as he yelled.

"We've been tasked with locating the survivors of the Wormwood impact. We only want to make sure we have an accurate estimated population count so the appropriate amount of resources can be allocated to the area."

Everett yelled back. "Okay. We're two people. We don't know of anyone else that survived. So if that's it, we should be free to go."

Everett watched as four armed GR peacekeepers exited the Typhoon from the rear doors. The man who had been speaking through the loudspeaker now yelled up the ridge to Everett. "Yes, well. We do have to ensure that you have your Mark."

"And if we don't?" Everett inquired.

"We will implant you right here, and you can be on your way. Trust me, I have no desire to spend any more time here than I must. I have a quota of 100 persons from the outlying areas to implant, then our team will be reassigned off this wretched hemisphere. I have no reason to lie to you. But let me be clear, the quota is to implant or eradicate. Obviously, it's easier for us both to implant you. I do not wish to transport your bleeding corpses back to the outpost, but I want my reassignment. Do we understand each other?"

Everett's face held a grave expression as he looked to Courtney. "We're going to have to run. We'll leapfrog backward. One lays down cover fire, the other moves."

She looked deeply concerned. "Then what? We don't have enough ammo to do that all the way back to the landslide?"

Everett watched as six more peacekeepers got out of the vehicle. "They left the back doors open. Let's try to lead them in a spread-out circle. If we can get back to the Typhoon before they do, the vehicle is ours."

"It's not a great plan." Her voice was distressed.

"Okay, what do you suggest? They're heading up the hill."

"Not a great plan, but it'll do. Cover me. I'll run first." Courtney got in position to move.

"If you want to live to see that reassignment, you should leave us alone!" Everett was sure the statement was made in vain, but he had to give the easy way one last try.

"I can't do that." The man began leading his squad up the hill with weapons drawn.

Everett took aim at the one he assumed was the

commander. "Go!" He pulled the trigger, dropping his target and causing the others to dive into the snow, and scurry for cover.

Courtney sprung up from her position and ran while Everett fired three more quick shots at the positions where he'd seen the men jump.

"Set!" Courtney yelled to Everett.

He waited for the first GR troop to stick his head up, then joined Courtney in firing at him to keep him pinned down. Everett slung his rifle around his back and began hustling up and beyond Courtney's position. "Set!" He leveled his rifle and began firing so Courtney could advance to the next position of cover.

They repeated the maneuver four more times. As Everett readied his weapon, he called out to Courtney. "Come to me." He opened fire in the direction of their pursuers while she ran up the mountain toward him.

Once she arrived at the burnt stump where he was positioned, he asked, "Did you hit any of them?"

"I think I winged one in the shoulder."

"Then we better start circling around. If they send wounded back to the vehicle, it will ruin our plan. As far as I know, the only one I've hit so far was the boss. The rest of them don't seem eager to get shot."

She fired two rounds at one of the peacekeepers who was preparing to make a run toward them. "Yeah, but they're not giving up either."

Everett scoped out the path they would take. "When I start shooting, you keep going all the way to that knoll. Once I get to your location, we'll be in position to get between them and the Typhoon."

"Okay, ready when you are." She got into position for her sprint.

Everett laid down a volley of heavy fire, quickly changing magazines before the GR troops could pop back up. "We could all still walk away and call it a draw."

A peacekeeper called out in reply, "You shot the boss, mate. We can't go home without your scalp now."

Through his sights, Everett saw the barrel of the man's gun rising from the cover of a charred log. He breathed steadily, waiting for the man's head to be visible. Everett pulled the trigger, and the shot echoed off the barren landscape. The peacekeeper slumped onto the log, and crimson blood streamed down onto the brilliant white snow.

Courtney's rifle rang out from a distance, letting Everett know that she was in position. He let off another short volley of rifle fire, then dashed through the snow toward his wife.

"Okay." He gasped for breath when he arrived at her location. Trudging through the snow proved to be much more challenging than their morning runs with Sarah. "You head straight back from me, then start curving down the hill toward that group of stumps. But not too much. I don't want them to figure out what we're doing until we're between them and the MRAP."

"Got it!"

Everett whispered, "Go!" and began providing cover fire for Courtney's retreat.

"Set," she yelled from a distance. The remaining troops were still following and appeared to be losing steam. Everett bolted from cover and tromped across the snow as quickly as possible.

When he got to Courtney, his heart was pumping like a locomotive. He breathed in his nose and out his mouth to regulate his respiratory system.

"You're huffing hard. We should rest so you can catch your breath."

"No." He shook his head. "I'll be okay. Besides, it's all downhill from here, and they're out of breath also." Everett inhaled deeply and raised his rifle. "Go."

Courtney ran, and Everett began shooting.

Soon, one of the peacekeepers caught on to their predicament. "She's going for the truck!" he yelped.

Everett wanted to yell *gotcha*, but he knew it was too soon to get cocky. He heard Courtney's rifle begin firing. It was his cue to run like he'd never ran in his life. This was the final leg of the race. And unlike most contests of speed, the prize for this one was life. Everett left the safety of the seared tree trunk and charged toward the armored vehicle.

Yelling and gunfire broke out behind him. Courtney continued to shoot back, but the GR troops seemed to have renewed vigor and an undaunted determination to stop Everett from reaching the Typhoon.

Just before he reached the vehicle, he stumbled, dropping his weapon.

"Come on, Everett!" Courtney unleashed a hail of bullets from behind a snow drift on the side of the road. "We're almost there, but these guys are right on top of us!"

Everett reached out to grab his rifle, then struggled to get back on his feet. "Go! Get in the truck!"

Courtney turned to dart toward the open door of the MRAP. Everett rushed behind her. She climbed in the back door. Everett jumped in as bullets peppered the heavy metal door. "Give me cover!" He lay on the floor of the vehicle waiting for Courtney to shoot.

She fired three rounds, and Everett reached out to grab the door handle of the armored vehicle. He had to use the weight of his entire body to move the cumbersome chunk of steel hinged to the rear of the truck, but he got it closed. "Check the latches on the front doors. Make sure they're locked!"

"Roger." Courtney hurried up the aisle to the front of the vehicle, slamming the security latches shut.

PING, PANG. PONG. The sound of bullets hitting the truck rattled inside the vehicle like a marble in a soda can. Everett soon realized the rifles of the GR peacekeepers were no threat to them at all. "Thank you, Jesus!" He held his hands heavenward in praise. He looked to the sky. "Now, Lord, just let the keys be in the ignition."

Everett made his way to the driver's seat. His smile slipped slightly as he looked at the vacant slot where the keys should have been.

Courtney looked over his shoulder. "I don't suppose you know how to hotwire a military truck, do you?"

He shook his head. "No, do you?"

"What kind of girl do you think I am?" She feigned a look of uncertainty.

He started to grin at the jest but saw peacekeepers approaching the left side of the vehicle. He drew his Sig from his side arm holster and quickly located the latch for the driver's side gun port. He stuck the pistol out and fired two rounds, hitting one of the assailants in the knee. "We have to keep them back from the truck. If we let them get close, they could build a fire and smoke us out real quick."

Courtney changed magazines and readied her rifle to fire out the passenger's side gun port if the GR troops tried to get close."

"Patrol nine, respond." The radio chirped with the voice of a British man.

"That ain't good," Everett said as he dug his last full magazine out of his pack.

"Respond patrol nine. I'm dispatching three backup units to your location, but it would be very helpful if we knew the particulars of your situation."

Courtney shook her head as she watched Everett pick up the mic.

He gave her a smile that said he understood her objection, but that it had been overruled. He pressed the talk key and made a very poor attempt at a New Zealand accent. "We've just returned to the vehicle. No need for backup. Thought we saw some activity down in the valley, but it turned out to be a garbage bag blowing in the wind."

"Very good to hear, patrol nine. Just give us today's authentication code, and I'll recall the additional units."

Everett set his teeth together tightly as he strained to think of how he could possibly bluff his way through this one. "Password."

"What was that you said, patrol?"

Courtney dropped her head into her palm.

Everett tightened up his fake accent and doubled down. "Password."

The voice became very hostile. "You are in violation of crimes against peacekeeping forces of the Global Republic, for which the punishment is death. I hereby command that you release control of the vehicle you are in and surrender yourselves."

Courtney cut the power to the radio. "Password?"

Everett lifted his shoulders. "Do you know how many people use *password* for their computer password?"

"This is a military authentication code. Not someone's personal laptop."

Everett huffed and pointed to the rear of the truck. "Look around and see if you can find any 5.56 ammo. The hospitality team is on their way, and I'm on my last mag."

"Yeah, me, too." She began searching compartments as Everett scanned the rearview and watched both sides of the truck for anyone trying to sneak up on him.

"This looks like some kind of gun for implanting chips. I guess he wasn't lying about this being a mobile station for giving people the Mark."

Everett fired three more shots out the driver's side gun port. "Yeah, yeah. How's the ammo situation?"

"Boom!" she exclaimed. "Full AR mags!"

"5.56?" Everett didn't want to take his eyes off the outside of the truck long enough to look.

"Roger that," Courtney replied. "And here's a breaching shotgun."

"Good, good. Bring me some magazines, then look around and see what other goodies you can find." Everett saw a man trying to sneak up from the back. He sprinted toward the back door, opened the rear gun port and fired several rounds from his HK rifle. "These guys are as persistent as a bunch of hyenas trying to get into a rabbit cage. You gotta work fast so you can help me keep an eye out."

"I'm moving as quickly as I can." She continued to rummage through the various compartments. "Berkey water filter. It's specifically for arsenic. Ration bars."

"Great, I could use one of those, but we need to get our mags loaded first"

She dumped the AR-15 magazines out of the ammo box and began stripping out the shells.

Everett pulled all the empty mags for his HK G36 out of his pack. "Here comes another one!" He rushed to the passenger's side and fended off yet another attempt by a GR troop to get close to the vehicle.

Courtney opened a ration bar and took a bite. She held it up to Everett's mouth. "You burned a lot of calories running up and down the mountain."

"Thanks." He kept his eyes peeled as he bit into the tasteless nutrition bar.

Courtney began loading Everett's magazines

while she chewed. "Here's a full mag. Why don't you change it out for the one in your rifle?"

Everett took the mag she handed him and exchanged it for the one in his gun. He scoured the mirrors and windows for any sign of movement.

Courtney diligently loaded 5.56 bullets into Everett's spent magazines as well as her own. "How long do you think we have until their backup comes?"

"It sounded like he'd just dispatched them. I know they're not coming out of Winchester. Tommy would have probably heard something if they had an outpost in Martinsburg. I'm assuming they're farther out than that."

She passed him two more full magazines. "We don't know they're coming from the north. They could have been on their way back south after reaching the end of their patrol."

"They definitely didn't drive across the landslide."

"No, but they wouldn't have to. The patrol may have originated out of Harrisonburg and went west into West Virginia, then came back through Wardensville."

He kept a steady lookout. "That would have been a convoluted way to get here, but I suppose it's possible. More likely though, is that they came out of Hagerstown or Fredrick. If that's the case, we're probably looking at an hour and a half until backup arrives.

"And I don't mean to sound grim, but they know we're in the MRAP, so they'll be coming with heavy weaponry."

"Like what?" Her forehead puckered.

"I don't know. Something big enough to defeat this armor."

"We need a plan before they get here." Her statement was insistent.

"I'm open to suggestions." Everett stuck his rifle out the gun port and fired several rounds at the burned-out tree trunk the GR troops were using for cover.

Courtney huffed. "I don't know. I don't see any fragmentation grenades or explosives in here."

"That wouldn't matter. They'll be coming in heavily armored vehicles."

The minutes crept by slowly as the two of them struggled to come up with a plan. They said a quick prayer asking for wisdom and protection. They took turns eating and drinking water so they'd have the strength to take advantage of any opportunity that God might provide.

Everett looked at his watch. "It's been over an hour. All the magazines are topped off. We've done all we can. Whatever happens, know that I love you forever."

"And I love you, Everett. I can't imagine going through the Tribulation without you. As hard as it's been, you've made it one of the best times of my life."

Everett could hear engines approaching. He took Courtney's hand to hold for what could be the last time.

She smiled at him. "Our lives are in God's hands." She looked up. "Thy will be done."

Everett made his way to the rear of the vehicle.

He prepared to stick his rifle out the rear gun port in the direction of the approaching threat.

Courtney remained in the front, watching the rearview mirrors. "I see something."

"What is it?"

"Those aren't armored vehicles. It's a Jeep and a big four-wheel drive pickup truck." She sounded perplexed.

"That can't be the GR. No way they'd come after us in civilian vehicles." Everett returned to the front of the vehicle to get a better look at the rearview mirror. Excitement welled up inside him as he exclaimed, "That's Tommy's truck!"

"Thank you, God!" Courtney squealed like a wild monkey.

Everett had to fight to control his own optimism. "Let's not get ahead of ourselves. The Global Republic backup team is still on their way. And they'll be here any minute."

Gunfire broke out between the remaining peacekeepers and the occupants of the approaching vehicles. Everett waited for his opportunity, then swung the heavy rear door open. Using the armored door as a shield, he took out two GR troops from behind. Shooting from just inside the back door of the MRAP, Courtney eliminated one other hostile.

"Is that you, Everett? Are you alright?" Tommy's low voice echoed out from the big pickup truck.

"Yeah. Thanks to you," he yelled.

Tommy walked over to Everett's position. "When I saw you were running late, something told me you were in trouble. I rounded up the boys to come look for you."

"We're not out of the woods yet. GR sent backup. They'll be here any minute." Everett patted Tommy on the shoulder.

"It'd be a cryin' shame to leave a fine vehicle like that one behind." Tommy stopped to look the MRAP over.

Everett shook his head. "It's got GPS. Besides, there's no time. We need to get out of here."

"Devin, see if you can locate the GPS and remove it from this truck here."

"You got it." Devin wasted no time in gathering some tools from the Jeep.

Tommy called out to the other men. "Preacher, you and the rest of the boys start stripping these uniforms from the dead whilst we wait for Devin. And find them keys."

Everett clinched his jaw. "Tommy, I don't think we have time for all of this."

"The sooner we get it done, the sooner we can skedaddle. You can waste time arguing or you can help out so we can get goin'. Either way, I ain't leaving without that truck and those uniforms."

Courtney huffed as she began walking toward one of the deceased peacekeepers. "I suppose you want the weapons also."

Tommy chuckled and glanced over at Everett. "See there, she's got the right attitude."

The uniforms were soon stripped and loaded into the bed of Tommy's truck along with the battle rifles from the fallen troops. Devin held a small black plastic box with two wires hanging out of it. "GPS is gone."

"Let's get moving then." Tommy made a quick about face and hurried to his vehicle.

Courtney jogged alongside Tommy. "We think they might be coming out of Hagerstown or Fredrick. We wouldn't want to run right into them."

Tommy glanced over at her as he continued walking. "No. We wouldn't want to do that. We'll head west when we get to Wardensville. I know some good folks in Kirby that'll let us lay low for a while."

Tommy tossed a set of keys to Everett. "Think you can drive that monster."

Everett caught the keys. "I guess we'll find out."

Everyone was loaded into the vehicles in a matter of seconds. Everett took the driver's seat of the Typhoon. Courtney sat next to him in the passenger's seat.

He stuck the keys in the ignition. "Automatic transmission. Imagine that."

"We've got to start moving, Everett. That convoy is going to be on top of us any second now."

He put the vehicle in drive and punched the gas. "It's got good traction in the snow."

"It should, these things weigh three tons."

Everett followed the Jeep, which was behind Tommy's truck. "Once we get through Wardensville and start heading west, I'll feel better."

"Yeah, me, too. Let's just hope we're right about the backup team coming from the north. What did you think about Tommy gambling with our lives for a truck and a couple of guns? I thought he was supposed to be saved."

Everett sighed. “Saved doesn't mean perfect. It just means forgiven. That outlaw-hustler’s mentality may die hard for him. Or, in this environment, it may not die at all. In fact, it may be something of a blessing, times being what they are.

“But no, I didn’t appreciate him taking risks with our lives.”

Courtney looked out the window. “I guess I’m being ungrateful. If he hadn’t shown up when he did, we’d be gone.”

“That’s true.” Everett focused on the vehicle in front of him. “Still, it seemed like a foolish wager.”

Everett and Courtney both let out a deep breath as they exited Wardensville, heading west on US 48. Eight miles later, Tommy turned off onto a gravel road, which snaked through a series of steep hills. He pulled into the parking lot of an old coal mine.

“I guess this is where we’re hiding out for a while.” Everett cut the ignition. He and Courtney exited the MRAP and joined Tommy.

Tommy pulled two rifles out of the truck bed. “Y’all got anything to eat in that big ol’ truck? These folks is gettin’ by mighty poorly.”

“There’s some ration bars. No MREs or anything,” Everett replied.

Tommy nodded with a smile. “They’ll appreciate it. They don’t have much of nothin’.”

“I’ll get them.” Courtney walked back to the Typhoon.

A frail old man, a thin middle-aged man, and an emaciated teenage boy emerged from the mine. All three carried shotguns. “Tommy, is that you?” the eldest asked.

"I brought you a little something, Cotton." He handed the rifle to the old man.

Cotton took the weapon and placed his shotgun near the entrance of the mine. "AR-15?"

"It's called a MARS-L. I reckon it's about the same as an AR-15 though. This one's for Jeb." Tommy passed the other rifle to the middle-aged man.

Cotton admired the rifle. "Fraid I ain't got nothin' to swap ya fer it, less'n you want some coal. Always's got plenty of coal."

"Don't need nothin' 'cept a place to hang my hat for the evenin', me and my friends here."

"I wouldn't charge you nothin' fer that, Tommy. You know that."

Tommy tipped his hat to Cotton. "Well, the rifles are a gift then."

Courtney walked up with a box of ration bars and handed them to Tommy.

Tommy passed the container to the teenage boy. "And here's a little something to fill your bellies."

The boy's eyes lit up like it was Christmas morning. Everett looked on in shame. He remembered how he'd grumbled about not having anything fresh to eat in the past couple of months, and here was this group of people right up the road from him on the cusp of starvation.

Tommy made introductions and Cotton invited everyone to come inside the mine whenever they wanted.

"We'll be along directly." Tommy waved as the others went inside.

Everett and Courtney stayed outside with Tommy.

"I reckon we can have our little pow wow inside your fancy new vehicle." Tommy pointed to the MRAP.

"Okay, but it's not our vehicle. You rescued us. You earned it." Everett led the way to the Typhoon.

Tommy was the last one in and closed the door behind himself. "So. What was so important that you risked getting yourselves killed over?"

Everett spent the next twenty minutes explaining how Elijah and Moses had returned. He told Tommy about the seven quantum computers at the old NSA Utah Data Center, which made up Dragon, the supercomputer, which ran the Global Republic's digital currency system, defense system, logistics, Mark embeddable personal identification system, and all other aspects of the world order. He laid out the weakness John Jones had identified in the water pump station, which supplied the cooling system and regulated the temperature of Dragon's server stacks.

Tommy listened, asking for additional information from time to time. Once Everett finished his discourse, Tommy nodded pensively. Finally, he looked up. "I'm in. I wouldn't miss it for the world. I'm pretty sure Preacher will be game. Devin, too. The rest of 'em, I can't say for sure. But you'll have a good ten to fifteen of us."

Everett shook Tommy's hand with a firm grip. "Thank you. This means a lot to us."

"Yes, sir. Glad to help." Tommy got up from his seat. He had to duck down to keep from hitting his head on the ceiling of the armored personnel carrier. He turned as he exited the vehicle. "Why don't you let me fill the boys in. I've got a way with talkin' to folks about these kinds of things."

"Sure, Tommy." Everett smiled and got up to follow him out. Courtney walked behind Everett.

CHAPTER 4

Have not I commanded thee? Be strong and of a good courage; be not afraid, neither be thou dismayed: for the Lord thy God is with thee whithersoever thou goest.

Joshua 1:9

One week later, Everett stood next to Tommy's truck. Like everyone else, he was kitted out in full battle rattle. And, like everyone else, he carried an AR-15 rather than his HK. He wasn't as comfortable with the AR-15, but standardization in battle rifles meant that anyone could lend an extra magazine to anyone else in the squad. That single advantage could mean the difference between life and death.

His load bearing vest held his Sig, four pistol magazines, six magazines for his AR-15, a radio, flashlight, and a rudimentary medical kit. He looked over Kevin's shoulder to see the map Tommy was holding on the hood. "So, you think we're good logistically?"

Kevin rubbed his beard. "Utah is a long way. Over 4,000 miles round trip. We've got a 500-gallon water trailer about three-quarters filled with gas. The tanks of all three pickups are topped off. That will get us there."

Tommy said, "I had to beg, borrow, and steal to get that much fuel. Well, I didn't steal, unless you count what I siphoned out of some GR vehicles." Tommy looked at the Dodge Ram crew cab next to his pickup. "And we've got a 500-gallon trailer full of water."

Everett looked at the assortment of bicycles affixed to the luggage racks of the two pickups with toppers. "I sure wish we had enough fuel to get home. We've got the Berkey arsenic filters that we scavenged from the GR vehicle. It's a slow process to gravity filter water for twenty people, but as long as we can find fresh water, we won't die of dehydration. Still, we'll never be able to carry enough food to get back. Best-case scenario, it'll take us five weeks to return on the bikes."

He looked at Courtney who was talking to Sarah over by the third truck in the convoy. He was willing to buy a one-way ticket for himself, but taking his wife on a suicide mission was another thing altogether. He sighed, wishing there was another way.

Kevin's eyes turned toward Sarah as he put his hand on Everett's shoulder. "I know exactly how you feel."

"It ain't too late to back out." Tommy folded up the map and stuck it in his rear pocket. "I'm only goin' on this trip because you asked me to."

Everett shook his head as he looked down at the dirt. "No. That's not an option for me. Elijah needs me to do this. I have to go. If God wants us to come back, He'll get us home. If not, then we'll have done our duty."

Tommy cupped his hands over his mouth and hollered, "All right, boys." He looked over at Courtney and Sarah and smiled. "And, girls. Let's load up and roll out. Backup drivers, make sure you get some sleep. We'll be driving straight through, and it's a thirty-hour trip under the best of conditions. I might remind you that it's been more than three years since we've seen anything that remotely resembles the best of conditions. I expect it'll take us about forty hours if we don't have any unanticipated trouble.

"A moving target is harder to hit than one that's sittin' still, but a three-truck convoy is going to get noticed. If we run into a GR patrol, we'll have to fight to the death. We'll never outrun their radios. So that means everyone stays geared up until we get there. It ain't gonna be comfy wearing all this gear, but neither is gettin' shot.

"When we get there, we'll rest up for a day. We'll be laying low on the east side of the Wasatch Range of the Rocky Mountains. Early the next morning, the diversionary team will hit the military base with a few little attention getters that I'm bringing along. Everett's team will take down the water pumping station.

"We've been over the plan. We've drilled, and everyone knows what they're in for. I'm not gonna sugarcoat it. If you live to take it, the trip home is gonna be brutal. If you want to tap out, now is the time."

Everett looked around at Preacher, Devin, and the rest of Tommy's men. They all appeared to have a very strong resolve. And like Tommy, they seemed to be ready to die if necessary.

"Okay, mount up." Tommy got in his truck with four other men. His was the only one without a topper. Instead, he had a blue tarp covering an assortment of heavy weapons that he'd traded for or scavenged on raids against the GR. The other two trucks would each hold four men in the crew cabs and three or four in the beds of the trucks covered by toppers. Preacher, Everett, and Courtney rode in the bed of the Dodge Ram for the first leg of the trip. Kevin drove with Sarah as his relief driver. The middle-aged man from the coal mine, Jeb, and his teenage son, Michael, would be in the back seat of the Dodge. Kevin and Sarah would switch with Everett and Courtney after the first leg of the journey.

The convoy departed from the compound with Tommy in the lead. The truck with the fuel tank drove between the other two trucks as it was the most important vehicle to protect. The Dodge was in the rear of the convoy, so Everett, Courtney, or Preacher had to be watching for vehicles approaching from behind at all times.

"I can take first watch if you two want to get some rest," Preacher offered.

"Thanks, but I'm not the least bit tired." Courtney smiled.

Everett positioned his assault pack against the wheel well and reclined on it. "Me either."

Preacher leaned against the cases of MREs stacked at the front of the bed. "Did Elijah leave yet?"

Everett replied, "No. They'll wait until Tuesday morning to leave. Hopefully, Dragon will be down, and they'll be able to get out of the country."

Courtney added, "If we're delayed or unsuccessful, they should be able to tell that Dragon is still online. In that case, they'll hang around the airport for a couple of days."

Preacher took out a compact Bible and opened it up. "One way or the other, they have to get out." He held the book in the air. "Not one prophecy written in here has ever failed." He lowered the small Bible and began to read.

Everett nodded. "Yeah. You're right."

"It's a blessing to be a part of it all, don't you think?" Preacher glanced up from his reading.

"No doubt." Courtney took Everett's hand. "A little scary at times, but it is an honor."

"And it's definitely not boring." Everett squeezed her hand. "We were feeling a little cooped up in our cave. While not the ideal outing, it's still better than living like a mole."

The three of them chitchatted for the next hour, then Courtney put her head on Everett's shoulder and nodded off to sleep. Preacher continued his reading. Everett prayed silently, asking God to grant them success and to bring Courtney home safely.

The convoy moved slowly through rough roads with deep potholes left by the debris field of Wormwood. They'd take the back roads through West Virginia, Ohio, Indiana, and Illinois. They would then pick up I-80 west once they'd passed Chicago. While it didn't guarantee that they wouldn't have trouble, taking this route greatly reduced the odds of running into a Global Republic patrol.

The first scheduled stop was outside Salem, West Virginia. The team unloaded to stretch their legs and relieve themselves. The trip had taken four hours so far and would take another four for them to arrive at the second scheduled stop, two miles north of Chillicothe, Ohio.

Once they passed the small town of Chillicothe, Everett and Courtney changed places with Kevin and Sarah. They would be the drivers through the next leg of the journey.

Everett greeted the two men in the back of the truck as he got in the driver's seat and started the engine. "Jeb, Michael, I can't say how much you coming along means to us."

Courtney fastened her seat belt. "And we really appreciate your family watching our pets."

Jeb replied, "We're honored that you'd have us. And we're forever in your debt for the food you provided for my wife and daughters."

"And grandpa," Michael added.

"And grandpa," Jeb confirmed. "Cotton wanted

to come with us, but he ain't as fast as he used to be."

"So, your family; you're all Christians?" Courtney inquired.

A tone of regret could be detected in Jeb's voice. "We are now. Wasn't none of us church goin' folk before."

"Obviously." Michael's voice had a note of sarcasm.

Jeb continued. "My mother-in-law, Cotton's wife, she read the Bible every day. Had my oldest boy and one of our daughters readin' it too. Them three, our youngest daughter and my baby boy were all taken in the rapture.

"Course, we figured it out right quick what happened to 'em. The rest of us who was left, we all converted, and got to studyin' grandma's Bible. That's why I say it's an honor to be comin' along with you; to be a part of fulfillin' prophecy and all."

Courtney turned toward the back seat. "I'm sorry for your loss, but you'll be reunited soon."

"Yes, ma'am. It was hard when they disappeared, especially my youngest daughter and the baby. But I'm glad they were spared the hardships we've had to abide."

"Mama took it harder than anyone. Had a real hard time for the first year. She's better, but she's anxious to get on to Glory so she can see her babies." Michael's was the voice of a young man who'd seen his mother suffering great anguish and could barely handle it.

Everett considered all the pain and heartache brought on the world by the Tribulation. With the constant chore of surviving disaster after disaster, the emotional aspect of it all was often overlooked. He said a short silent prayer, thanking God that he and Courtney had not been subjected to the pain of losing a child in the rapture.

Everett followed the convoy as they skirted mid-sized towns and major cities that had the potential to be infested with desperate people willing to do anything for the few supplies they carried with them. The team passed between Dayton and Cincinnati, heading west to Indiana State Road 44, which would take them across the dusty and barren farmland that had once been filled with corn fields. Sunset was a welcome event as the darkness of night served to shroud the hopeless scenery.

The members of the convoy avoided Martinsville Indiana, then having put sufficient distance between themselves and Indianapolis, proceeded north to US-36.

The team stopped at an abandoned bar when they reached the intersection US-36 and Illinois Route 32. The darkness and the building offered visual cover for the team to relieve themselves in an otherwise wide-open and sterile landscape. Sarah and Kevin took the front seats while Everett and Courtney returned to the bed of the truck. The convoy would take Route 32 north to keep away from Decatur.

In all his travels since leaving early that morning, Everett had not seen one single person besides the other members of his team.

Once the convoy was back on the road, Everett lay back on the unrolled sleeping bag. “I think I’ll close my eyes for a while if you don't mind keeping watch, Preacher."

"Rest easy. I'll keep an eye out for trouble." Preacher smiled.

"Wake us if you see anything, or if you start feeling tired." Courtney put her head on Everett's chest and closed her eyes.

"Will do. Sleep tight," Preacher said.

Everett awoke to the sound of Kevin's voice. "Hey, buddy. Think you can drive for a while?"

Everett felt stiff from sleeping on the hard bed of the pickup. "Where are we?"

"Avoca, Iowa."

"That doesn't tell me much." Everett sat up.

"Half an hour from Nebraska," Kevin said.

The sun shined brightly, maybe brighter than Everett had seen it since the ash cloud of Wormwood had darkened the sky. He shielded his eyes. "How long have we been out?"

"A good eight hours," Preacher replied.

Sarah tittered as she crawled into the bed of the truck. "I hope we can sleep that good."

After a cup of cold instant coffee and some long-expired granola bars, Everett and the rest of the team were back on the road. The sunlight once again revealed the desolation of the country, which had once been the world's richest and most prosperous. Now, it was little more than an afterthought of history. The hours crept by as Everett had nothing more to look at besides the truck hauling the fuel tank in front of him and the utter emptiness on either side.

The drivers switched one last time outside of Cheyenne, then continued to their final stop at Bear River State Park just outside of Evanston, Wyoming. The park would serve as the forward operating base.

They arrived at 8:00 PM according to Everett's watch. They'd leave the Dodge, the water tank, the fuel tank, and all the bicycles at the state park, which was one hundred miles from the objective.

Monday would be spent recuperating from the drive. Then, long before dawn on Tuesday, Tommy's team would cram into his truck and go directly to their assault position. Everett, Courtney, Kevin, and Sarah would take the other vehicle straight to the water pump station.

CHAPTER 5

Jesus said unto her, "I am the resurrection, and the life: he that believeth in me, though he were dead, yet shall he live: And whosoever liveth and believeth in me shall never die. Believest thou this?"

John 11:25-26

Everett could see his breath by the ambient light of the truck headlights. He finished his breakfast and glanced at his watch, which had been synchronized to the Mountain Time Zone. "Two thirty. We need to be on the road by three. It could take us two hours to get through those mountains."

Tommy chugged the rest of his coffee. "Yeah. It's gonna be a long day. Come on over to the truck and pick out what you need."

Everett and Kevin walked with Tommy. They watched as he pulled the tarp back from the bed of his pickup and shined his flashlight on a large assortment of rocket-propelled grenades and a few tube-fired weapons. "This here is an AT-4, anti-tank missile. I've got six of these."

"What about that big one?" Everett pointed to the single tube in the middle of the bed.

"That's my pride and joy." Tommy ran his hand over the large green tube.

"That's a Javelin," Kevin said. "It's an anti-everything missile."

Tommy gingerly lifted the giant tube up and stood it on its end. "It cost me a pretty penny. I got all this stuff before Jesus saved me. Well, most of it anyways." He hoisted the Javelin out of the truck and set it at Everett's feet. "I'm giving her to you." He glanced up at Kevin. "You know how to fire one of these, I assume."

"I shot one once in training. It's been a while, but I can figure it out."

Tommy looked like a man who'd just lost his favorite pet as he pulled his hands away from the weapon. "It should take out the wall of the pump house. I expect it'll take down most of the pumps as well, but you'll have the AT-4s to clean up any of the pumps that remain. You said the pump station has four pumps, right?"

"Yeah. That's what Jones had on his diagram." Everett passed the heavy tube to Kevin.

Tommy reached into the back of the truck and extracted four AT-4s, handing the first two to

Everett.

Everett took one in each hand. "Wow, these are a lot lighter."

"And a lot cheaper on the black market. I think they're around fifteen pounds each. That Javelin is about thirty-five pounds." Tommy carried the last two AT-4s over to the pickup Everett would be driving.

Everett followed with the first two shoulder-fired missiles. "That only leaves you two."

"I've got thirty-five RPGs. They don't make quite as big a hole, but I'm just lookin' to create some smoke and racket."

"RPGs will certainly do that." Kevin lugged the large Javelin missile over to the truck on his shoulder.

"We appreciate everything you're doing, Tommy." Everett carefully placed his weapons in the back of the truck.

The big man helped Kevin lower the Javelin into the bed. "It's all for the glory of the kingdom, right?"

"Yes, sir," Everett said.

"I had Devin put just enough fuel to get my truck and this one to the objectives and back." Tommy pointed at the Dodge. "I had him put the rest in the Ram. It's got a full tank. That will get us to Cheyenne. It's still gonna be a long road home." He paused. "For those of us who get out alive."

Everett understood that twenty people weren't going to fit in the Dodge. He knew Tommy's math had already figured on some of them not coming back from the raid.

Tommy looked at the dirt for a moment, then back up. "If you're followed, don't bring 'em back to the state park. You gotta lose your tail before you come back. We'll do the same. If everyone isn't back here at the same time, whoever's first will give the other team twenty-four hours to get back. Remember, if somebody has to shake a tail, they might run out of gas and have to hump it back on foot."

"Agreed." Everett nodded.

"Good. Let's get movin'," Tommy said.

Everett put his hand on the tall man's shoulder. "I think we should pray before we go."

"I think you're right." Tommy turned toward the other men. "Y'all gather round. We're gonna ask the Lord's blessing, then we're gonna go kick some new-world-order tail!"

The men hooted and hollered as they made their way over and formed a circle. They stood with arms locked and grew reverently quiet.

Everett bowed his head and held Courtney's hand. "Father God, we are here to do your will, so we know that your will shall be done on this day. We only ask you for courage, strength, and a good measure of confidence so we might faithfully execute the high honor to which we have been called on this morning. We pray that you will watch over these warriors, and the ones they've left at home. Grant us your perfect peace until you call us home and our worries in this world are no more. Amen."

"Amen." Kevin echoed as he patted Everett on the back.

"Let's go shut down Dragon!" Sarah held her rifle in the air as she marched to the truck.

Everett waved to Tommy and the rest of the team as he, Courtney, Kevin, and Sarah drove off to the pump station. They drove through the mountains, exiting I-80 onto US-40 south to avoid Salt Lake City. Kevin reviewed the plan as they drove.

Once they got closer to Lake Utah and the location of the pump station, Everett slowed his pace, giving Tommy's team ample time to get into position for the diversionary attack on the GR military base.

Kevin rode shotgun. He glanced at his watch. "Tommy's team is supposed to launch their assault at 6:00 AM. We should be in position by 5:45."

"Roger that." The anticipation grew in Everett's stomach as he got closer to the pump station.

Sarah leaned forward. "Let me make sure I've got this straight. We'll fire the Javelin from the truck. From there, we each have to carry an AT-4 to the pump house. Then, we fire an AT-4 at any of the pumps that aren't destroyed. What if we're taking fire? I'm sure they'll have at least a small security force defending the most important water pumps in the world."

Kevin turned to face the back seat. "Then Everett and Courtney will lay down cover fire, and we'll carry two AT-4s each. We'll have our rifles slung over our backs. If it's more than the two of them can fend off, we'll shoot until we thin out the hostiles, then continue with the mission.

"But one way or the other, those pumps have to be taken out. Even if it costs all of us our lives."

Everett glanced at the rearview to see his precious wife in the back seat. He was ready to sacrifice himself. Sarah and Kevin were also acceptable losses, but not Courtney. Somehow, some way, the mission had to be accomplished, and Courtney had to live.

The pump station was on the north side of Lake Utah. Every possible approach forced Everett to drive through neighborhoods, which he did not want to do. The abandoned homes, stranded vehicles, and deserted streets were the perfect ingredients for choke points, traps, and ambushes.

"Everybody, look alive." He kept his attention on the forsaken community roadways, watching for potential roadblocks. "Every one of these dilapidated houses is a potential snare for would-be bandits."

"I'm watching the houses, you just keep driving." Kevin held his rifle with his left hand, ready to fire out the window at the first sign of trouble.

"And keep moving fast," Sarah said from the back. "Don't give anyone an opportunity to hit us."

Everett eventually emerged from the residential streets, turned onto I-15, and followed it four miles to the north side of the lake. He maintained a high speed when he exited and drove to the road which would take them straight to the pump station. He slowed down as he got closer. "How are we looking on time?"

"It's five thirty," Courtney said. "We've still got a half an hour."

"Good. That gives us time to make a quick drive-by." Kevin continued to watch out the window.

Everett proceeded down the perimeter road which followed the contour of the lake. "Look, a sign that says *Pump Station.* They couldn't have made it any easier. I told you, you can't underestimate human complacency and stupidity."

"That's the service road." Kevin pointed ahead. "But let's keep going forward. According to our map, there should be a bridge going over the Jordan River just ahead."

"Crossing the Jordan to take the promised land!" Courtney exclaimed.

Everett pressed his lips together. "Wrong Jordan."

"Wrong promised land, too," Sarah added.

Seconds later, Courtney pointed ahead. "There's the bridge, and a perfect view of the pump station!"

Lights illuminated the concrete building, which had been constructed across the Jordan River like a bridge.

"Correction," Sarah said. "A perfect *shot* to the pump station."

Kevin nodded. "Those are the four intake valves, going straight into the river. From this distance, I should have no trouble hitting the station dead center. No question that the two middle pumps will be out of order. I'm sure it will disable the outer two pumps, but we'll have to get inside to be sure they're beyond repair."

Everett kept driving across the bridge. "What if you try for a direct hit on the third valve? We'd be certain to eliminate that pump, plus the second and fourth pumps on either side. Then, we'd only have to worry about the first water pump. We could hit it with two AT-4s for good measure."

Kevin turned to look at Everett. "I think that could work. But we'll still have to get inside to confirm they're all down."

"Okay." It wasn't for his own sake, but Everett was feverishly trying to reduce the risk for Courtney. "I'll turn around at this park. We can get everything ready, and be back on that bridge at exactly 6:00 AM."

Everett pulled into the parking lot of the inlet park just a few hundred feet away from the bridge.

"I'll take the scope down to the water and see if I can get a visual on any guards around the pump house." Sarah got out of the truck.

"I'll come with you." Courtney was next out of the truck.

Everett and Kevin exited the vehicle, opened the topper and dropped the tailgate.

Kevin prepared all the shoulder-fired missiles for deployment. "Sarah and I will ride on the tailgate, tubes ready to fire. I'll shoot the Javelin, then she'll set off the first AT-4. I'll hit the first valve with a second AT-4 to be certain. We'll toss the tubes on the ground, jump in the truck, and you can drive straight down the service road."

Everett didn't like it, but military decisions were made by Kevin, and he didn't argue.

Minutes later, the girls returned from the bank of the lake.

"Did you see anything?" Everett asked.

"No," Sarah replied. "The river splits as it's emptying into the lake. The pump station isn't even on this fork."

Everett gritted his teeth. "So, we're going in blind."

"Livin' by faith!" Courtney said exuberantly.

"Or stupidity," Everett mumbled.

Kevin looked at his watch. "Time to roll."

"Let's get it over with." Everett got in the truck and started the engine.

Kevin slapped the side of the truck once everyone was in position with their weapons ready.

Everett eased out of the parking lot, careful not to send Kevin and Sarah sliding off the tailgate. He crept onto the bridge, stopped, and looked at his watch. "5:59."

He heard a faint boom in the distance.

"That must have been Tommy's team initiating their attack on the GR military base," Courtney said.

Everett nodded and watched as Kevin lifted the large launch tube, pointing it at the pump house. Kevin fired the weapon, and a bright flash of light and flame flared out of the tube with a loud *whoosh*. The Javelin missile careened into the building, at precisely the point of the third intake valve.

Unable to look away from the spectacle, Everett closed one eye to preserve his night vision on that side.

BOOOOM! A flash of fire and smoke billowed out from the side of the building, mushrooming toward the night sky like an enormous lantern. Brilliant red, shining yellow, and radiant oranges glowed from the center of the cloud. The sound of metal and concrete dropping into the river below could be heard over the echo of the roaring explosion.

Sarah fired the AT-4 at the first intake valve. The missile left a much smaller trail of illuminated smoke as it flew toward the remnant of the pump house. It struck the wall, just above the valve and exploded into a shower of spark and debris. While much less impressive than the Javelin, it too created a bright blast and rumbling clamor. Kevin wasted no time in sending the second AT-4 missile to the target. Another thundering eruption, and another dazzling cloud of flame and smoke.

Sarah and Kevin jumped into the cab of the truck. Kevin yelled, “Drive!”

Everett killed the headlights and sped to the service road. Immediately after turning onto the gravel drive, he saw the beams of several flashlights pointed toward the smoldering pump station. One flashlight turned toward the noise of Everett’s pickup truck rolling across the gravel. It was instantly joined by a second flashlight, then another.

Everett threw the truck into reverse and floored the accelerator.

“What are you doing?” Kevin snapped.

“I’m not running headfirst into a brick wall. If we’re going to do this, we have to be smart about it.” Everett backed onto the perimeter road and let the vehicle roll to a stop. “We can hit them from the bushes on the side of the service road. As long as they keep their lights on, we can see them, but they won’t see us.”

Kevin scowled at Everett as he pushed his door open. “Okay, I guess we’re doing things your way.”

Everett tucked low and led the team toward the brush. The ambient glow from the flashlights revealed the faint forms of six GR peacekeepers jogging up the gravel drive in the direction where the truck had been.

Sarah was the first to take a shot. Everett, Courtney, and Kevin all joined her. Pop, Crack, Crack, Pop, Pop, Crack! The team opened fire and the six peacekeepers were dead before they could locate the source of the rifle fire.

"Should we cross over to the other side of the road and use those bushes as cover to get closer?" Everett looked at Kevin.

"It's your show now, boss. You wanted to lead, now lead." Kevin fumed.

Everett huffed. "Cross one at a time with the other three providing cover. I'll go first, Courtney next, then Sarah, then Kevin." Everett made his way to the edge of the shrubbery, then darted across the road. Courtney followed, then Sarah.

Everett threw his hand up to signal for Kevin not to come. The beams of at least a dozen more flashlights were advancing from a building behind the pump house. "Get down!"

The team lay down in the bushes and waited for the peacekeepers to get in range.

Everett was first to fire, striking the peacekeeper closest to him in the head. The other team members unleashed a barrage of rifle fire on the GR troops. This time, however, the peacekeepers not killed in the initial wave of the assault zeroed in on the muzzle flashes coming from Everett's side of the road.

"Courtney, Sarah, fall back!" Everett continued to shoot, intending to draw the enemy fire while the girls melted into the brush.

Kevin stood up on the other side of the road and screamed as he opened up, killing three more peacekeepers. He'd made himself a more obvious target than Everett, and was now the focus of the GR troop's gun sights.

The flashlight beams shined all over Kevin's body, illuminating the splatters of blood as bullets ripped through his torso, legs, and arms. Kevin continued to pull the trigger as his body dropped into the shrubs on the other side of the gravel drive.

Everett's heart sank as he watched his brother-in-arms and his brother-in-Christ fall to the cold earth below. "Oh no, Kevin."

Everett shot two more troops, leaving three flashlights still moving around and soon pointing straight in Everett's general direction. Quickly, he began to move backward. He continued to take pot-shots as he retreated, in hopes of luring the remainder of the GR force to himself and away from Courtney.

He turned around and began sprinting through the tall grass in the opposite direction from the truck. Pow! POP! Pow! Zing! Everett heard a bullet sail right by his ear. He felt the wind caused by the projectile breeze across the back of his neck. He rolled to the ground and spun about to engage his pursuers from a prone position. Crack, crack, crack! His rifle spit out round after round, dropping two of the GR troops. The last peacekeeper was still barreling right for him, firing at Everett as he ran.

The man was nearly at point-blank range and the peacekeeper's weapon ceased with a tell-tale click of his rifle bolt locking open.

Everett looked the man in the eye. For a brief second, neither of them moved. Everett lay in the tall grass, with the barrel of his gun pointed up at the man standing six feet away. In turn, the peacekeeper stared at Everett, the man now holding his life in his hand. He stood motionless.

Suddenly, the peacekeeper hit the magazine release button, dropping the spent mag to the ground. He instantly reached for another magazine on the front of his vest.

POOOOW! The shot from Everett's rifle rang out and echoed into the darkness. The man lurched forward, falling directly in front of Everett. The hole in the peacekeeper's head landed just inches from Everett's nose. Blood streamed out of the dead man's head. Everett rolled aside to see the headlights of a Humvee turning off the gravel road and rushing in his direction.

"Oh, no. They've got a man in the turret with a fifty-cal and a spotlight. I'll never outrun them. And I've got nowhere to hide." Everett quickly changed his magazine and prepared to fight it out to the end.

The man in the turret worked the spotlight, shining it on each dead peacekeeper's flashlights strewn about the field where they'd fallen. The spotlight went from one troop to the other, like a game of connect-the-dots. The final dot was Everett, and they were closing in fast. Everett lay still in the tall grass waiting. Soon, the light shined straight at him.

Everett fired, taking out the light. He released a volley of bullets and took out the man in the turret before the fifty-cal started shooting, but now the vehicle was right on top of him. Someone else would soon be in that turret, and a flood of troops would come pouring out the doors of the Humvee. Everett didn't stand a chance.

BOOOM! Light, fire, smoke, ash, rubber, and metal shot into the air as an intense flash of white-hot heat sent the Hummer into flight, flipping it upside down. The Humvee sailed over Everett's head. Instinctively, he put his face down into the grass and covered his head with his hands. The seconds felt like hours as the vehicle was suspended a few feet above his body. Finally, he felt the earth rumble beneath him as the Humvee landed on its rear bumper two yards from Everett's feet. He looked behind him. The truck was vertical, like a pillar of Stonehenge, in suspended animation. He could hear the distressed metal creaking as the giant monolith lurched to fall, but in the darkness, he could not tell which way it would drop.

Everett wasted no more time in speculation. He jumped to his feet and lunged away from the descending mass of iron. SWOOP! The Humvee accelerated as it came crashing down to a more stable position. SMASH! The impact was enough to cause Everett to lose his footing and fall to his knees. The vehicle lay on its back, resting right where he'd been only moments before.

Everett breathed a deep sigh of relief. He looked up to see two figures racing in his direction. "Oh, no! My rifle! It's under the Humvee!" He rapidly drew his Sig from the holster on the front of his load bearing vest. It was no match for rifles, but he wasn't about to surrender without a fight.

"Everett!" One of the figures running toward him was Courtney.

The other was Sarah. She still held the spent tube of the AT-4 she'd used to take out the Humvee.

He lowered the pistol and sat back on his feet while he caught his breath.

The two girls arrived at his location. "Are you okay?" Courtney asked.

"Yeah, are you?" He looked her over in the light of the burning fuel from the Hummer.

"We're good. We have to find Kevin," Sarah answered.

Everett looked back at the blazing inferno of the Humvee. "My rifle, I need my gun."

"Forget it. Here, take one of the peacekeeper's weapons." Sarah grabbed a rifle from the nearest soldier.

Everett took it from her as he stood up. "I'll need their magazines then." He hurried to discard the remainder of his magazines and quickly collected several from the fallen troops, stuffing them into the pouches on the front of his vest.

"Did you see where Kevin went?" Sarah asked as they began moving back toward the GR compound.

He couldn't speak. His voice was gone, like in a dream when one tries to scream but can't. *Maybe it is a dream*, he thought.

"Everett, I asked you a question. Are you okay?" Sarah paused and turned to look him in the eye.

Everett forced himself to open his mouth but once again, nothing came out. He dropped his head and wagged it from side to side.

"Everett! What are you saying?" Sarah's voice grew frantic. "Everett?"

He looked back up at her with compassion.

"No!" she yelled. "No," she pleaded. "No," she moaned. Her eyes welled up with tears. Her rifle dropped to her side, then she let go of it and let her weapon fall to the ground.

Everett felt horrible for her, but a terrible thought crossed his mind as he watched her pain. A thought he couldn't control, one that came like a reflex when the doctor hits the knee with a mallet. *I'm glad it wasn't Courtney.*

Then a thought far worse came. It too came without invitation or will. Unstoppable, unavoidable, a dirty little voice from the darkest part of his soul said, *I'm glad it wasn't me*.

The first thought was understandable, forgivable even. But not the second. It was reprehensible, shameful, and wicked. Suddenly Everett could not stomach being in his own skin. Instantly, the self-loathing set in, and he wished it had been him who'd died. Kevin was at peace. Everett was wracked by guilt and dishonor. No bullet could ever inflict the pain that Everett's own psyche imposed upon his being in that moment.

Sarah was paralyzed by grief, Everett was frozen by shame. Courtney grabbed Sarah and pulled her head to her chest. "Shhh. Sarah. We have to keep going. We have to wrap this up. We'll find Kevin, but we have to finish what we came here for."

Sarah grimaced in utter agony. She wiped her eyes with her wrists and nodded her head. Everett also found the resolve to keep going forward. Courtney led the way back to the edge of the brush and knelt down.

Everett shook off his self-hatred long enough to resume the lead. He peered around the corner of the shrubbery and down the gravel drive. All was silent and motionless. "We'll proceed with extreme caution. You two stay back at least fifteen feet from me." If anyone else was going to get shot on this mission, Everett was determined that it should be himself.

Twice, Everett had to go back and tell Courtney to stay off the road and inside the concealment of the brush.

"But you're out in the road," she argued the second time.

"Just stay in the bushes. Don't worry about me," he scolded.

"But I am worried about you!"

He turned away and kept advancing. Lights were on inside the building next to the pump station, but he saw no movement. He crouched down and waited for the girls to reach his position. "I'll go in and clear the building. You two stay outside and take down out anyone I flush out."

"No way! You're not going in by yourself. We've never trained like that, and we're not going to do it now," Courtney demanded.

"Fine. Stack up behind me at the door." Everett scowled.

The three of them made entry and cleared the

building room by room. The door at the end of the hall was locked. Everett looked in the window but saw no one. "There was an open gun safe in the front office. We'll fall back and see if they have a shotgun to breach this door. It's locked for a reason."

Sarah led the way back to the office, Everett watching their six and Courtney in the middle. Once in the room, Everett checked the safe. "Riot gun." He slid the pump on the shotgun backward, ejecting the shell. "Double-aught buck. It ain't a slug, but it should knock that lock off."

He racked the pump forward, sliding another shell into the chamber, and led the team back to the locked door. Everett held the barrel at a 45-degree angle up and out from the lock. "Boom!" He struck the keyed door knob with the butt of the shotgun and the fragments fell away.

Everett dropped the shotgun and held up his rifle as he led the entry team into the room.

"Stop! Stop! We surrender!" Four hands appeared from behind a desk.

"Step out!" Everett ordered.

Two men came out from behind the desk. Both wore casual pants and polo shirts. Neither looked like GR troops, and neither had the distinct accent of foreigners from other English-speaking countries that the Global Republic liked to send to police the former United States.

Everett looked at the badges hanging from the lanyards around their necks. "GRSA. You two worked for NSA before?"

"Yes, sir. We were the engineers who ran the

pumping facility," one said.

"Non-combatants," the other added.

Everett chuckled as he leveled the rifle. "I worked for CIA." He nodded toward Courtney. "She sub-contracted for NSA. There may be such thing as naive, stupid even. But don't kid yourselves, just because you don't carry a weapon doesn't make you a non-combatant. Especially when you enable that hideous thing up the river from here."

One man shook his head. "We don't want to know where you worked or anything about you. Just take what you need and go. We didn't see you, and we won't say a word."

"I'm supposed to trust people who knowingly support a system that beheads Christians? Even if I did believe you, you're engineers. You'd help bring this beast, Dragon, back online. And we simply can't have that. Do you both have the Mark?"

The two men seemed to not understand why he'd ask such a thing in the midst of the assault. They each showed the raised bump on the back of their hands which held the pico projectors of their Mark implant systems.

"Then we don't have anything else to talk about, I'm afraid." Everett fired two rounds in quick succession and dropped the two engineers dead where they stood.

He lowered his rifle and turned to Courtney and Sarah. "If there were any other troops who wanted to engage us, they'd have done so by now. We'll remain cautious, but most likely, all the peacekeepers are dead, or they've fled the scene.

"Let's go check the pump house." Everett kept his rifle at a low-ready position as he led the team to the pile of rubble that had been the pumping station. The glowing embers of the wood-framed roof provided enough light to confirm that all four pumps were no longer operational, and were indeed, totally annihilated.

Sarah looked on at the destruction. "So, we could have just hit it and run. Kevin died for nothing."

"Don't say that." Courtney put her hand on Sarah to console her.

"Let's find Kevin and get out of here." Everett knew exactly where his friend lay. The valiant soldier had been called home, while the man who thought such disgusting things like *I'm glad it wasn't me*, still disgraced the Earth with his presence.

Everett's pain, shame, guilt, and heartache hit him like a tsunami when he saw Kevin's lifeless body lying in the shrubs where he'd fallen. Waves of sorrow overtook him. He knelt down by the man who'd become a brother over the past three years. He hugged Kevin's corpse.

Sarah bawled like only a widow could. Courtney sobbed softly as she comforted her friend. Everett dried his eyes and hoisted his fallen friend on his shoulder. Courtney helped Sarah walk behind, like an anemic funeral procession.

Everett placed the body of Kevin in the bed of the truck.

Sarah grabbed Everett's arm and pleaded with him desperately. "Maybe God will bring him back to us again, Everett. Maybe if you ask him, He'll listen to you."

Everett knew that if God would listen to anyone on the planet right now, it certainly wouldn't be him. He shook his head. "No. I can't"

Sarah squeezed his arm tighter. "Why not? Why won't you try?"

Everett looked at Courtney as if to beg for help. "Because. God won't listen to me." Confronted by his own shame, he began to cry again.

"Everett, just pray. Just ask. If God says no, so be it, but we have to ask." Now Sarah's pleas were like those of a small child who wanted to believe so badly.

Everett dropped his head. Unable to cover up his sin, he confessed. "God hates me. You don't know what I've done. You don't know the thoughts I've had. I don't even know if I'm a Christian."

"What could be so bad?" Sarah asked.

Everett hated to disappoint Courtney. He looked up at her with self-condemning eyes and divulged his trespasses. "I couldn't stop the thought, but after Kevin died, something inside me said, I'm glad it wasn't Courtney."

Sarah put her arm around him. "Oh, Everett. She's your wife. Don't you know that's normal?"

His head sunk lower as he whispered the next dreadful phrase. "Then the voice said *I'm glad it wasn't me*. Kevin was twice the man I ever was. I don't deserve to live."

Sarah shook her head. "You snap out of it, Everett. That's so common in battle. I had to go through counseling when I came back from the desert. I watched a couple of my buddies die, I thought the same thing you thought, and I went through exactly what you're going through. It's reactionary. It's a reflex. It's that deep-seated instinct of self-preservation. You can't stop it. Don't do this to yourself. You don't really believe those things, or you wouldn't be feeling so guilty. Don't you see that?"

Everett quickly did the math in his head. She was right. If he was truly glad that it was Kevin and not him, he wouldn't be in the undone state in which he now found himself. Everett cleared his head. Still distraught, he nodded. "Okay. We'll all pray together."

They each put a hand on Kevin's body. Everett began, "Jesus, you are the resurrection and the life. He that believes in you, though he shall die, yet shall he live. We pray that you would send our brother back to us. We know that you can."

Courtney prayed a short prayer asking God to once again, resurrect Kevin.

Sarah prayed last. "God, you've been too good to us. I thank you for our second chance, for salvation, for bringing Kevin back before, for restoring my leg. But God, he's all I have on this earth. Yes, I cherish the friendship of Everett and Courtney, but Kevin was mine, and I was his in a way that only husband and wife can be. Please God, I would gladly give you back my leg to have him by my side for just one more day." She sobbed, and they all waited quietly to see what God might do.

Minutes later, Sarah looked up with sad eyes. "God's not bringing him back. I can feel it in my spirit."

Courtney hugged her tightly.

Sarah nodded as she cried. “But somehow, I can feel that God is going to give me the grace to get through it.”

Everett put his arm around Sarah. “Thank you for not hating me for my evil thoughts.”

“I don’t hate you, Everett. I never could. And for what it’s worth, you were right to back the truck out of the drive when we were being identified by the peacekeepers. Don’t let the devil tell you that this wouldn’t have happened if you’d stuck to Kevin’s plan. I’ll love him for eternity, but he was wrong on that one. And if he were here, he’d admit it. So, don’t feel like you left on a sour note. We’re family. Families disagree. Sometimes they even fight. And that’s okay. It doesn’t mean they don’t love each other.”

Tears ran down Everett’s cheeks as the Holy Spirit used Sarah to comfort his soul.

Courtney pointed to the remaining AT-4 in the bed of the truck. “What about this? Think we could use it to eliminate that electrical substation by the pump house? It’ll take them that much longer to get Dragon back online if they have to bring in a load of transformers in addition to a new pump facility.”

“Let’s do it for Kevin.” Sarah dried her eyes and smiled.

“For Kevin.” Everett nodded and closed the tailgate.

They all loaded into the truck and drove up to the substation. Once there, they exited the vehicle. Everett took the AT-4 out of the bed and offered it to Sarah. “Would you like to do the honors?”

She gave a slight smile and took the tube. She aimed it at the center of the substation and launched the missile.

BOOM! Transformers exploded into a shower of sparks and dazzling blue flames.

Sarah tossed the spent tube to the ground. "We better get out of here."

Everett made his way back to the driver's seat. "Yeah, I'd say we've officially worn out our welcome."

Everett started the engine and began to drive away.

"Wait!" Courtney exclaimed from the passenger's seat.

Everett took his foot off the accelerator. "What is it?"

"Those two cars in the lot. I bet they're the engineers' cars."

Everett looked over to see a Volvo wagon and a Subaru Outback. "Let me guess. You want to get their gas."

"Every gallon we get is about 20 miles we don't have to bike in the middle of winter." Courtney released her seat belt.

Everett tightened his jaw. "I'm worried that a security force is going to show up any minute."

"Ten gallons of gas could shave four days off our trip home." Courtney's hand was already on the door handle.

Everett drove up to the side of the two vehicles and put the truck in park. "We've got to move fast."

All three of them exited the vehicle.

"We need containers. I'll check inside." Sarah

started toward the building.

"I'll go with you." Courtney jogged behind her.

"I'll stand guard. Hurry!" Everett kept watch and removed the gas cap of the truck while he waited for the girls to return.

Less than a minute later, the two girls returned with a collection of receptacles ranging from coffee cups to small plastic organizer totes.

Everett lay on the ground and slid beneath the Volvo. "Hand me a container."

Courtney passed him a water pitcher. "We found this in the fridge."

Everett took the pitcher and positioned it near the low point of the gas tank. He drew his pocket knife and slammed it into the tank. A slight trickle of gas began to leak out. Everett wedged the blade deeper into the tank and pried the hole to make it larger. Soon, a steady stream of gas poured from the tank. "Quick, give me another container!"

Courtney slid a large Tupperware bowl to Everett.

He quickly switched the bowl for the pitcher and passed it to Courtney. "Have Sarah pour this into the truck and bring it back."

Everett was unsure how much fuel they'd obtained when the tank finally ran dry. He quickly slid beneath the Subaru and repeated the process.

Ten minutes into the second tank, Sarah called out, "The truck is full."

"Just keep giving me containers. We'll figure out what to do with it once the tank is tapped." Everett continued to pass the full containers to Courtney.

Everett was down to the office coffee pot when

the tank gave its last drop. He squirmed back out from under the Subaru and sat up. "How much do we have left over?"

Courtney looked at the various containers lying about. "It looks like about four gallons."

Sarah turned back toward the building. "The water cooler! The bottle on it was five gallons."

Everett quickly retrieved his medical kit from his assault pack and dug out the duct tape. When Sarah returned with the giant water bottle from the office cooler, she dumped out the water. Then, the three of them poured the remaining gas inside it. Everett made a make-shift cap from the duct tape, placed the bottle in the truck, and hurried back to the driver's seat.

"I hear vehicles!" Courtney shouted as she slammed her door. "They're coming from the north. We'll have to go the other way."

Everett sped out of the lot, turning toward the inlet park and away from the direction they needed to go. Everett pointed to the passenger's side visor. "The map is right there."

The sun was coming up, so they were quickly losing the cover of darkness. Courtney opened the map and studied it for a moment. "Hang a right here and a left on 68!"

Everett made the maneuver at the highest possible speed. "Sarah, hang on to that bottle with the gas. Don't let it tip over."

"I've got the gas. Just worry about getting us out of here," she replied.

Everett took the next left turn and stomped the gas pedal. "How far out of the way is it going to take us to get around the lake?"

Courtney inspected the map a little longer and looked up. "I'd guess about fifty miles, but at least we have plenty of gas."

Everett looked in the rearview to see if they were being pursued. "We don't really have plenty of gas, but if we get out of here without being caught, it'll be a net gain on the fuel situation."

He kept the speedometer near 120 down the long straight stretch of road. The truck could have gone faster, but at any second, he could happen on a pothole left by Wormwood's debris field or a fissure created by one of the many quakes. Seventy miles per hour was no longer considered a safe speed, so 120 was pure madness. Nevertheless, Everett chose to take his chances with the dilapidated roads rather than a squad of GR peacekeepers.

He continued to look in the side view mirror. Not seeing anything, he slowed to a hundred miles per hour to give himself more time to brake if he were to happen upon a seriously damaged section of road.

Sarah leaned forward. "We're going to have to bury Kevin when we get back to Bear River."

Everett nodded.

Her voice was sad. "If you feel like it's safe, like we're not being followed, I'd appreciate it if we could stop so I could ride in the bed of the truck. I'm not going to get much of a chance to say goodbye."

Everett's heart broke for her. "Okay, once we get to the south side of the lake, I'll look for a place to pull over."

"Thank you, Everett."

Fifteen minutes later, Courtney pointed ahead. "This should be US-6. Take a left there. It might be a good place to pull over."

Everett took the turn, then pulled off to the side of the road. Sarah quickly got out and went back to the bed of the truck to spend a few precious moments with Kevin before they committed his body to the earth.

CHAPTER 6

For he shall give his angels charge over thee, to keep thee in all thy ways. They shall bear thee up in their hands, lest thou dash thy foot against a stone.

Psalm 91:11-12

Absolute exhaustion hit Everett as he tossed the last shovel of dirt out of the hole, which would be Kevin's grave. He'd volunteered to do the digging, so Courtney could help Sarah with getting Kevin cleaned up.

Sarah selected the peaceful resting place near the Bear River, just a few hundred yards from the staging area where they were to meet Tommy and the rest of his crew.

Everett looked toward the park entrance as he climbed out of the hole. No one from Tommy's team was back yet. "They should have been back hours ago." Everett walked over to the edge of the river and rinsed his face and hands, being careful not to get any of the water in his eyes or mouth. Arsenic levels out west were nowhere near as high as they were back home, but he still wanted to limit his exposure.

Everett carried his shovel back to the truck, where Sarah sat with Kevin's head resting in her lap. "Are you ready?"

"No." Sarah stared at Kevin's face. "But I probably never will be, so we can go ahead. Besides, the more I look at him like this, the harder it will be to remember him as he was."

"Okay." Everett's voice was solemn. "I'll drive the truck over to the grave site. You and Courtney can stay in the back with Kevin."

Sarah nodded as she stroked Kevin's hair.

Everett drove the truck to the pit in the earth, then he walked to the rear of the vehicle and opened the small Bible he carried. He read the 23rd Psalm, then prayed for God to comfort Sarah.

Next, he, Courtney, and Sarah used several strands of paracord to lower Kevin's body down into the hole. Sarah stared blankly at the grave, then began to weep bitterly as Everett started to fill it back up with the dirt he'd excavated just a short while earlier.

Once the grave was covered, Sarah asked, "Do you two mind if I stay here alone until Tommy and the others return?"

"Not at all. We'll be over by the pavilion if you need us." Courtney gave her a hug, then got into the truck with Everett.

Once back to the staging area, Everett and Courtney ate two MREs. "You look tired," Courtney said as she ate.

"It's been a long day."

"We won," she said. "We accomplished what we came here to do."

"This victory doesn't seem very sweet." Everett continued eating because he had to, not because he wanted to.

"Even if he knew it would be the last thing he ever did, Kevin would do it all over again. He'd see it as a win. I think we owe it to him to acknowledge the success. We owe it to Kevin to keep on living our lives." She took his hand. "And we owe it to each other."

Everett turned to her and smiled. "Yeah, you're right." He set the rest of his meal on the tailgate and hugged her. "I'm so glad I've still got you."

That evening, the sun set behind the mountains to the west, and Tommy's team still didn't return. Everett finished securing the fuel tank trailer to the back of the water tank trailer, which was hitched to the Dodge crew cab. He looked up to see Courtney returning from the grave site alone. "Is she alright?"

"She's fine, but she wants to sleep there tonight. She'll never get a chance to visit his grave again."

"I can understand that." Everett knew they'd all be reunited in less than four years, but that fact wouldn't have eased his sorrow if it had been

Courtney who died, so he wouldn't act as if it should for Sarah.

"How long will we wait for Tommy tomorrow?"

"The agreement was twenty-four hours. So just after sunrise." Everett hurried to get the gas drained from the truck they'd taken on the raid. He wanted to finish before dark. "They must have gotten in some real trouble. They had a shorter drive than we did."

Courtney helped him by pouring the gasoline into the fuel trailer and returning the receptacles to Everett. "Tommy would give us a little more time if we weren't back by dawn."

"We can wait until noon, but if they're not back by then, it's likely that none of them survived."

The next morning at sunrise, Everett read his Bible, then prayed that God would bring Tommy and the others back safely. Courtney took an MRE to Sarah down by the river, then returned. The morning hours inched by as Everett kept watch for Tommy.

"It's noon, I guess we should get going, huh?" Courtney asked.

Everett nodded in disappointment.

"I'll go tell Sarah it's time to go." Courtney headed toward the river one last time.

Everett evaluated the items they were taking with them and the ones they were leaving behind. He wanted to be sure they had everything that might be of value in case they got the opportunity to trade for gas. But at the same time, he didn't want to carry extra weight that would cause them to expend additional fuel.

Everett heard a faint clip-clop in the distance. It took a moment for the subtle sound to register in his mind. "Horses." Everett drew his rifle and looked to see who was coming. He saw two riders near the park entrance. One was large in stature. He lifted his rifle to look through the scope. "Tommy!"

Everett lowered the weapon and sprinted toward his buddy. He soon recognized Preacher as being the other rider.

"Thanks for waiting," Tommy yelled as they drew closer.

"Where's everybody else?"

"Dead." Preacher slung his leg over the saddle and stepped down. "All of them, Devin, Jeb, Michael, everybody."

Tommy's horse looked like it was ready to drop. Tommy looked worse. "Are either of you injured?" Everett looked them over for apparent wounds.

"No." Tommy slowly got down from the horse. "But I could do with some water."

"Of course. You're probably hungry also." Everett led the two men back toward the vehicles.

"Did you shut it down?" Tommy asked.

"We cut the water pumps. I've scrolled through the radio stations a few times, but I can't pick anything up, so I don't have any way of confirming that Dragon is down." Everett offered filled canteens to Tommy and Preacher.

"How's your team?" Tommy took a long drink.

"Kevin was killed. The rest of us made it out."

Courtney and Sarah arrived back at the truck.

"Is everyone else coming?" Courtney asked.

Preacher finished his canteen and gave it to Everett to refill. "We hit the base hard and took off. We made it back into the mountains and thought we were home free, but then four Humvees caught us. They shot out our tires, so we had to stick Tommy's truck in the ditch and take off into the mountains. Everyone else was gunned down. The peacekeepers finally gave up on us, I guess."

Tommy tore into an MRE. "If we took down Dragon, they'll resume the search today. They'll widen the perimeter, too. We best be getting on our way."

Everett nodded. "Okay, let me rig up two more bikes to the cargo rack on the Dodge. Otherwise, we're ready to roll out."

Ten minutes later, the team was on the road. Everett drove, and Courtney rode shotgun, with Sarah in the back seat. Preacher and Tommy slept in the bed of the truck as they'd been traveling all night long. Everett kept the speed at 55, both to watch for potholes, and to maximize fuel efficiency. Because of the slower speed, they didn't reach Cheyenne until after dark. They used flashlights to fill the gas tank.

Tommy and Preacher drove for the next leg of the journey while Everett, Courtney, and Sarah slept in the back of the Dodge.

Everett woke up after a long ride. The sun was up and the vehicle wasn't moving. He heard voices talking outside. Everett's heart raced, and he reached for his gun. He peeked out the side window of the topper to see Tommy and Preacher speaking to five well-armed men, all wearing overalls. Everett couldn't make out what they were saying, but the interaction didn't appear to be hostile.

He nudged Courtney and Sarah. He whispered, "Girls, something is going on outside. I don't think it's trouble, but I'd rather be safe than sorry. Get your guns."

Courtney and Sarah each grabbed their weapons. "What's happening?" Sarah asked.

Everett described the scene out the window. "Tommy and Preacher don't have their weapons drawn, neither do the other guys. Tommy's turning his back on them and walking this way."

Tommy opened the back window of the topper. "Good mornin'."

"Everything okay out there?" Everett asked cautiously.

"Better than okay." Tommy smiled. "I'm swapping our excess food, ammo, and weapons for ethanol; enough to get us home. These fellas started converting their surplus corn into fuel after the initial false flag attacks on the oil refineries way back when.

"Can you slide all the boxes of MREs except one to me? And I need Courtney's rifle. Everett and Sarah, I need your side arms. Magazines too, please."

"Nope. You said extra. That rifle and these two pistols are not extra," Sarah protested.

Tommy's reply was patient but direct. "They're extra because we'll be home tomorrow instead of next month."

Sarah looked at Everett. "You've got to tell him,

we need our weapons to get back safely."

Everett looked at Tommy. "What weapons are you guys keeping?"

"I'll hang onto my rifle and Preacher will have his pistol. Everyone will still have a firearm for the trip home. But I had to do some heavy negotiating to get the price down to what we have. They wanted all the rifles."

Sarah scowled. "What about supply and demand? They don't have many customers to sell to. Why can't you ask them to just take the food and extra ammo for trade?"

Tommy chuckled. "The way they understand supply and demand is that ain't no more corn gonna grow in arsenic ridden soil. On top of that, they see a truck with empty gas tank more than a thousand miles from home. We don't exactly have the strongest hand at the table."

Tommy looked at Everett and winked. "On top of all of it, it seems the Mark payment systems are experiencing some technical difficulties, and these folks think that might mean more demand for their fine product."

Courtney put her arms around Everett's neck and kissed him on the cheek. "We did it! We took down Dragon!"

Everett took a moment to drink in the elation of success. He then looked at Sarah. "I have to agree with Tommy on this one. I'd rather take our chances with a limited amount of firepower. We'll be totally exposed the whole trip home if we have to travel a thousand miles by bike. Not to mention, we'll have to choose between carrying food or weapons anyway. And once we get home, we've got an entire cave full of weapons and ammo."

Sarah continued to pick the plan apart. "This engine won't run on pure ethanol, especially in the winter."

"Winter ain't gonna matter," Tommy said. "We ain't gonna turn the motor off long enough for it to get cold. And I'm not worried about long term damage. I'm more concerned with gettin' home than the resale value."

"Fine." Sarah drew her pistol and passed it to Tommy.

Courtney handed Tommy her rifle and spare magazines. "This has to be a miracle from God. How did you know they had fuel?"

Tommy collected the items to be traded. "Hand painted sign on the side of the road back there said *Ethanol for serious trade*."

Everett considered Courtney's words as he passed the remaining boxes to Tommy. She was right. This had to be a gift from the Almighty.

CHAPTER 7

And Ruth said, Intreat me not to leave thee, or to return from following after thee: for whither thou goest, I will go; and where thou lodgest, I will lodge: thy people shall be my people, and thy God my God: Where thou diest, will I die, and there will I be buried: the Lord do so to me, and more also, if ought but death part thee and me.

Ruth 1:16-17

The team arrived safely back to Tommy's compound Friday morning. Tommy gave Devin's Jeep to Everett to take home from his farm. Everett pulled the distributor cap from the Jeep when they reached the landslide area to keep it from being stolen. Then, he and the two girls rode across the debris field and back to the cave on the last remaining quadrunner.

The sun had not yet risen when Everett, Courtney, and Sarah returned to the cave. Everett was exhausted, but he was also filthy. He pushed himself to go through the laborious process of drawing bathing water from the well, which was up the ladder, and down a long, narrow corridor. Once there, Everett had to draw the water up by a string tied to a five-gallon bucket, which was weighted on one side, so it would tip over into the water, once it reached the well. Next, the water was poured into a funnel, which fed into a series of PVC pipes that the team had scavenged from various places. The pipes used gravity to pull the water through the corridor, and down into a fifty-five-gallon drum sitting at the base of the ladder. Once the drum was full, they had water for cooking, drinking, and bathing. If anyone desired something besides the frigid cave water for bathing, heating the water was another long process. On this day, Everett settled for an icy cat-bath.

Sarah was more concerned with the lack of armaments. Immediately after returning home, she climbed to the storage corridor to dig out replacement pistols, rifles, ammunition, and magazines.

Courtney plopped down on her sleeping bag and went right to sleep.

Everett awoke late Friday evening to the sound of Courtney and Sarah heating water for bathing. The closest thing the cave dwellers had to a proper bath facility was a five-gallon camping shower hung around a stalagmite in a remote corner of the cave. An old sheet draped between two more stalagmites served as the shower curtain. And regardless of how hot the shower water was, the surrounding air was piercingly gelid.

Courtney took her shower first, then came over to the living area of the great room in the cave referred to by the team as the cathedral. She shivered as she got dressed. Next, she crawled back into her sleeping bag to warm up. "I hate going through this in the winter."

Everett snickered. "The cave is the same temperature all year round. It's always cold."

She covered her head and mumbled through the sleeping bag. "Yeah, but in the summer, you can go outside and warm up."

Minutes later, Sarah returned, also shivering. She repeated Courtney's method of getting warm.

Everett looked on at Kevin's empty spot, illuminated by the old battery-operated lantern sitting upon a stack of empty buckets. The five-gallon containers which had been filled with supplies three years ago now served as make-shift furniture. Four of them held a panel of plywood which made a table. Six more buckets surrounded the table for chairs. Moses, Elijah, and Kevin's chairs were now vacant.

Everett had to do something to dispel the void left in the dreary cavern created by the absence of his friends. "I'm going to go get Sox and Danger tomorrow. If no one has any objection, I'm going to take ten buckets of food over to Cotton's family.

With Jeb and Michael gone, they'll have a tough time surviving."

Courtney sat up. "I'll go with you."

Sarah popped her head out of the covers. "Then I'm going, too. I can't stay here by myself. I'm not ready for that."

Everett understood. "Okay."

He offered Sarah a smile, but it was more than she could do to return the gesture.

"What's that?" Courtney shined her flashlight at the corner of the cave where Elijah's sleeping area had been.

Everett turned to gaze into the dark region of the cavern. "A walking stick?"

"No." Courtney crawled out of her sleeping bag and stood up. She walked to the back section of the room and retrieved the object. "It's Moses' staff!"

"Like I said, a walking stick," Everett said.

"Everett, this is the staff he used to part the Red Sea, to call the plague of locusts, to summon the plague of frogs, to bring down hail and darkness on Egypt!" She stood mesmerized by the staff. She looked up at Everett and Sarah. "And most importantly, to turn water to blood!"

Everett shook his head. "Why do you say most importantly?"

"Because!" she exclaimed. "Revelation 11 says the two witnesses will have the power to make it not rain, to strike the Earth with plagues, and to turn the water to blood! What if Moses needs his staff to turn the water to blood? God gave him that power when he was here before. Elijah had the power to make it not rain, and Moses used his staff to turn the water to blood. Everett, we have to go to Jerusalem! We have to take Moses' staff to him!"

Everett exhaled deeply and rolled his eyes. "He doesn't need his staff. For all we know, he may have left it here for us."

She pleaded, "Everett, you are not being reasonable. Don't you see, he has to have this staff to fulfill the prophecy."

Sarah looked on, listening intently.

Everett pulled out his Bible and thumbed through the pages to Exodus. "What version are you reading? The Message? The NLT? Because the King James doesn't say anything like that."

"Everett, I'm reading the New King James. It's not that different." Her voice sounded insulted, as if she was being accused of reading some perverted text or being charged with heresy.

Everett shined his flashlight on his Bible. "Okay, Exodus 4, God tells Moses to cast his rod on the ground, and it turns into a snake. But this is when God is giving him his commission. That one was for Moses, so he'd believe."

"Yeah, then he throws it down as a sign to Pharaoh." Courtney stood holding the staff as if she were afraid of dropping it and the stick becoming a serpent.

Everett held up a finger. "Next, we have Exodus 7:10. *Aaron* cast *his* rod down, and it became a snake. Then in verse 19, Moses tells *Aaron* to strike the waters and turn them to blood."

Everett flipped the page. "Exodus 8:5, God instructs Moses to tell *Aaron* to hold *his* rod over the water to summon the frogs."

"Are you serious?" Courtney carefully leaned the staff against the wall of the cave and retrieved her Bible.

"I wouldn't kid around about the Bible." Everett scanned the page. "Verse 17. *Aaron* stretches out *his* rod and turns the dust into lice."

Sarah joined the conversation. "What about the Red Sea. That was the rod of Moses. I know it for a fact."

Everett held up his hand as if to stop traffic. "Ah, that's the Hollywood version, not the Bible." Everett thumbed past the pages. "Exodus 14:21. Moses holds up his *hands* and God causes the sea to part, doesn't say anything about a rod or a staff. Same thing when the sea comes back on the Egyptians. God tells Moses to just stretch out his *hands*. Verse, 26 and 27"

Courtney flipped through her Bible, carefully studying the text. "I can't believe I got all of that wrong."

"The Devil has been making people think God's Word says something it doesn't since the beginning of time. Eve, in the garden. Satan comes to her and asks, 'hath God said?' And of course, she gets it wrong. God said not to eat of the tree or they'd die. She comes back with 'we can't eat it or touch it, or we'll die.' She started adding to God's Word.

"Then Satan gets her to believe that God's Word doesn't mean what it says. He tells her that she won't die. She believes him over God's Word. And here we are, 6,000 years later, hiding out in a cave, avoiding the wrath of God."

"Why did you say it like that?" Courtney crossed

her arms.

"Say what?" Everett sensed he was in trouble, but he wasn't sure for what.

"Of course she got it wrong." Her lips tightened. "Because she was a woman?"

"No, no." Everett shook his head and laughed. "Look how many pastors were still here after the rapture. They were mostly all men. They got it wrong. I said *of course* because it's human to get it wrong. I'm sure I get lots of stuff wrong, but it's because I read it and misinterpreted it for myself. I'm sure God will be much more tolerant of me than the people who got it wrong because they listened to some pastor who told them what they wanted to hear instead of studying the Bible for themselves."

"Ah-ha! I knew I wasn't crazy." Courtney looked up from her Bible. "Check out Exodus 9:23. 'And Moses stretched out his rod toward heaven; and the Lord sent thunder and hail, and fire darted to the ground. And the Lord rained hail on the land of Egypt.' See, he used his rod."

Sarah seemed to be distracted from her grief. She joined in also. "Yep, 10:13, also. Listen to this, 'So Moses stretched out his rod over the land of Egypt, and the Lord brought an east wind on the land all that day and all that night. When it was morning, the east wind brought the locusts.'

"He used his rod there. Maybe Courtney is right. Maybe we should take it to him."

Everett quickly flipped through the pages. "Okay, both of those instances. Back it up one verse, 9:22, 'And the Lord said unto Moses, Stretch forth thine *hand* toward heaven.' And 10:12, 'And the Lord said unto Moses, Stretch out thine *hand* over the land of Egypt for the locusts, that they may come up upon the land of Egypt.' Maybe we're seeing a pattern here. Maybe Moses is beginning to change God's Word in his head. Like I said, it's human to do so."

"I think you're making a mountain out of a molehill." Courtney closed her Bible.

"Maybe and maybe not." Everett thumbed through his Bible. "In Exodus 17, God tells Moses to take his rod to the rock in Horeb and strike the rock so water will come out."

"Now you're proving *her* point," Sarah said.

"Hang on." Everett flipped past several more pages. "Turn to Numbers 20, verse 8. 'Take the rod, and gather thou the assembly together, thou, and Aaron thy brother, and *speak ye* unto the rock before their eyes; and it shall give forth his water.'

"Verse 11, 'And Moses lifted up his hand, and with his rod, he smote the rock twice: and the water came out abundantly, and the congregation drank, and their beasts also. And the Lord spake unto Moses and Aaron, because ye believed me not, to sanctify me in the eyes of the children of Israel, therefore ye shall not bring this congregation into the land which I have given them.'

"Moses didn't get to go into the promised land because he *smote* the rock instead of speaking to it. The details of God's Word are important. That's why I'm leery of the new translations."

Courtney's brows tightened together. "Everett, changing *thee* and *thou* into *you* and *yours* doesn't change the meaning of God's Word. Jesus didn't speak in the King's English. He spoke Aramaic."

"If that's all they did, that would be fine, but to get a copyright, you have to change a certain amount of the text so it's significantly different. What if the translators ran out of *thees* and *thous* and had to start making changes just to hit their quota for the copyright? Sounds dangerous to me."

"You could make the same argument over the King James." Sarah closed her Bible.

Everett shrugged. "There's no copyright on the King James."

"Because of a little thing we like to call the American Revolution." Courtney pressed her lips together. "Of course, none of them have an enforceable copyright under the Global Republic. They're all outlawed."

Everett closed his Bible as well. "This is the one I trust. Westcott and Hort, the guys who headed up the translations for most of the newer versions, didn't even believe it. Westcott didn't believe in the authority of the Bible, nor did he believe that it is infallible. Hort believed in evolution."

"Yeah, yeah, I heard Elijah talk about all of that. But the New King James and the MEV have nothing to do with those guys. They come from the same texts as the King James." Courtney sounded like she was ready to keep going on the topic.

Sarah seemed ready to change the subject. "So, we're not going to take Moses his staff?"

"I don't think he needs it. In fact, he may have left it here on purpose. Maybe he thinks the thing has gotten him in enough trouble already." Everett felt mildly disappointed. He would have welcomed any excuse to get out of the dreary cavern, but at the same time, he was in no hurry to expose his wife to unnecessary peril.

Everett awoke early Saturday morning to the sound of Sarah stirring about the cave. He felt for his flashlight and turned it on momentarily to look at his watch. "Four thirty." He put his head down to go back to sleep.

Sarah continued to move things around. Everett lay motionless, confident that she'd soon cease from her activities. A minute later, he gave up on returning to his slumber. *I'm wide awake now*, he thought. He rolled over to see what all the commotion was about.

Sarah stuffed clothing and MREs into her large military ALICE pack, then placed Moses' staff into a large, black duffle bag. Everett lifted his head off the pillow. *That's strange, why would she be doing that*? When he saw her begin rolling up her sleeping bag, he got up and walked over to her. He whispered so not to wake Courtney. "What's going on?"

Sarah shook her head. "I've gotta go."

The statement caught Everett off guard. "What?" His response was louder than he intended it to be. "Go where?"

"Jerusalem."

Everett looked at Moses' rod laying in the unzipped duffle. "Is this about the staff?"

"No. It's about me. I have to get out of here."

"I don't understand." Everett put his hand on her arm.

Courtney awoke and got out of her sleeping bag. "Why are you going to Jerusalem?"

"Because there's nowhere else to go."

Everett gripped her arm tight. "That's a suicide mission, Sarah. Jerusalem is the new ground zero. With New Atlantis destroyed, Jerusalem will be the focus of the coming judgments."

"It's not a suicide mission, Everett. It's an anti-suicide mission. I know how I get. I can't sit around here and stare at the empty walls of the cave. I'll just get more and more depressed until I can't take it anymore. I have to do something. I have to go somewhere, and there's nowhere else to go. This hemisphere is shot. I didn't particularly like the idea of sitting around here for the next three years waiting to die. But, with Kevin, I could have gotten by. Not without him. I can't do it. And no offense, but watching you two together just makes it that much harder. I have to go. I love you guys, and I'll miss you, but I have to get out of here. I hope you'll understand."

Courtney stood with her arms crossed. Her look of shock soon deteriorated into an expression of loss. "Sarah, no. You can't leave us. We need you. It's only been four days since Kevin died. Give it some time. It'll get better. We'll make a point of getting outside every day. Winter is almost over; the weather will be mild. Maybe the rain will cleanse the soil, and things will start to grow again.

"Please don't leave me." Courtney wrapped both arms around Sarah's neck and pulled her close.

Sarah held her friend in the embrace for nearly a minute, then pulled away. "I have to, Courtney. You don't know what it's like. Being all alone in this horrible cave."

"But you're not alone," Courtney pleaded.

Sarah wiped a tear from her eye, then used her sleeve to dry the eyes of her friend. "I have to do this. But I'll be with you in spirit. I'll never forget you guys."

Courtney's voice grew more desperate. "If you leave, you will be alone. We won't be there for you, and it won't bring Kevin back."

"I'll find Elijah." Sarah packed several magazines for her AR-15.

Courtney shook her head and turned to Everett. "We have to do something. We can't let her leave. It's too dangerous."

At a total loss for words, Everett lowered his gaze to Sarah's rifle. "She's a grown woman. I can't physically restrain her. If her mind is set on leaving, we can't stop her."

"Then we'll go with her!" Courtney didn't phrase the statement as a question.

"No." Everett grabbed Courtney's hands. "We've worked very hard to put everything together so we can ride out the apocalypse right here in this cave. If we leave, we walk away from all of our provisions, all of our security. We have shelter, food, water." He pointed at the entrance of the cave. "People are killing each other for those things out there."

"Well, I'm going with her. You can stay here with your provisions if you want, but Sarah needs us, and I'm going to be by her side." Courtney abruptly walked away and began packing a large-frame backpack.

"Courtney, you absolutely are not going!" Everett's eyes grew wide.

She didn't turn away from her task. "You can't stop me."

"You're going to leave me?" He was stunned by her actions.

She paused and let the pack fall over. She sat next to her belongings, silent and still for several moments. Then she broke down and began to bawl.

Everett pulled her close to his chest. "Shhhh. It's alright."

She took a deep breath and looked up. "It's not alright. I won't leave you. You're my husband. But I won't be happy. I won't sleep knowing that Sarah is out there by herself. It'll just be the two of us. I love you Everett, but we'll drive each other nuts being cooped up in here for three years alone."

He bit his lower lip. He knew she was right, but he was in no way prepared to follow through with the next statement that he blurted out of his mouth. "Okay, we'll go with her."

"You mean it?" Courtney's countenance changed in an instant.

Immediately, he regretted what he'd just said. "Sarah, can you give us a couple hours to pack some supplies?"

"Sure." She ceased her activities.

Everett looked around the cave. "And we'll have to take some more supplies over to Cotton's mine than the ten buckets I'd originally intended. It looks like they'll be keeping Sox and Danger permanently."

"Whatever we do, it has to be done in one trip.

The Jeep has less than an eighth of a tank of gas." Courtney went through her belongings, selecting the few items she'd take on the journey.

Sarah unrolled her sleeping bag and sat back down on the floor. She turned the radio on and listened to it at a low volume.

Everett slowly began to pack his rucksack. Of all the supplies they had in the cave, he could only carry a few pounds worth. Everything in the cave was essential for survival. Choosing what to bring would be a monumental undertaking.

Sarah held up the radio. "I don't mean to sound ungrateful, but if you guys are coming with me, we've gotta be gone by this time tomorrow. According to the GR Press Secretary, Athaliah Jennings, Dragon will be back online in two days. We'll only have one day to get out of the country."

Everett grunted. The added pressure did not assist him in making the difficult decisions of what to bring and what to leave behind. "Did you have any idea how you're going to get to Jerusalem?"

"No," Sarah said plainly.

"Well, they're not going to just let us walk onto a plane headed for the new GR capital." Everett picked up his HK G36. The rifle was one item definitely on the *take l*ist.

"Maybe they will let us walk right on." Courtney seemed to think it was a good plan. "We could just make a fake Mark with a Sharpie."

Everett shook his head. "The Mark's embedded pico projector actually elevates the skin on the back of your hand slightly."

He paused for a moment. "Unless..."

"What?" Sarah let the radio rest on the ground while she waited for Everett to finish his sentence.

"Unless we actually implanted a deactivated pico projector in our hands. They had a mobile implant gun in the MRAP we took from the GR."

Courtney dropped what she was doing. "Seriously? You're considering taking the Mark?"

"It's not the Mark. It's just a small piece of equipment that isn't activated. We wouldn't be connected to Dragon, we wouldn't have a GR number assignment, and most importantly, we wouldn't be taking the pledge to Luz."

"I'm not doing it. No way, no how. I don't care if it is deactivated." Courtney waved her hands in the air to express her adamant position on the matter.

Sarah said, "The pico projector is about the size of a piece of rice. Why couldn't we just sterilize a piece of rice and stick it under our skin?"

"Maybe." Everett considered the idea. "Perhaps if we were dressed as peacekeepers, the authorities would pay less attention to our Marks."

"I don't know about that." Courtney frowned.

"We have the uniforms from the skirmish on the way to Tommy's," Everett said.

"Tommy has the uniforms," Courtney clarified.

"He'll let us use them if it's for a good cause," Everett rebutted.

Sarah looked at Courtney. "Everett's right. We need a plan, and I can't think of anything better."

"Sounds risky." Courtney's brows pulled together.

"This whole quest is risky." Everett laughed. "And if we get out of the country alive, we'll have successfully made it out of the frying pan and straight into the fire. I hope you both realize the level of absolute peril we're getting into here."

Undeterred by the caveat, Courtney nodded. "Okay, we'll pose as GR peacekeepers with grains of rice implanted under our skin."

Sarah asked, "From where?"

"South Africa, mate." Courtney did a phenomenal South African accent.

"Aw royt theen." Sarah tried her hand at the cadence.

"That sounds a little more Australian than South African, but we can work with it." Courtney chuckled.

Everett continued packing. "Hopefully, if we can pass as peacekeepers, our food and water will be supplied."

Sarah looked at Everett's rifle. "If we're going as South Africans, we'll have to use those Vektors Tommy salvaged from Winchester. That means your G36 will have to stay here."

Everett collapsed the stock of the HK rifle and stowed it in his backpack. "No one will ever know it's here."

"Careful you don't let that gun turn into a security blanket like Moses' staff. I'd hate to see it get you in trouble." Courtney chided him.

"I think we're all in more danger from that rod than this rifle." He looked up and glared at the smoothly carved piece of wood. "It was that stupid stick that started all of this business about going to Jerusalem."

CHAPTER 8

Thou shalt tread upon the lion and adder: the young lion and the dragon shalt thou trample under feet.

Psalm 91:13

Everett examined the smoothly cut stones poured out on the coffee table. Some were small, a quarter carat or less. Most seemed to be between a half and one carat. One was easily over two, while several others were well above a full carat. He counted them as he placed them one by one back into the small black velvet pouch. "Fifty. It seems like an awful lot of diamonds for the supplies left in the cave."

Tommy sat back in his easy chair. "250 million Americans have died in the last four years. Half of them were women. Most of them had at least one diamond. The market isn't what it used to be. On the other hand, ammo, solar panels, weapons, and dry goods are getting tough to come by. Access to a freshwater supply alone is worth a fist full of diamonds."

"If I'd had any idea that you were going to be so generous, we'd have carted the supplies over to your house." Everett pulled the string to the pouch and tied it securely.

Tommy put his arm around his wife, Daisy. "We won't even go get it unless we have to abandon our place or we get robbed. I'm thinking of it as an insurance policy. And like I said. I'm only laying claim to half of it. The rest still belongs to you. Won't nobody else ever know the whereabouts of your little cavern 'cept me and Daisy here."

Courtney had been hypnotized by the glittering jewels. Now that Everett had put them away, she returned to the land of the living. "That's very kind of you, Tommy. But I seriously doubt we'll ever make it back."

"I know. But if you do, you've got a place to hang your hat." His entire beard seemed to smile. "We'll miss your friendship. We've had some good times together, and we've been there for each other when things got rough."

Sarah finished blousing her trousers over her boots to make sure the black, Global Republic peacekeeper uniform looked as proper as possible. "Yeah, we've been blessed to know you. And I really appreciate all you've done for us."

Tommy kissed Daisy on the lips. "I'm gonna

walk 'em out to the truck. I'll be right back."

"Y'all be safe." Daisy waved as Everett, Courtney, and Sarah walked out the front door.

Each of them bade her farewell as they proceeded to the MRAP.

With God's providence and a little planning, Tommy had managed to save his home from the Wormwood debris field. With a front-end loader, he'd piled up earth on the sides and rear of the house. He reinforced his roof and covered it with several inches of dirt as well. None of it would have mattered if the roof had taken a direct hit by any meteors larger than a basketball, but God had spared him from those.

Everett examined the stitching on the front of his black GR uniform shirt where a bullet hole had once been. "Thank Daisy for us again. She did a great job getting these clothes cleaned up."

"She was glad to do it. She likes to stay occupied." Tommy nodded. "You'll tell Elijah I said hello when you see him."

Courtney smiled as she stepped up into the giant armored vehicle. "Of course we will."

Everett waved as he fired up the engine. He was sad to be saying goodbye to yet another friend.

As they made their way down the road, Everett glanced down at the red patch on his arm. "Anyone know what rank we are?"

Courtney looked at her own name and rank patches. "Bekker. The rank patches look like they're loosely based on the old UN insignia. "I think I'm a corporal." She looked back at Sarah. "That's a sergeant, maybe." Courtney studied

Everett's name and rank patches. "I'm not sure what you are, Mr. Smith, but you outrank us both."

The Typhoon had roughly a quarter tank. Everett was sure this would not be enough to get them to DC. The team would be relying on motor oil drained from abandoned vehicles to supplement the diesel fuel.

The highways were littered with vehicles which had run out of gas. They made their first stop at a deserted pickup truck outside of Berryville, then the second stop at a Toyota just west of Arcadia Farm. Courtney stood guard while Everett drained the oil and Sarah poured it into the fuel tank. The next vehicle was on the shoulder of the road near Leesburg on State Road 7. The cars were spread out, and each one yielded roughly a gallon and a half of fuel. It added up quickly.

"We've still got a quarter tank and we're just a couple miles from Dulles." Everett breathed easy. "Makes me feel better than rolling up on an unpredictable situation sitting on empty."

"It's good to have options," Sarah added.

Everett drove up to the gate which was manned by a squad of twelve GR peacekeepers. His heartbeat quickened as he rolled down his window. He offered only a nod, waiting for the guard to speak first. If the man sounded like he was from South Africa, Everett wasn't about to test out his fake accent on a native.

"Got papers?" The man sounded Canadian. He was the first GR troop Everett had encountered from North America.

"Who's got papers? We've been relying on this

confounded device." Everett flicked his wrist as if trying to activate the interface on his Mark implant.

The guard rolled his eyes. "Where you coming from, aye?"

"Harrisonburg. We were reassigned to Jerusalem."

"Like everyone else from around here. Where's the rest of your platoon?"

"We had an uprising when the system went down. Everyone else was killed. We didn't leave many survivors though."

The guard looked in at Courtney and Sarah, then gave the vehicle a quick once-over. "Follow this road to the old parking garage. The garage is no longer operational as it was hit by a large meteor, but the south end is undamaged, and they're using it as offices for issuing temporary papers."

"The system is supposed to be back online tomorrow. Why bother?" Everett kept up his accent.

The guard looked at him as if he were crazy. "Tomorrow? That's propaganda. Dragon won't be back online for weeks."

"Rubbish!" Everett feigned exasperation over the inconvenience. "Do you know if any planes are leaving today?"

"No. We've got no planes here. Supposedly more C-130s are coming in tomorrow, but they'll be landing at Reagan if they show up at all. We don't have any runways in good enough condition to land large cargo planes. I hate to be the bearer of bad news, but it's starting to look like we might be left behind. All the brass was shipped out weeks ago, and they seem less and less worried about getting us grunts out of this cursed location."

"Yes, well, we'll be on our way then. Thanks for your help." Everett pulled through the gate and proceeded to the location he'd been told.

Once at the temporary papers office, he cut the engine, and the three of them got out of the vehicle.

Sarah led the way to the desk. A pile of papers sat atop the desk, but no one was around. She looked the papers over without touching them. "Follow my lead," she whispered softly to Everett and Courtney as a young woman wearing the traditional black uniform of the Global Republic approached the desk.

"You all just keep tricklin' in, don't you?" She sounded British, and she sounded annoyed. She picked up a small passbook and a pen. "Regiment, battalion, company, rank, name."

"South African Regiment, 3rd Battalion, Foxtrot, Sergeant, Sarah Fourie."

"Sergeant Major." She glanced up at Sarah.

Everett slowly slid his hand down to his side arm. If the woman went for a radio, he'd have to put her down fast.

"Be specific about rank while you're on the Dulles airbase. It might not matter at the whistle stop outpost where you've been, but it does here." The woman looked back down at her desk and continued to write. "Fourie, that's French, isn't it?"

"Lots of South African names are," Sarah said plainly.

"Yes, the Huguenots. I suppose they are, aren't they?" The woman stamped the passbook with the seal of a blood red dragon which had seven heads.

"Some of your countrymen were through here yesterday. Bravo Company, I believe." She looked up with a sour grin and handed the booklet to Sarah. "But I guess we're all countrymen now, aren't we?"

Everett stepped forward. "South African . . ."

"Yes, yes, 3rd, Foxtrot, Second Lieutenant. I'm not stupid. Just your name." She didn't look up.

"Everett Smith."

"Ahh, Smith. That's English." She glanced up and looked Everett over. She offered him a warmer smile and bit her lower lip. "A *fine* English name, Lieutenant."

Everett returned the smile as he took the booklet. "Second Lieutenant."

Courtney's jaw was clinched. Almost too tightly for her fake accent. "Courtney . . . Bekker."

Everett fought back a chuckle. He could see that it was eating her up. He knew just how badly she wanted the woman to know that while it might not be *Smith*, she had the same *fine last name* as Everett.

"Do you know if we can get a transport to Jerusalem?" Sarah inquired.

"I just fill out the papers. I'm surprised they trust me with that." She stamped Courtney's passbook with a great deal of animosity.

Sarah tilted her head and pursed her lips as she looked at Everett.

He picked up the clue. Sarah was recommending that he might get more flies with honey.

Everett said, "Have you heard anything? Will there be more planes?"

She crossed her arms gingerly on the desk. "I've

not seen much activity. A convoy of thirty or forty trucks left out of here yesterday. It looked like they were hauling supplies somewhere. The trailers were all those metal containers, like they load on a ship. I suppose they were heading to the port."

"Norfolk?" Everett quizzed.

The British woman shrugged. "I suppose. The acting commandant of the Dulles airbase has his office set up in the first office building west of the terminal. You could file a transport request to the port, perhaps you can be included in the next convoy. But then again, he might transfer you here permanently." She batted her eyelashes. "And wouldn't that be a shame?"

"Our orders are from Jerusalem." Everett clarified.

"The commandant can override them." She leaned forward.

Everett paused as if he were considering it. "And what is the good commandant's name?"

"Miller."

"Thanks, you've been very helpful." Everett smiled and turned to join the girls.

"See you around," the woman said.

Courtney mocked the GR clerk silently as she bobbed her head and mouthed the words *see you around*, under her breath.

Once back in the MRAP, Everett started the engine.

Courtney crossed her arms and looked out the window. "So, are we off to the commandant's so we can get reassigned here permanently?"

Everett bit his tongue to keep from laughing.

"No, but I thought it might come in handy to have a name to drop if we ask for fuel. We'll never make it to Norfolk on a quarter tank. And we can't keep adding motor oil unless we get some diesel."

Everett continued around to the terminal. He waved down two peacekeepers crossing the road. "Pardon me, but can you direct me to the quartermaster."

The first looked at the other like Everett was some kind of a hick. He reluctantly turned to Everett. "What is it you need?"

"Diesel."

The other man shook his head vehemently. "There's no diesel on the base." He pointed at the MRAP. "You'd best make whatever you have last."

"Yeah, thanks." Everett offered a flippant wave and a smirk, and carried on.

"Now what?" Courtney asked.

"Drive around to the runway. This thing will run on jet fuel," Sarah instructed from the rear.

Everett found his way to the tarmac. He located a refueling truck and barreled toward it. Once there, he rolled down the window. "Hey, buddy. Think you can fill me up?"

The driver, who had been sleeping, lifted his ball cap. "How much fuel is your requisition form for?"

"Commandant Miller sent us here personally. We have orders to get to Norfolk, double time."

The driver sat up straight and repositioned his hat. "I don't care if your orders came from his Most High and Prepotent Majesty himself. No form, no fuel."

"I'll make sure the commandant understands

your adherence to protocol. Hopefully, he'll be impressed rather than upset that you're delaying his personal commands," Everett grunted. "We just got here. Can you tell us where to get the requisition form?"

The man seemed to be in no hurry to show up on the commandant's radar. He lost his disdainful look and his tone became more considerate. "Typically, you'd have to go to the energy quartermaster's office by the main fuel tanks, but I have a couple of blank forms in the truck." He exited the vehicle and handed a piece of paper up to Everett's window.

"You can fill it out, have the commandant or his secretary sign it, then bring it back to me. If I had the authority to just give you fuel, I'd do it. But this ain't the worst gig on the base and I don't want to lose it."

"I can understand that. I appreciate your help." Everett took the form and drove away.

"Now what?" Sarah asked.

Everett passed her the form. "Start filling it out. I'll look for the next available fuel truck." He raced down the airstrip and around the terminal. At the far end of the next terminal, he saw another refueling truck.

Everett pulled up to the truck. "I don't see anyone around."

"Then let's just help ourselves," Courtney suggested.

Everett pushed his door open. "Good plan. Let's strike while the iron is hot. I'll get the oil bucket. Sarah, you pull the fuel hose to the truck. Courtney, you remove the fuel cap."

Each of them scurried to perform their individual tasks. Sarah opened the valve releasing the fuel into the bucket while Everett poured the jet fuel into the funnel, which Courtney steadied over the tank opening of the Typhoon.

After the fourth bucket of fuel had been transferred a man yelled, "Whoa, whoa, whoa!"

Everett spoke softly to the girls. "Keep going, I'll handle him."

"What's the problem?" Everett snarled.

"You can't just take fuel! You need a requisition form." The man stepped close to Everett's face. "Tell them to stop, or I'll call security."

Everett reached into the cab of the MRAP and pulled out the form. He shoved the paper into the man's chest. "Yeah, you do that. Call security and tell them you abandoned your post and that a team on special orders from Commandant Miller had to pump their own fuel."

He stepped back from Everett and glanced over the piece of paper. "I had to go to the bathroom. The porta potty is on the other side of the airport, and they don't want us driving over there. We gotta conserve fuel. What was I supposed to do?"

Everett turned his back on the man. "I'd recommend keeping a bottle in your cab during working hours."

The man followed Everett, still trying to explain himself. "It wasn't nothing I could do in a bottle, if you know what I mean, Lieutenant."

Everett turned on his heel and glared at the man. With his teeth showing he said, "Then get a bucket!"

Obviously familiar with this degree of inhumanity from his superiors, the man walked over to Courtney and Sarah. "You can get back in your vehicle. I'll finish up for you."

To maintain the ruse, neither of the girls thanked the man or even acknowledged his existence. They simply walked away.

Everett stepped up to get back in the driver's seat. "And make sure you wipe out my oil bucket before you put it back in my vehicle. I don't want jet fuel fumes filling up the cab."

The man said nothing but complied with Everett's demands.

Minutes later, they were back on the road. Everett was careful to exit via the same gate he'd entered through so not to encounter more peacekeepers than necessary.

Sarah squatted in the aisle between the driver and the passenger seat. "We've already burned half the day. It'll be evening by the time we get inside the port."

Courtney asked, "What if we don't find anything in Norfolk? Shouldn't we have a backup plan?"

Everett kept his eyes on the road. "If it's God's will for us to go, something will open up. From what Elijah said, and from the feeling I got back at Dulles, it sounds like most all key personnel have been evacuated out of North America. Our best bet is to try hitching a ride on a military vessel."

Sarah added, "Still, we might want to keep the tank as full as possible so we have options."

"Yeah, we'll stop as we have opportunities." Judging from the amount of fuel they'd used so far,

Everett felt confident that ten gallons of motor oil would be enough to get them home if the plan to catch a ship from Norfolk fell through.

They drained a Civic near Woodbridge, then found a Volkswagen Bug and a Kia less than one hundred feet from each other, past Fredericksburg.

After draining four more vehicles along the way, Courtney leaned over to look at the fuel gauge. "What do you think?"

Everett glanced down, then back up at the highway before him. "That should do it."

"Five thirty." Courtney looked at her watch as the Typhoon drove up to the guard gate outside of the Global Republic Naval Station Norfolk.

Everett rolled down his window and handed his passbook to the guard.

The man kept his hand out until he'd collected the passbooks from all three people in the vehicle. "Where are you headed?"

"Jerusalem."

"Do you have assignment papers?"

"No. We were assigned there before the system went down. All of our orders are locked up."

The man waved for the other guards to open the gate. "You'll need to go straight to the personnel department to register. They'll have to write up temporary assignment papers."

The man turned to point down the road. "It's the last building on your right before you reach the piers."

Everett took the passbooks back from the man. "Who should I ask for?"

"Lieutenant Colonel Pender."

Everett waved and pulled through the gate.

Once at the building, the team exited the vehicle. Everett led the way into the characterless, concrete, two-story government building.

A receptionist who looked bored out of her mind greeted them. "Can I help you?"

"Lieutenant Colonel Pender, please," Everett said.

"Do you have an appointment?"

"No. We've just arrived on base."

She picked up a radio. "Colonel, three peacekeepers are here to see you."

"It's after five. What's it about?" The radio chirped.

She held the radio out toward Everett and lifted her brows as if that should suffice for relaying the inquiry.

"We need passage to Jerusalem."

She released the talk key and Pender's voice came back. "Send them in."

"Second door on your right." She looked back down at her doodling.

No gratitude seemed to be expected, so Everett didn't show any as he led the way down the hall.

He opened the door and held it for Sarah and Courtney, then walked in after them. Despite the concrete block walls with no drywall and the one-foot-by-one-foot, white-with-black-specs linoleum tile floors, Pender had managed to furnish the large room quite nicely. The office seemed to have been intended as a larger meeting room rather than one man's personal workspace, but Pender was obviously accustomed to taking certain liberties.

Everett saluted the lieutenant colonel as did Courtney and Sarah.

"At ease, please take a seat." Pender waved his hand at two plush white couches.

Everett and the girls followed the directive.

"How may I assist you in fulfilling your duties this evening?" He held a glass in his hand, and a bottle of whiskey sat open on his desk.

"We're seeking a transport to Jerusalem, Lieutenant Colonel." Everett sat up straight, despite the comfy couch.

"I'm afraid you've caught me at the end of my work day." He topped off his glass. "We don't have any naval vessels leaving to Jerusalem or anywhere else anytime soon."

He pushed some papers around on his desk. "But I can't have you stay here. I've got my share of idleness on this base as it is. Filling that void with menial tasks for the disengaged peacekeepers around here has proven to be the bane of my existence since His Majesty began shifting operations to Israel."

He held up what looked to be a ship's manifest. "Ah, yes. Here we go. I've got a container ship scheduled to leave at dawn tomorrow morning, the Madison Maersk. I was supposed to have two squads to provide security for the vessel. Both were supposed to be here no later than end of business on Friday. So, they're both late. One was out of Fayetteville, the other out of Roanoke. My guess is that the one out of Roanoke was killed by insurgents, and the ones coming from Fayetteville have deserted."

He sipped his whiskey. "The rumor mill is that the GR is completely pulling out of the Americas. We've had bands of peacekeepers just deciding that they'll stay behind and make their own government. I don't know what they think they'll govern."

He laughed and took a long drink. "They'll fight over scraps, kill for water, and wish for food. That's what they'll do."

"And the Republic doesn't go after the deserters?" Everett knew Tommy regularly dealt with disenfranchised peacekeepers; this was the first he'd heard of mass desertions.

"No," Pender said. "They're not worth the resources needed to hunt them down. And they know it. That's why they desert.

"Anyway, let's see your papers. Let's get your orders written up while I'm still seeing only one of everything."

Everett and the girls handed him their passbooks, and Pender pulled out a folder with some forms. He began filling them out.

"And this vessel, it's going to Jerusalem?" Everett inquired.

"No, Mersin."

"Turkey?" Sarah asked.

"Yes, that's right. The ship is carrying Humvees, MRAP's, bulldozers, Hesco barriers, radios; equipment that won't be needed on this continent."

Pender looked up. "How many are with you?"

"Just the three of us." Everett wouldn't give any additional information unless asked.

"Three?" Pender seemed torn between wanting

more details and his desire to get back to drinking alone. He glanced over at his bottle, which seemed to have won out. Pender returned to writing. "I'll have to find at least one other squad to accompany you. Mersin isn't the best neighborhood these days."

"Oh?" Everett wanted to keep the lieutenant colonel talking. The whiskey was obviously loosening Pender's lips, and it seemed like a waste to not milk him for all the info he could.

"No. The Shia Muslims see His Majesty Angelo Luz as the returning of the Twelfth Imam who disappeared in the ninth century. Therefore, the Sunni categorically reject him. Even if the Sunni saw His Majesty as their legitimate Caliph, they'd never admit it as long as the Shia see him as the Twelfth Imam.

"It's a crying shame that it wasn't the other way around. Shia make up less than 20 percent of the Muslim population. The other one and a half billion are Sunni."

Pender exchanged his pen for his whiskey glass. "Well, that number has been significantly culled by recent cataclysms. It's probably closer to 700 million, but that's enough to cause a stir. At any rate, the Global Republic is shifting all available assets to that region. And you're lucky enough to get a front row seat to all the action."

Pender gave a sinister grin as he handed the papers to Everett. "Your ship is the Madison Maersk, a huge container vessel docked at the last loading crane of the international terminals. You'll actually leave the naval base, then enter through another guard gate for the international terminals. It's the next row of piers to the south."

"And it's just us and one other squad to provide security at a potentially hostile port? No military escort vessel?" Courtney inquired.

"No. We don't want to tip our hand that the ship is carrying military equipment. The radical Sunni would be sure to go after the cargo if they knew. Just make sure the captain doesn't stop the vessel for any reason once he's passed the Strait of Gibraltar. Good luck."

Everett stood with his papers and a concerned look on his face. "Thanks."

"You're going to need it." Pender raised his glass as Everett and the girls left the room.

The team returned to the vehicle and drove around to the docks. Everett had no trouble finding the ship as the giant container lifting systems towered into the sky. "The loading cranes look like snow walkers from Star Wars."

"Such a nerd, Everett. No one would see that but you." Courtney chuckled.

"No, I see it, too." Sarah looked up at the huge apparatus hovering over their ship. "It looks like an AT-AT."

"A what?" Courtney quizzed.

"All Terrain Armored Transport. That's the technical name of a Star Wars snow walker." Sarah grabbed her rifle and her rucksack.

"You're a bigger nerd than he is." Courtney rolled her eyes as she exited the vehicle.

Everett parked the Typhoon out of the way at the far end of a row of shipping containers so its presence wouldn't become an issue until after the ship had departed the next day. He wanted to keep it close enough in case they needed it for a hasty escape.

The team strolled casually down the corridor between the large metal boxes stacked three high. When they arrived at the gangway, Everett led the way up.

"Welcome aboard." A young Asian man greeted the team as they entered the Madison Maersk. "I'm Chief Steward Lui."

"Thank you." Everett handed the stack of papers to Lui.

"Okay, I show you to your quarters. Follow me." Lui led the team to the large tower in the center of the ship. "Your staterooms are on Deck D, which is same deck I live. Mess is on Deck F; fitness room and rec room is on Deck G."

Everett looked at Courtney as they walked. Compared to the conditions they'd been living in, anything with windows was an upgrade, much less recreational facilities.

Lui directed Courtney and Sarah to a large cabin with two full beds. "Maybe you can have own room if we don't get more passenger. But, you happy to share for now?"

Courtney paused before she responded. "Happy to share," she finally answered with a nod.

Everett's room was diagonally across the hall. The large cabin also had two full beds.

"Supper served at 6:30, so you don't have much time if you want to eat. Breakfast at 5:00, lunch at noon. You don't have much to do until we get close

Morocco. After that, Captain Petrov expect two peacekeepers on bridge at all time. 'Bout Saturday evening, you need work out security schedule.

"GR send more peacekeeper?" Lui looked concerned.

Everett lifted his shoulders. "Pender said he'd assign another squad, but they intentionally want to keep a low profile. I assume you have some idea what the cargo is."

"Yeah, I know, I know." Lui waved his hands as if he didn't want to think about it. "But Alboran Sea not safe for travel, even if you have only empty ship. Everybody worried 'bout go through there."

"We'll do what we can." Everett attempted to sound confident.

Lui pressed his lips tightly together. "If we make it through Alboran Sea, then gotta make it past Tunisia. After that, smooth sailing in Mediterranean until get to Turkey. Once we there, probably wish we died at Gibraltar." Lui dismissed himself and headed for the stairwell.

Everett stood in his doorway looking at Courtney and Sarah diagonally across the hall. "Sounds like we're going to get more of an adventure than we bargained for."

"At least we'll get some R and R for the next six days." Sarah turned to go in her room.

"I wouldn't bet on it." Everett knew better than to count those chickens before they'd hatched.

Courtney waved. "You going to dinner?"

"Yeah, as soon as I found out if this ship has hot water. I haven't had a hot shower in years."

"Don't even get my hopes up. I couldn't stand

the disappointment." Courtney turned to go in her cabin.

"See you in ten minutes." Everett closed his door and looked for a place to stash his rifle. None of the cabinets in his room locked. Even if they did, he figured Lui and everyone else on the ship probably had a key. He fastened the door and quickly looked around. He found a shaving cream can in the bathroom. He wedged it between the deadbolt lock and the doorknob, preventing it from being unlocked from the outside. At least no one would be walking in on him while he took a shower.

The water ran hot almost immediately. Everett stepped into the shower and all his muscles relax. "Thank you, God! This feels absolutely amazing!" He didn't want to get out, but neither did he want Courtney out of his sight any longer than necessary, and he certainly had no intentions of missing supper.

Minutes later, Everett was dressed. He placed his rucksack and rifle in the closet, locked his door, and crossed the hall. He gently knocked on Courtney's door.

"Who is it?" Sarah's voice came from the other side.

"Smith."

"Why come right in, Lieutenant." Sarah's South African accent was improving. "Corporal Bekker is still in the shower."

"She must hurry then." Everett played along by staying in character. He wrapped on the bathroom door. "You can come back and sit in there all night after we eat, but we need to get to the galley."

"I'm coming." The water stopped running and Courtney emerged from the bathroom cloaked in a towel. "We should have stowed away on a ship a long time ago."

Everett sat on the side of the bed. His forehead puckered. "The sea hasn't been that inviting, with the tsunamis, meteors, earthquakes, and all. Which is pretty much why we took up cave dwelling in the first place."

Courtney quickly finished dressing. "Right again, Lieutenant Smith."

"Second Lieutenant." He winked. "Leave your rifles here, wear your side arms and make sure your backup guns are easy to get to in case we get disarmed for any reason. Sarah, I know you've been wearing your backup on your ankle. I'd keep it in your waist if I were you."

"Roger that." Sarah dug through her pack and retrieved a very simple inside-the-waist holster.

Everett stood and opened the door. "Be courteous, but not too chatty. We'll stay to ourselves as much as possible."

"Yes, sir." Courtney faked a salute and marched out the door.

Everett also felt slightly more chipper after a hot shower and the promise of a meal at an actual table, but he wasn't about to let his guard down.

Once they arrived in the dining area, Lui introduced them by last name and rank to Captain Vasily Petrov, Chief Officer Maria Lopez, Second Mate Nate Williams, and Lars Andersen, the chief engineer.

"How do you do?" Everett shook hands with

everyone and led the way to the table farthest from the captain's.

Lui assisted Chief Cook Ana Garcia in serving enchiladas with salad. Though it was simple, Everett couldn't remember eating a more perfect meal. He so wanted to relax, to take in the luxurious experience of being waited on, of sitting in a chair, at a table, next to his wife. He wanted to take her hand, but he couldn't. The mission depended on the charade.

After dinner, they returned to their rooms. Everett visited with the girls and fell asleep, snuggled next to Courtney.

CHAPTER 9

And Asa cried unto the Lord his God, and said, Lord, it is nothing with thee to help, whether with many, or with them that have no power: help us, O Lord our God; for we rest on thee, and in thy name we go against this multitude. O Lord, thou art our God; let no man prevail against thee.

2 Chronicles 14:11

Everett and the girls ate breakfast at 5:00 AM with the rest of the crew. Powdered eggs, real bacon, and pancakes were served. Pancakes were a staple for Everett's team during their time in the cave, but the bacon and eggs were a welcomed addition.

As they finished eating, Everett turned to Lui who was clearing the table next to his. "Still no other security team?"

"Not yet, but Captain said they coming. We still got 'bout 45 minute before ship leaving."

"Thanks." Everett stood up from the table. "Tell Chef Ana that breakfast was excellent."

"Yeah, sure. I tell her. See you at lunch." Lui handed a stack of dishes to another of the galley hands and began wiping down Everett's table as they left.

"Thanks, Lui." Courtney waved.

"What's next?" Sarah followed Everett toward the stairwell.

"I don't know about you guys, but I'm going back to bed. It's been months since I slept on a mattress." Everett led the way up the two flights of stairs to Deck D.

"Sounds like a plan." Courtney stayed close behind him.

Sarah followed them to their room. "Maybe I'll read a little. I wouldn't have had that third cup of coffee if I knew you guys were going back to sleep."

Everett awoke in Courtney's bed well rested at 10:00 AM. The girls were looking over Everett's small Bible together. It was the only copy they'd brought, both to conserve space, and because getting caught with a non-GR-authorized version like the King James meant certain death.

Courtney saw him roll over. "Everett, you're up."

He stretched his arms and legs. "Yeah. I slept like a log."

"Good, what do you say we do some exploring?" Courtney walked over to the bed and sat down.

"What do you want to explore?" He sat up.

"The rec room. I'd like to see if they have a ping pong table. I wouldn't mind getting some fresh air also," Sarah said. "I can't stay cooped up too long. I start thinking about Kevin."

"Sure." Everett slipped his uniform boots on, then attached his pistol belt. "Side arms and backup guns. We don't want to let our guard down. We still have to meet the other security team. But even if they decide to run around in flip-flops and Bermuda shorts until we get to Gibraltar, we'll stay in uniform any time we leave the rooms."

Courtney put on her pistol belt as well. "Uniform or no uniform, I can still whip all of you at ping pong."

"We'll see about that." Sarah tucked her backup gun in her waist.

Everett led the way out of the room. Lui was entering his cabin. He looked curiously at Everett coming out of the girls' stateroom, but waved and said nothing.

Courtney teased Everett as they jogged down the stairwell. "You're gonna have quite a reputation, Lieutenant Smith."

Everett held the door open for the girls when they reached the G Deck. The three of them found the rec room unoccupied. It indeed had a ping pong table as well as a pool table. It also had a thick glass window that looked out onto the open ocean.

Everett stared out at the blue water that extended into forever as the girls began playing a game of ping pong. The sea showed no scars from the vicious assault against the planet. It had no scorched surface from the fire, no crimson stains from the raining blood, no tears or rips from the mega-quake, and no pock holes from the meteors. The ocean was smooth and even, unblemished by the first three years of the tribulation. Everett allowed his mind to drift back to a time when the whole planet had looked just the way it was supposed to, just like the Atlantic as he gazed at her beauty.

"Earth calling Everett," Courtney quipped. "You look like you're in a trance. Sarah beat me, are you going to take winner?"

"Huh?" He was instantly brought back to the rec room, the ship, and the broader mission at hand. "Oh, sure. I'll play."

"Prepare to be smoked!" Sarah volleyed the ball with her paddle.

Everett picked up the other paddle. "Give me a little time to warm up. I haven't played since college."

"Sorry. No mercy." Sarah served the ball hard and fast.

Everett reflexively countered her shot.

Sarah returned the ball with a firm strike. The two of them soon had the ball bouncing back and forth. Finally, Sarah missed a shot that Everett had sent to the far corner of the table.

She turned to pick up the ball. "I thought you hadn't played since college."

"I may have neglected to mention that I was

really good in college." He resumed his stance as she served the ball again.

Minutes later, the rec room door opened. Everett looked up for a second to see who it was, and the ping pong ball went flying past him.

Even though the four men were wearing the same uniform, Everett's heart jumped at seeing peacekeepers walk in unexpectedly.

"Ah, the other security squad," One of the men said in a distinctly South African accent. He was slender with thin black hair and a sharp nose. He inspected the ranks of Everett, Courtney, and Sarah. "Although, you're really not a squad. Three peacekeepers would hardly qualify as a fire team, much less a squad. My squad is twelve. So, we are fifteen altogether.

"Being that I'm a First Lieutenant, I suppose I'll take the liberty of issuing the watch schedule when we approach the Moroccan coast."

Two of the men eyed Courtney and Sarah as they walked to the pool table. One asked, "Do you girls want to play doubles?"

"No, thanks." Courtney was polite but firm.

Everett looked at the man's name patch. "Our squad works together, Lieutenant Baard."

Baard's eyes slowly traveled from Courtney's feet up to her face. He tilted his head and smiled at her. "I'll decide who works with who. But seeing that we're all countrymen, I can assure you it will be amicable for everyone."

Everett clinched his teeth and took a deep breath through his nose. He was unhappy about the way Baard was looking at his wife. To make matters worse, the man was sure to sniff out their fake accents.

"What part of South Africa are you from, Corporal Bekker?" Baard stepped closer to Courtney.

"Cape Town," she replied. "Yourself?"

"Pretoria." Baard then said, "Jy is baie mooi. Maar ek is seker jy reeds weet dat."

Courtney smiled. "I don't speak Afrikaans."

"No?" Baard furrowed the thin white skin on his elongated brow. "That's very odd. Bekker is a classic Afrikaans name. And most everyone in Cape Town speaks Afrikaans."

"My father was from Cape Town; he met my mother in England and we only moved back when I was in high school."

Everett knew Courtney's excuse wouldn't do more than buy them another minute or two. He sized up the man next to Baard who was listening intently to Courtney's explanation. Everett eyed the other two who were engrossed in their pool game except for the occasional glances at Sarah and Courtney's back sides.

Baard turned to Sarah. "Perhaps your friend can translate for you then."

With one fluid motion, Everett drew his pistol and pulled the trigger. The bullet caught Baard from the rear side, under the cheek. The exit wound from the hollow point shell excavated a tennis-ball-sized crater in the front of Baard's face, relieving him of his upper lip, nose, and left eye. The Lieutenant's body went limp, and he collapsed forward onto the floor.

Everett turned the gun to the other man and shot him between the eyes. At such close range, head shots were the most economical solution.

The two pool players dropped their cue sticks and ducked behind the table. By now, Courtney and Sarah had each drawn their weapons and were assisting Everett in gunning down the peacekeepers behind the pool table. The two remaining troops got off two shots each before they slumped onto the linoleum floor and into growing pools of their own blood.

Everett looked Courtney over. “Are you hit?”

“No. I don’t think so.” She turned to her friend. “Sarah, are you okay?”

“I’m a little shaken up, but otherwise, I guess I’m fine.” She looked up at Everett. “I wasn’t expecting that.”

“Yeah.” Everett quickly put a fresh magazine in his pistol. “None of us were.”

Courtney looked at the four dead men strewn about the rec room floor. “Good job, Everett. You did the right thing. Baard was about five seconds away from getting the drop on us.”

“Let’s not celebrate just yet. We’ve still got eight more to deal with.” Everett bent down and retrieved Baard’s side arm. “And let’s get these pistols. The last thing we need is for the crew to get a hold of their weapons. We’ll have a whole new crop of combatants.”

Sarah and Courtney bent down, stripping the weapons and ammunition from the other peacekeepers. Courtney tucked the peacekeeper’s pistol in her back waistband and the mags in her side cargo pockets. "Now what?"

"I don't know. I'm kind of making this up as I go along."

"I hope no one heard the shots." Sarah looked out the window of the rec room door. "But either way, we need to find the other peacekeepers before they find us."

"Yeah, and I'd rather have a rifle than a pistol for that mission. Let's get back to the room first." Everett cautiously walked out of the rec room, then led the team up the stairs to Deck D.

Everett had the girls stand guard while he retrieved his Vektor, magazines, and his load bearing vest from his stateroom, then the three of them crossed the hall to the girls' cabin.

Courtney put on her load carrying vest and placed the rifle sling over her shoulder. "Lui. He knows what rooms the other peacekeepers are in."

"Good thinking. We'll take a stroll down to Lui's room. Courtney, you ask nicely to see him. I don't want to have to shoot our way into his cabin."

"How nice?" She puckered her lips.

"Not too nice." Everett pressed his lips together. "Sarah and I will stay on either side of the door so he can't see us through the peephole. Stand close so he sees your face rather than your tactical vest."

The three of them proceeded quietly down the hall to the Lui's cabin. Courtney stood inches away from the peephole and tapped lightly on the door. She whispered as if she had a secret to tell him. "Lui, are you there? Sorry, to disturb you, but I need to talk to you."

"Corporal Bekker, come in." Lui's door flew

open. The chief steward lost his smile as Sarah and Everett stormed in from each side of the doorway, pushing Lui into the room.

"Sorry about this, Lui." Courtney closed the door behind them.

"Don't shoot! Don't shoot!" Lui raised his hands and turned away from the weapons which were trained on him.

"Nobody wants to hurt you, Lui. Just calm down." Everett spoke in a soft tone.

"Why you come in room with rifle? What Lui do wrong?"

"Nothing yet." Everett patted the frightened man on the back. "We had a little issue with Lieutenant Baard. I need to know where his men are staying, and I need the keys to all of their rooms."

"All room keys hanging inside door of cabinet."

Sarah quickly opened the cabinet. "Looks like a ring of master keys for the whole ship."

"Yes, all keys for ship. You take! Lui don't say nothing." He covered his head with his hands.

"Where's the other security team sleeping?" Everett inquired.

"E Deck. Lieutenant took all room on E Deck for his men."

Everett counted off the doors on his floor. "So, eight rooms? They have eight rooms for twelve people?"

"Yes, Lieutenant have own room. His squad leader have room next to his. E1 and E3. Other ten men share remaining six room. I don't know who go where."

"Do you have any zip ties or duct tape?"

Courtney asked gently.

"All in Engineering Department."

Everett took out his knife and began cutting strips of cloth from Lui's bed sheets. "You can secure him with these."

Courtney explained, "This is to keep you safe, so you won't do anything that I'd have to kill you for. I don't want to kill you, Lui."

"No, I don't want you kill me either." Lui frantically shook his head.

Sarah and Courtney bound Lui's hands and feet.

Everett questioned Lui while the girls finished tying him up. "Does the captain or anyone else have a gun on the ship?"

"Not supposed to, but captain keep shotgun locked up in cabinet in his quarters."

"No one else?"

"Not that I know 'bout."

"What's the total number of crew on the Madison, including yourself?"

"Ten. It's skeleton crew."

"Does everyone show up for lunch?"

"Everyone except officer of the watch. One person stay on bridge. For lunch, probably First Mate Lopez."

Everett nodded. "If you're honest with me, I'll make sure you're not hurt. But, if you lie to me, you become a problem. We're only three people; we can't afford problems. Problems have to go overboard, Lui. Do you understand."

Lui nodded his head as it was the only part of him not bound with strips of the sheet. "I don't lie to you. Lui will not be problem. I assure you."

"We'll be back, and we'll let you loose," Sarah said as they made their way to the door.

Everett looked at his watch before leaving Lui's cabin. "11:15. We need to get to E Deck and eliminate all the other hostiles before the rest of the crew makes their way to the galley for lunch."

He glanced at the carpet beneath his feet. "The noise from the rifles will travel through the stairwell louder than from floor to floor. If we can get rid of them before people start moving between decks, it'll greatly reduce our odds of being heard. I'm estimating that we have about a half an hour."

"So, what do we do? Go from room to room, saying *housekeeping*, then slay everyone in the cabin?" Courtney huffed.

"That'll work on the first room. I'd imagine the occupants of the others will come out to see what all the fuss is about." Everett turned the knob of the door.

"I was joking!" Courtney's brows pulled close together.

Everett looked at the girls before walking out the door. "If Lui is being honest with us, we don't have to worry about E1 and E3. But, we'll have to clear those rooms to be sure. Then, we'll clear E2, E4, and work our way up. I don't want shooters coming out in the hall from both directions."

Sarah closed Lui's door softly as they exited to the stairwell. Everett opened the door from the stairs to the hall of E Deck. He nodded toward Cabin E1.

Courtney gently placed the master key into the door and turned it. "Housekeeping," she said softly and pushed the door open. Everett rushed in, followed by Sarah.

Everett looked past his rifle sights but saw no one in the cabin.

Sarah checked the bathroom. “Clear.”

Courtney checked beneath the bed. “Clear.”

“Let’s hope God will bless us, and they’ll all be sleeping in the last room at the end of the hall.” Everett looked down the hall before leaving the room.

They quietly made their way to E3.

“Housekeeping.” Courtney pushed the door open. Everett and Sarah rushed into another empty room.

The team repeated the process for cabins E2 and E4.

Everett waited for the girls to stack up behind him before proceeding to the next room. “Four to go.”

“Housekeeping.” She gently slid the key into the lock of E-6.

“We just got here today. We’re fine.” A voice called out from the other side.

“Someone called for fresh towels.” She pushed the door open.

“It wasn’t . . .” The man turned and looked curiously at the flash of light emanating from the barrel of Everett’s Vektor. POW! He was dead before he knew what was happening.

Sarah rushed in behind Everett, killing two more peacekeepers before they knew what was going on.

Courtney closed the door and secured the bathroom while Everett and Sarah dealt with the cabin.

A fourth peacekeeper dropped behind the bed, but Everett sent a steady stream of green-tipped 5.56 rounds through the mattress, which offered the man only visual concealment. Everett walked around the side of the bed and put two more rounds in his head.

"Travis! Who is shooting over there? Are you guys crazy?" A man rattled the door knob, then pounded on the door.

Everett tried to envision where the man's center of mass would be on the other side of the entry door, then opened fire, forming a pattern of perforation in the wood. Dead or alive, the man on the other side no longer seemed concerned with Travis nor the gunfire.

Everett changed his magazine, then worked his way up to the door. He could see the cabin across the hall through the bullet holes.

A man came running out with his rifle drawn. "Coetzee. What's the situation?"

Everett pressed the barrel to the door and unleashed another barrage into the man's sternum.

"Two more peacekeepers left." Courtney looked distressed.

Everett grunted, "And two possible rooms where they could be.

"Wherever they are, I'm sure they know we're here by now." Sarah changed magazines.

Everett pulled the punctured door open, then peered into the hallway. "We've gotta keep moving."

Everett took the keys from Courtney. "I'll stick

the keys in the door. You two give me cover fire. Courtney, you fire at the door I'm going in, and Sarah, you fire at the one across the hall."

"How am I supposed to do that?" Courtney quizzed.

"Door knobs on the left, you shoot on the right." He started out the door.

"What if I accidentally shoot you?" Courtney sounded perplexed.

"Just don't." Everett's eyes were wide with anxiety. Keep your rifles close to the door. When I say *now*, stop shooting until I push the door open."

"I don't like this plan." Courtney's voice was high pitched and hushed.

"Me either, but we're going with it." Everett led the way to the next room.

His hands shook as he held the keys by the lock. "Go!"

Sarah and Courtney opened fire at the two doors from point blank range. Everett shoved the key in the lock, turned, and pushed it open. Courtney and Sarah rushed past him with rifles leveled.

Everett didn't hear shooting as he followed them in.

"It's clear." Sarah returned from checking the bathroom.

Everett paused to catch his breath. "The pea has to be under the last shell."

"They're ready for us." Sarah's eyes showed her concern.

"Maybe not." Everett thought quickly. "This time, you two go into E5 and spray rifle fire into the walls toward E7. Drywall won't even slow down green-tipped 5.56. I'll go to the door and unlock it. Then, we'll go in and clean up. Start firing for five seconds on my mark. Sarah, you pull out after five seconds. Courtney, you lay down another five seconds of cover fire. When we hear you cease fire, we'll go in."

Sarah nodded. "Okay. Let's do it."

Everett gave the girls two seconds to get into position, then yelled, "Go!"

"RATATATAT! The Vektors barked out an even flow of ammunition.

Everett held his breath as he turned the key. "Four, five."

He kicked the door open and leveled his rifle at the inside of the cabin. Rifle fire erupted from inside the room, spraying erratically at the walls and toward the door. Everett knew if he waited for Courtney, she'd go in first, so he took aim at the general direction of the gunfire inside the room and rushed towards it.

He squeezed the trigger and continued to fire until his bolt locked open. He pulled the trigger several times, but nothing happened.

Courtney's rifle fired once more from behind him, and Sarah's gun, twice more.

"Clear." Sarah lowered her weapon and changed magazines.

Everett was in a daze. He looked at the bullet-riddled wall to his left, then around the room. One peacekeeper was dead on the floor behind him, and the other lay prostrate at his feet, eyes still open. Everett twitched and stepped back from the corpse.

"Change your magazine, Everett." Courtney

switched out her mag, tossing the empty one on the floor and refilling the pouch on her vest with a magazine from the tactical vest of one of the hostiles on the bed.

Everett also salvaged a magazine from the load bearing vest on the bed. He checked the ammo. "Green tip. We're good to go."

Sarah leaned against the wall to let Everett resume the lead. "Next time, we say we're Canadian."

"Agreed." Courtney fell in line behind Everett.

"Where to next, boss?" Sarah asked.

Everett hustled to the stairwell. "We need to get to the engineer maintenance room. We need those zip ties and duct tape. We need a way to restrain the crew."

"Little chance that no one heard all of that." Courtney followed him down the stairs.

Everett looked through the window in the hallway of F Deck as they passed it. He looked again as they descended past G Deck. "Not a creature is stirring." And again, when they reached H Deck. "Not even a mouse."

Chief Engineer Lars Andersen met them coming up from the ground level. "What is all that racket you people are making?" His Scandinavian accent was thick.

Everett took a deep breath. "Training. Don't blame us. Lieutenant Baard insisted because our two squads have never worked together before."

"But this is a ship. You can't train with live ammunition inside a ship! If you need to target practice, you take it out on the aft deck and shoot over the stern." Andersen took a deep drag from his cigarette, then threw it on the floor.

"You'll have to talk to Baard." Everett shrugged as if there were nothing he could do about it. "He actually sent us to ask you for some duct tape and zip ties."

"What for?" He scowled.

"Couple of the men's gear is loose."

"That's not my problem." Lars started to push past them.

"It will be if we get hit at Gibraltar." Sarah stepped aside as if she were going to let him walk by.

He paused and looked at her. "Okay. I'll get them after lunch."

Courtney curled one side of her lip. "We need them now. Baard isn't going to break for lunch until we get these guys tightened up. And if the crew doesn't wait for him to eat, he'll pitch a fit. That'll create a bad atmosphere for the rest of the trip."

"Let's get it over with then." Lars turned back.

Everett followed him into the engineering maintenance room and waited for him to scrounge up the materials.

Lars handed the requested items to Everett.

Everett didn't take them. "Just set them on the table, then go ahead and place a couple zip ties on your feet."

Lars shook his finger. "No, no. You'll not get way with this."

"You may be right, but you're not going to be the one who stops me." Everett leveled his rifle at Lars and took two steps back.

"I'm the engineer. You won't make it to Gibraltar without me. Go ahead. Shoot me. I dare you."

Everett took aim at Lars' forehead. "Like you said, we probably won't get away with it anyway, so why should it matter if we have an engineer or not? The only question is, will you still be alive to see us when we get caught, or will you be fish food at the bottom of the Atlantic?"

"Grrff," Lars grunted, picked up a pair of zip ties, sat on the chair in the corner of the room and tightened them around his feet.

"Courtney, get his hands." Everett kept his rifle trained on the burly fellow.

Seconds later, the team had the needed supplies. With Lars detained on the floor, they headed off to the galley.

CHAPTER 10

To every thing there is a season, and a time to every purpose under the heaven: A time to be born, and a time to die; a time to plant, and a time to pluck up that which is planted; A time to kill, and a time to heal; a time to break down, and a time to build up.

Ecclesiastes 3:1-3

Once the team had reached the landing of the third flight of stairs, Everett checked his watch. "Twelve oh five. Let's hope everyone is in the mess room. We'll speak calmly. If we're calm, they'll be calm. But, if someone steps out of line, we have to take them out."

"Roger that." Sarah stacked up behind Everett.

Courtney stood behind Sarah with her rifle at a low-ready position. "We need to keep some people alive. I don't know how to drive a container ship."

"Agreed. But the most important people to keep alive is us." Everett took a deep breath and opened the door to the hallway of F Deck.

The team stayed close as they approached the galley. Everett walked in first. Most of the crew were sitting down, but they seemed concerned.

Ana, the chief cook approached Everett as he walked in the room. "Have you seen Lui? He's never late for his shift, and he's not answering his phone."

"Lui's fine."

Captain Petrov stood from his seat. He held a pump action shotgun in his hand but did not point it at Everett or the girls. "What about Lars?" His thick Eastern European accent added to his menacing scowl. He checked his watch. "He's always on time for lunch. And where are other security personnel? Some of the crew told me they heard gunshots. If you are training with live ammunition, I need to be made aware of it beforehand."

"Lars is fine also." Everett nodded in an unruffled manner. "But I am going to ask you to relinquish your weapon, Captain Petrov."

Petrov put his other hand on the shotgun's pump. "No. This will not happen. This is my ship, and I will maintain control. You put it down your weapons."

Everett quickly took aim at Petrov's head before he had a chance to raise the shotgun. "Captain, you can't win this one. Drop your weapon."

"If you kill me. You never make it to shore."

Everett spoke to the girls. "Secure the door. No one leaves."

As Courtney and Sarah stepped in front of the doorway and lifted their rifles, the atmosphere grew tense. The rest of the crew froze like a room full of ice sculptures.

Everett continued to try reasoning with the man. He knew if he took him out, the entire situation would quickly deteriorate. This was the man the rest of the crew looked to for leadership. "Captain, I'm going to ask you one more time to put your weapon down. These people need you. You'll make a bad situation much worse if you force me to kill you."

"No. You make already situation worse. I don't play this game. I am leaving; going back to bridge. If you want shoot me, just do it. But you have to shoot me in back, right in front of whole crew. If you do this, they never help you get anywhere." Petrov walked to the kitchen, intending to bypass the door being blocked by Courtney and Sarah.

"If you walk through that door, I'll drop you before your foot crosses the threshold!" Everett commanded.

Whether Petrov thought Everett was bluffing, or whether he had a death wish, Everett did not know. The one thing Everett did know, was that Petrov was right about the effect shooting him in the back would have on the rest of the crew.

"So just do it and shut up about it." Petrov continued through the door.

Everett gritted his teeth as he squeezed the trigger. The bullet made a clean hole in the back of the captain's head, and the man toppled like a tree, face first into the kitchen.

Everett spun around to face the screaming and horrified crew. He pointed the gun at Second Mate Nate Williams, the next highest-ranking officer in the mess room. "Do you want to live or die? I need an answer right now."

Williams stammered. "Live."

"Then instruct these people to calm down right now. Tell them to lie face down on the floor with their hands on the back of their heads. Their lives are in your hands at this extremely volatile moment."

In his distinctly British accent, he said, "Do what the man says." Williams slowly got down on the floor.

Everett pointed to a deckhand and the messmate. "You two. Get up, get the zip ties from the ladies at the door, then secure the rest of the crew. Make sure it's tight. If you intentionally leave them loose, you'll be viewed as a problem to me. In the given situation, I only have one recourse for dealing with problems. Do you understand?"

They both mumbled, "Yes, sir." The two men kept their heads low and proceeded to get the materials as instructed.

Everett shouted, "Look at me! I need to know that you hear me perfectly. This is literally life and death for you two gentlemen."

They stopped and turned to Everett shaking in fear.

Everett repeated his question. "Do you understand?"

It seemed to be all they could do to look Everett in the eyes. “Yes, sir,” both said firmly, and almost in unison.

“Second Mate Williams.” Everett wanted to establish to the crew that some semblance of their world still existed by showing the ship’s command hierarchy remained in place, even if only as a puppet regime ultimately commanded by himself. He needed them to continue functioning in their assigned roles for the ship to cross the Atlantic. “Explain to your crew that all is well and that we’ll all live through this less-than-ideal experience, as long as we play by the new rules.”

Williams kept his head low but looked up around the room. “Everything will be okay. Just do what the man tells you.”

Everett personally tested the zip ties of each crew member. He looked at the name tag of the messmate. “Mr. Fernandez. What’s your first name?”

“Juan,” he answered plainly.

“Good. Juan, I need you to come with me. We need to go make sure the chief officer is going to be okay with the new arrangement.” Everett instructed Juan to get some zip ties, then led the way up to the bridge.

Everett nodded to Sarah as he walked out of the room. “Watch the crew. Courtney, come with me. We’ll be right back.”

“I’ll be here,” Sarah said.

Everett and Courtney followed Juan up to the bridge. Juan walked in.

Chief Officer Maria Lopez turned to him “Que

paso, Juan?"

"English please." Everett smiled politely.

Juan spoke nervously. "The man wants me to put the zip ties on jour hand and jour feet."

"Whatever for?" She turned to Everett. "What's the meaning of this? I've done nothing wrong!"

"We've had some issues. I'll explain everything once it's all straightened out, but for now, we need you to let Juan secure you. It's for your own safety."

"For my safety, please. Don't insult me, Lieutenant."

Everett offered a faint smile as he nodded to Juan to begin restraining her. "I assure you, my safety is not the one in jeopardy here. Trust me when I tell you, it truly is for your safety."

Juan placed the ties on her hands as she held them out reluctantly. "Where is the captain? Does he know about all of this?"

Everett waited for Juan to finish securing her before answering. "The captain made some bad choices. You're now the commanding officer of the Madison, so the lives of your crew are your responsibility. If anything happens to them, the blame rests on your shoulders."

"No, no, no! You killed Vasily? What have you done? What is going on? I demand that you tell me right now!"

Everett motioned to Courtney. "Go back downstairs. Cut the restraints off the second mate's feet so he can walk, and bring him up here. She's not going to be the one to help us get where we're going."

Courtney looked at him. “Don’t kill her. She’s not threatening us.”

Everett lowered his eyebrows, disappointed Courtney would think that he’d kill the woman simply to get rid of her. “I won’t. Bring the messmate with you when you come back. We’ll have him and Juan take her downstairs.”

“Who are you people?” Lopez asked.

Everett looked at her hand where the Mark had been implanted. “Who we are doesn’t matter. The only thing you need to be concerned with is whether you’re going to do things the easy way or the hard way. Yes, we need help to get across the ocean, but we’ll get it from someone. Team players are going to have a much better experience than those who resist.”

Everett looked out over the stacks of containers at the vast Atlantic. The trip wasn’t going to be the relaxing pleasure cruise he’d originally hoped for.

Minutes later, Courtney arrived with Nate Williams, the messmate, and the deckhand. Everett looked at the messmate’s name badge. “Hill, what’s your first name?”

“Clark.”

“Good. Clark, you and Juan need to get Mrs. Lopez down to the galley with the rest of the crew.”

“Miss.” She snapped her head. “It's Ms. Lopez.”

“Thank you for bringing that to my attention.” Everett made another mental note for his naughty and nice lists. “Courtney, leave Clark and Juan with Sarah, then bring Lui up to the bridge. You can cut the restraints on his feet so he can walk. I don’t think he’ll hurt you.”

"I'll be fine." She escorted the messmate and deckhand as they carried Lopez down to the mess room.

"And grab some walkies from the peacekeepers quarters on E Deck. We're gonna have to split up, but at least we can stay in radio contact."

Everett looked over the control panels, then turned to Nate Williams, the new captain. "Explain to me what I'm looking at."

"You've got the radars, and the ECDIS, or electronic chart display information system, which serves as our all-in-one-chart. Then the AIS, or automatic identification system, is what broadcasts our identification to other passing ships and eventually the port. The navigational controls that steer the ship and determine speed and direction."

Williams nodded to the comms unit. "That's the radio, obviously. Then you have a gyrocompass, magnetic compass, tachometer, which functions like the RPM gauge in an automobile, and an echo sounder to measure the depth, and watch out for obstructions in shallow water."

Everett nodded. It was a thorough answer. He took it as a sign that Nate Williams saw the wisdom in doing things the easy way.

Courtney returned with Lui and the walkie talkies in roughly fifteen minutes.

Everett took a radio, then cut Lui's hands loose. "Lui, we're gonna need your help." He nodded as he spoke to let Lui know that his statement was being phrased as a request, but really was more of a directive. "Captain Williams here, has been promoted. You'll essentially be the first officer.

He's going to teach you the basics of navigation. Teach you what you need to do to keep us on course, and how to know if something is wrong. I'm hoping the two of you will be our go-to-guys for getting us safely to port."

"I try Lieutenant, but dock ship take years of experience." Lui seemed eager to help but overwhelmed by the task before him.

"Captain Williams can get us into port, even if we have a couple scrapes and bumps. He's a smart man. I have full confidence that he'll survive the trip." Everett grinned at Lui. "Along with you, of course."

Lui smiled nervously. "Yeah, of course."

"Good." Everett turned to Courtney. "Any funny business, put a bullet in them. Anyone touches that radio, kill 'em. If someone calls in from another ship, just let it go, and don't answer. I'm gonna get Clark and Juan, and find a suitable place to hold everyone."

"We'll be fine." Courtney took a seat by the door.

Everett looked at Lui and the new captain with a steely expression. "No funny business. I'm not issuing warnings. First offense, you're going overboard."

Both men nodded, and Everett made his way down to the mess room. He passed a walkie to Sarah. "Channel three."

She turned on the radio, set the frequency, and clipped it onto her vest.

Everett pointed at the messmate and the deckhand. "Clark, Juan, come with me."

The two walked past Sarah and out the door into the hallway.

Everett looked them in the eyes. “To keep these people alive, I need a secure place to house them. Otherwise, I’ll have to cull the herd down to what can be managed by two guards. Between myself and the girls, one of us is going to have to sleep while the other two stand guard. You understand my predicament.”

Clark pointed down the stairs. “You could put them in a container on the lashing deck.”

“Those containers are locked.” Everett looked to Juan.

“We’ve got bolt cutters in the maintenance room,” Clark said.

“The maintenance room.” Everett had almost forgotten about Lars. “Okay. Show me.”

The three of them made their way down the stairs to the maintenance room. Everett instructed Clark to walk in first. He confirmed that Lars was still bound before entering himself.

“You can’t leave me like this.” Lars flopped around on the floor.

“Settle down before I put a bullet in your head.” Everett gave the man a light tap on the back of his head with the toe of his boot.

“What is going on? What are you doing?”

“I’m working on getting you up off that floor, so be nice!” Everett threatened to kick him in the nose.

Clark found the bolt cutters, and Everett led the way out.

Once out on the lashing deck, Everett looked up at the stack of containers piled one on top of the other, ten high. He looked back down at the containers on the first row. "What are these bars holding the containers on the first row?"

Clark pointed out the items as he spoke about them. "Lashings. The first three rows are secured with metal lashings, and the top rows are held on with twist locks, which attach at all four corners, top, and bottom of each container."

"Can the lashings be removed by hand?" Everett looked at the thick metal rods that hooked into the container at one end, and a metal brace on the ship at the other.

"Yes. The turnbuckles can be turned by hand. They loosen and tighten the lashings."

"Great." Everett pointed to the bottom three containers closest to the center. "Pull these lashings off, cut those locks, and let's see what's inside." He stood back and let Clark and Juan get to work.

Everett stood motionless. He looked on, counting the turnbuckles as the deckhand and the messmate removed them one by one.

Clark positioned the bolt cutters on the first lock. SNAP! Juan pulled off the lock, tossed it to the ground and lifted the lever to open the container. Everett pulled his flashlight out of his tactical vest and shined it inside. Floor to ceiling, the container was filled with cardboard boxes. "MREs. Let's go ahead and open the next container."

Clark popped the next lock, and Juan opened the giant metal box. Inside, stacked top to bottom, were wooden crates. Everett stepped forward to read the side of one. "M72 LAW. 66 mm, Rockets. Heat. Explosive. That might help us get through

Gibraltar."

He instructed the two men to continue with the next container. Once opened, Everett saw it contained a Humvee. "I guess that's not going anywhere. Remove the lashings of the container next to the MREs."

Minutes later, Juan and Clark had the doors of the metal box opened. Everett looked inside. "Radio equipment. Well, it'll be easier to unload than the Humvee. Why don't you two start clearing out the radio equipment? Go ahead and toss it all overboard. I don't want anyone to get tempted. Once that's done, clear out the MREs. Stack as many cases as you can into the empty spaces of the container with the Humvee. The rest, just stack up on the deck."

Everett radioed back to Courtney and Sarah. "I think I've found a place to put everyone, but it's going to be a while. Tell everyone to sit tight, and let me know if any of them start acting anxious."

"Roger that." Sarah's voice came over the walkie.

Courtney's voice was next. "Take your time. All is well here on the bridge."

Everett kept watch for the next four hours, allowing Clark and Juan to take breaks and eat MREs, but making sure they maintained their cooperative dispositions.

CHAPTER 11

And the fifth angel sounded, and I saw a star fall from heaven unto the earth: and to him was given the key of the bottomless pit. And he opened the bottomless pit; and there arose a smoke out of the pit, as the smoke of a great furnace; and the sun and the air were darkened by reason of the smoke of the pit.

Revelation 9:1-2

Everett's weary eyes looked out over the Atlantic from the bridge of the Madison Maersk. The faintest hint of dawn glistened on the horizon. He stood up to keep the blood flowing to his head. Williams slept soundly on a mattress that Clark had brought up to the bridge. Lui watched the instruments as he'd been instructed to do by the new captain. Everett felt ninety-nine percent sure that Lui wouldn't try anything, even if he were to accidentally drift off to sleep. But it was that one percent of uncertainty, and the horror it would bring which kept Everett vigilant about not closing his eyes.

Courtney walked onto the bridge with her rifle dangling from the single-point sling and a steaming cup of coffee in her hand. "Morning."

"How'd you sleep?"

"Surprisingly well, considering the day we had yesterday."

"Coffee smells great. Can I have a sip?"

She held her cup away from Everett and kissed him on the nose. "You're going to bed! And you need to get some rest, so no. The pantry has plenty. You can make more when you wake up."

"Okay." He kissed her forehead. "So, tell me the drill for the crew one more time."

"Everett, I'm not going to mess it up. Just go to bed."

"Humor me. I'll sleep better knowing we've reviewed the schedule one more time."

"I can let Clark and Juan out of container one at eight. They can use the restroom, then they need to take MREs and water to the chef and the two deckhands in container two. Afterward, they can eat what they want from the pantry, then they need to be back in their container by ten."

"Good. What about container three?"

She rolled her eyes. "It's maximum security. Nobody opens that door unless all three of us are there. And even then, only once a day for Clark to change their privy bucket, give them a fresh water bucket, and one MRE each.

"Everett, don't you think it's a little cruel and unusual to only feed them once a day?"

He shook his head. "Lars and Maria have the potential to be dangerous. We're keeping them alive, which is a huge risk to us. Feeding them more means they'll use their privy bucket more, which makes it that much harder of a job for Clark. It also reminds them that they failed to cooperate and despite all of that, they're still getting one meal a day. And as I explained to them, it can certainly go to zero meals a day if they start yelling, screaming, or being difficult. It's only for five days. They'll be fine eating once a day."

"What if the people in container two want to come outside?"

"No." This was exactly why Everett wanted to go back over the plan. He knew Courtney's compassion had the potential to get them in trouble, especially if he wasn't around to keep it in check. "They've got flashlights, mattresses, playing cards, books, all the MREs they can eat, and their privy bucket gets changed three times a day. It's a lot better conditions than Lars and Maria have."

"They didn't ask for all of this. We have to let them shower, Everett."

"Maybe we'll take them out one at a time to shower on Friday if they don't give us any trouble between now and then. They won't die from skipping a shower for two days."

Everett gave her a hug. "I'll see you in a while."

"Okay. Sarah is cooking breakfast in the galley. Stop by and get something to eat on your way back to your room."

"Maybe I will. Thanks." He blew her a kiss and closed the door. He made his way down the stairs, stopping when he reached E Deck. From there on down, the metal stairs, which had been painted gray many years ago, were stained red. Wide and uneven smears of blood marked the path where Clark and Juan had dragged the corpses of the captain and dead peacekeepers down the staircase, out onto the deck, and finally over the rail and into the abyss.

He marched past the morbid patches of dried blood and stopped by the galley. Everett took a plate of previously-frozen waffles offered to him by Sarah and returned to his room. Once there, he wedged the shaving cream can in between the deadbolt and the doorknob. If Courtney and Sarah were overtaken and someone wanted in, the added measure of security could eventually be overcome, but it would give Everett a chance to react.

He placed the waffles at the small table, which was by the window, and took his seat. The direct view was at the doors of a well-worn shipping container. Several more containers were stacked above it, as well as to the left and the right. But, if he looked past the rusty stacks of boxes, he could see the vivid colors of sunrise painting the sky, and the waves below reflecting magnificent hues of dazzling orange, neon hot pink, and pastel plum.

He bowed his head. "God, thank you for keeping us safe, and thank you for this meal. I pray you'll help me stay focused on the sunrise and not to get caught up in the grimy steel boxes of this world." He looked up and enjoyed his breakfast. Afterward, he took a long hot shower and went to sleep.

The next few days passed without incident. Juan and Clark proved to be reliable helpers in caring for the general needs of the rest of the crew. Captain Nate and Lui kept the vessel on course and were entirely cooperative.

Friday came and Everett made good on his statement about allowing the three crew members in the second container to shower. Everett, Courtney, and Sarah each worked a ten-hour shift. All three put in an extra hour to let the detainees in container two come out, one at a time, to bathe. Sarah watched the bridge while Everett and Courtney escorted Chief Cook Ana Garcia and the other two deckhands back and forth from the bathroom.

Garcia went first and took her time in the shower. Everett wanted to hurry her along, but Courtney insisted that he allow her an extra few minutes.

Next came one of the deckhands. He was in and out in ten minutes. The second deckhand also did not take advantage of the situation. He thanked Everett as the container door was closed and shut.

"Okay. I'm ready for a break." Everett let his rifle hang from the sling. He tipped his head from side to side, cracking his neck, and relieving the tension that had built up from the state of hyper-awareness required to deal with detainees roaming about the ship.

"How about I make you some hot cocoa?"

Everett opened the door to go back into the crew accommodations. "Sounds good."

His radio squelched. "Everett, Courtney, you better get up to the bridge as quick as possible."

Everett's relaxed state of mind quickly dissipated. He pressed the talk key. "Are you okay? The guys giving you trouble?"

"No. They're fine. But we heard something over the ship's radio. I think you'll want to hear it."

"On my way." Everett started up the stairs. "Can I get a rain check on that hot cocoa?"

"I could make it and bring it up to you."

"Just grab the packets from the galley and bring them up to the bridge. We've got a coffee maker up there to heat the water. Bring enough for Sarah, Lui, and Nate."

"Look who's going soft on the detainees now." She followed him up the stairs as far as the galley.

"If it's bad news, they'll need something comforting as much as we will. And nothing makes you feel better than hot cocoa," Everett said.

He was slightly winded from hustling up the stairs when he walked onto the bridge. "What's going on?"

Lui sounded frenzied. "So sorry, Lieutenant, but radio say big comet coming down. Probably gonna land in eastern Atlantic."

"That can't be good." Everett looked out at the sky. "Any idea where it's going to hit in relation to us?"

Williams shook his head. "No, sir. We heard it over the short wave. The transmission was grainy at best. If they gave latitude and longitude, we missed it. The report came from GRASA who said they initially thought it was a much smaller object. Thought it would burn itself out before it hit. Now, it's estimated to splash down in the Atlantic."

"Do we know when?"

"9:00 PM GMT."

"What time zone are we in now?"

"GMT minus three."

"So 6:00 our time. Right before dark." Everett adjusted his watch to the current time zone and inspected the calm ocean in front of the boat. "We've got about seven hours, so keep scanning the channels. We have to figure out where it's going to hit so we can modify our course. Nate, if you pick up any nearby ships on the radar, you can reach out to see if they have any other information. Make sure you put on your best Russian accent. Remember, you're supposed to be Captain Vasily Petrov."

"Yes, sir. I will."

"And don't even think about trying to sneak in a distress call. If we get found out, and peacekeepers try to board this ship, the only thing I can do with you is put a bullet in your head. There just won't be enough time to walk you downstairs and lock you up in a container. I'm sure you understand." Everett gave him an iron gaze.

"Yes, sir. I understand."

"Good." Everett turned back to the ocean. "Courtney is bringing hot cocoa up to the bridge for everyone."

Everett, Courtney, and Sarah all stayed on the bridge for the next two hours as Williams continued to scan through the shortwave frequencies.

Everett sighed. “I’m going to the galley. I’ll fix something for all of us. No use waiting around on an empty stomach.”

“I’ll let Clark and Juan out to do their afternoon chores.” Sarah followed Everett to the door.

Once they’d left the bridge, he looked back. “Why don’t you have them get enough food and water for the detainees to last three days. Regardless of where this thing hits, we’re going to have some choppy seas.

“All it takes is for one of us to lose our balance on the deck, then they’ve got the perfect opportunity for a full-scale mutiny.”

“Do you think Juan or Clark would do that?” Sarah stayed within a few stairs of Everett as they descended to the galley.

He paused and turned to look her in the eye. “If I were in their shoes, and I got the chance to overpower a guard and take his weapon, believe me, I’d take it. Wouldn’t you?”

“Yeah, I would. You’re right.”

“Everybody treats you good when you’ve got a gun pointed in their direction, but turn your back for one second, and that’s out the window.”

“Not everybody. Lars and Maria didn’t seem to care,” she said.

“They cared more than Petrov. But you’re right, there’s an exception to every rule.” Everett reached the galley level. “You be safe. Just tell Juan and Clark that we might have some inclement weather. They don’t need any more details than necessary. Tell them to get extra privy buckets with lids. We can toss them overboard when things settle down."

Sarah playfully chastised him. "GREPA would freak out if they heard you say that!"

Everett laughed. "With the next wave of judgments coming on this planet, trust me, a couple buckets of poop will be the least of their concern."

Sarah continued down the stairs, and Everett proceeded to the galley. Once there, he began rummaging through the shelves. "Maybe we better hang on to the dry goods. If we get hit too hard, we might lose power. Of course, if that happens, it means the engines have failed, and we're dead in the water."

He opened the door to the giant walk-in cooler. "Still, we might as well eat good while we can. It'll probably be MREs for the rest of the trip."

Everett pulled out a box with several individually-wrapped, vacuum-sealed steaks, and a bag of shrimp, both were marked as being the private stock of Captain Petrov. He found a sack of potatoes, washed them, salted them, and wrapped them in aluminum foil. He stuck them in the oven and set the thermostat to 475. "We probably won't eat like this again until we get to the Kingdom."

Everett continued to scratch up some marinade ingredients for the shrimp. His radio came to life. It was Courtney. "Everett, we've got the coordinates of the impact."

"Roger that. I'll be right up." He looked longingly at the ingredients to his perfect meal. Knowing it could be a while before he got back to the galley, Everett grabbed a bag of chips, a jar of peanut butter, and a loaf of white bread. He snatched a stack of paper plates and headed back up to the bridge.

“Talk to me.” Everett passed the food to Lui and made his way to the ECDIS screen where Williams stood.

Nate pointed at the electronic display chart. “We’re here. The comet, which they’ve named Apollyon, is set to strike about 300 miles off the coast of Portugal. Right around here.”

“So, that’s what… 500 miles from our location?”

Williams' face showed that he was absolutely petrified. “Yes, sir. Give or take.”

“So that’s good news. At least it isn’t going to hit us.” Everett tried to cheer the man up.

“I don’t know, sir. The wave, we don’t know how big it will be. GRASA has issued an evacuation warning for all coastal areas from Britain to Liberia.”

Everett found this piece of information quite disturbing but wanted to keep everyone else calm. “But they didn’t say how big the wave would be. That may just be precautionary. After the Las Palmas Tsunami, the GR operates with an abundance of caution on these matters.”

“No ships were recovered from the Atlantic after the Las Palmas Tsunami. We must hope that the wave is not nearly as great as that.”

Everett looked at the Mark on the back of Williams’ hand. Nothing he could say would comfort the man. “Yeah, let’s hope. Do we have a plan in addition to our hope?”

“We should turn the ship south, put as much distance between us and the impact zone as possible. Then, an hour before the impact, we'll turn around and set our course directly at the anticipated direction of the wave. We have to maintain forward momentum. We must keep the ship pointed at the wave. If it hits us from the side, it will roll us. Going straight at it is the only way through."

"Then that's it? We're home free?" Everett asked.

Williams stared at the ECDIS screen. "No. Just like throwing a pebble in a pond, smaller ripples will come after the initial shock wave. We'll have to maintain a steady course, head-on into the waves. The secondary waves could roll us just as easily if we get turned sideways."

"I suppose we should replace the lashings on the containers we've removed." Everett began to realize what a truly bad situation the wave represented.

"Yes, sir. I believe that would be prudent."

Everett called Sarah on the radio. "Go ahead and have Clark and Juan replace the lashings on all the containers but their own. Let me know when they've finished. I'll come help you put the last two on once they're inside."

"Roger."

Everett looked out on the deck of the ship. "What if we pulled the twist locks from the top couple rows of containers? Maybe when the wave hits them, they'd just float away. That might minimize the weight on top and reduce our odds of capsizing."

Williams shook his head. "If we were to do that, and the bow of the ship goes underwater, it would wash the rogue containers directly toward the bridge. We have very thick glass on the windows of the bridge, sir, but they won't stop a 2,500-kilogram metal container."

Courtney's brow was furrowed into deep rows. "Yeah, we need to keep the bridge intact. It's kind of an important part of the ship."

"And the twist locks, are they strong enough to hold the containers if we go under?" Everett stared out at the gargantuan would-be projectiles.

"Let us hope, sir. Let us surely hope."

Sarah called for Everett to assist in replacing the lashings on the remaining container. Once he'd finished that, he returned to the galley and resumed making what might turn out to be their last meal.

At 5:00 PM, Williams began bringing the ship about.

Everett watched the compass. "It's a slow process."

The acting captain nodded. "She's a big girl as it is. We're carrying more than 15,000 containers. Each shipping container is two and a half tons when it's empty. None of the ones on the Madison are empty."

Once the ship had been brought around, Williams began building up speed.

Everett stood next to Courtney with his arm around her. Until now, they'd not let it be known to Lui and Williams that they were a couple, but if these were to be their last moments on earth, Everett was determined to spend them arm in arm.

Minutes later, Everett stared at the early evening

sky. It was clear, soft like the petals of a powder-blue flower; like something from a painting. A pinhole of brilliant white pierced the perfectly even veil colored like a robin's egg. The pinprick grew, shining brighter. Everett picked up the binoculars from beside the AIS. The glowing object instantly became more menacing when magnified by the lenses of the field glasses. "This thing has a distinct red halo. I've never seen anything like it."

"Can I see?" Courtney reached for the binoculars.

Everett handed them to her. "Three years ago, I would never even have seen a shooting star. Now I notice the subtle color differentiations from one comet to the other."

"Welcome to the end of the world." Sarah took the binoculars next. "At least we've got good seats for it."

"You say that like it's a good thing." Everett took the field glasses once Sarah finished gazing at the meteor. It grew larger and the red halo burned brighter. Everett could see a clearly defined space between the white-hot asteroid and the radiant scarlet ring around it. It continued to descend from the heavens above, getting closer, and developing an elongated tail that penetrated the crimson halo. The comet's tail left a trail of smoke, also unlike anything Everett had ever seen.

"It's getting brighter." Courtney clutched Everett's arm as the meteor's center flashed vivid white. It faded over the horizon and out of view with no grand finale nor monumental spectacle.

"Everyone, strap down." Everett sat in the chair

next to Williams. All of the chairs on the bridge had been outfitted with rope from the engineering room for makeshift seat belts.

Sarah tightened the rope of her chair around her waist. "So, will the wave come crashing over us?"

"No. We're far enough from the impact that we won't be affected by the initial splash. And we're in deeper water than the impact zone," Williams replied. "A wave in the ocean functions just like a sound wave or any other wave in nature. As long as it has sufficient room above and below, it will transmit the energy evenly, crest to trough. A wave breaks when there is no longer room below the surface to maintain the distance between the crest and the trough."

Williams tightened his rope for a third time. "Our biggest worry will be the angle at which we're pulled up over the wave, and then when we come back down the other side."

Williams' constant fidgeting with his rope did nothing to ease Everett's nerves. It appeared to be contagious. Courtney retied her rope, tugging to check its security. Everett held the binoculars to his eyes, waiting, watching for the inevitable wave of destruction. "Apollyon," he murmured.

"What did you say?" Courtney quizzed.

"Apollyon, the name of the comet, it means destroyer." He continued to scan the horizon for any sign of the coming surge.

The bridge of the Madison Maersk grew deafeningly silent as all aboard awaited the inescapable fate ahead. Everett broke the soundlessness. "I see it." He passed the binoculars to Williams.

Williams stared out beyond the bow. His face paled. His body froze like a statue.

Everett snapped his fingers. “Stay with us captain. What’s going on? Are we on course?”

Williams pulled the field glasses away to reveal eyes as wide and round as the lid of a Mason jar. He stuttered. “Yes, no, I’m not sure.”

Everett took the binoculars back. The wave raced toward the Madison at a phenomenal speed growing larger and larger. Everett lowered the glasses and adjusted the wheel to aim the bow straight at the colossal mound of water barreling toward them. “Everyone shield your faces. If the containers break loose from the deck and come flying at the bridge, we could have shattered glass and water surging right for us.”

Everett braced for impact as the 150-foot wall of water rushed into the front of the ship. The bow disappeared into the ocean, which rose up and quickly blotted out the sky. The ship pitched upward as water flooded over the deck. The sound of the metal creaking against the pressure of the wave sounded hideous. The ship moaned with the songs of ghosts, a petrifying sonata of lost souls wailing a lamentation from beyond the grave.

Everett couldn’t help but watch. The bow emerged from the depth, pushing the entire vessel up at a one-hundred-degree angle. Everett felt the velocity of the gigantic ship being launched heavenward. He could once again see the sky. It lay right in front of him. Instantly, the wall of water on which the Madison lunged upward fell out from beneath them. The ship seemed to pause in suspended animation for a brief moment. The ship leveled out revealing a horizon with many more smaller waves charging toward the Madison.

Then, without warning, the ship tilted forward, rapidly falling downward until Everett was staring straight down at the surface of the ocean. Like a rollercoaster, the ship bolted down at a greater rate than free fall speed.

Everett's stomach churned, and his heart stopped as the bow of the Madison plunged into the ocean below. POP! POP! CRACK! SNAP! The force of the impact broke off several containers from the front of the ship, throwing them wildly off to the side. Water rushed over the deck as the ship leveled out once more.

"Water is over the third row of containers!" Sarah shouted as she pointed at the deck.

Everett sat silently, looking on, completely powerless to do anything about their situation. He observed the water running off the deck. The Madison Maersk remained right-side up and still afloat. "We made it." He let out a sigh of relief.

"Don't speak too soon. Here comes another one!" Courtney's voice sounded distressed.

Everett leaned back in his chair and held tight while the ship once again pitched up toward the sky. Again, it leveled out, and again, the ship raced down to the ocean below. The second wave measured more than ninety feet from crest to trough, plenty high to rip more containers from the front of the ship. Water washed over the first row of containers, and the ship dropped like a toy boat in a bathtub. The next wave approached from the starboard bow, washing over the deck and tossing the ship up at a slight angle.

Everett looked over at Williams who had his head tucked down and his eyes closed. "Captain, I need you to come back to us. The ship is turning. You need to get us back facing into the waves before the bridge becomes the basement."

Williams nodded and looked up, his eyes squinting and his face in a painful looking grimace. Williams took the wheel and pressed the throttle forward. The ship leveled out atop the wave, then came crashing down. Once more, containers were ripped from the bow. One washed around the side and struck the bridge castle, producing a shaking thud felt by everyone on the bridge.

Courtney looked at Williams. "You're doing great. Just stay calm, breathe, and keep doing what you're doing."

The wretched groans of anguish coming from the hull of the vessel being bent against the uneven sea continued like a phantom performing a concerto of death on a massive cello crafted in Gehenna. The metal creaked as if the wraith were dragging his bow across the instrument torturously slow, creating a hellish opus designed to steal the lives of men through trepidation and fright.

Everett watched Williams pull back on the throttle. "We've gotta keep the engine going. We're still sitting at an angle."

"Yes, sir, but when we level out on the crest of the wave, the propeller is sticking out of the water. If I push the throttle, we could burn out the engine."

Everett understood that they were at the mercy of the sea, at the mercy of God himself. Everett closed his eyes and prayed silently. *Jesus, I ask that you'll help us. Turn this ship, keep us afloat. But if it is not your will, I pray you will comfort us as you call us home. Keep us from fear and anxiety and help us to rest peacefully. While our bodies may die, we know that our spirits will live on because of what you've done.*

He looked up, determined to do all he could to prevent their demise. "And you've got the rudder cranked as far as it will go?"

"Yes, sir," Williams responded. "But, just like the propeller, the rudders aren't in the water while we're at the crest and on the first segment of each descent."

The ship crashed into the trough of the waves, water flooding over the starboard bow. The vessel listed heavily to the right, then quickly rolled to the left as the Madison began to climb the next wave.

"The waves are getting smaller." Courtney offered an encouraging fact.

Williams quickly deflated the hopeful comment. "Yes, but a series of fifty-foot waves could capsize us if we get turned perfectly sideways."

The acting captain stayed diligent in his efforts to bring the ship's bow back toward the wave. He throttled up while the ship was in the trough and in her assent, then pulled back for each crest and subsequent descent. Slowly, the ship began to turn.

Everett looked up and said aloud, "Thank you, Jesus!"

Lui and Williams both looked at him curiously.

Everett was sure they now understood why his team was at such odds with the Global Republic. He wanted to share the blessed hope he carried in his heart, but they each had the Mark. Too late; their souls belonged among the damned.

Everett kept watch on the bridge until the sun rose Saturday morning. Courtney tried to go down to her cabin to sleep, but she couldn't even make it down the first flight of stairs. The tempestuous seas also prevented Sarah from getting much slumber. Although, she did manage to nod off for a couple hours tied to her chair on the bridge, neither Lui nor Williams slept.

The sea eventually calmed to the point where the waves measured roughly twenty-five feet from crest to trough. Courtney turned to Everett. "We need to check on the people in the containers."

"We can't do it. Not until these waves get smaller. They probably got an inch or two of water in the containers, but it ran right back out. They'll be a little uncomfortable, but they'd survive."

"The containers on the bottom row were completely submerged."

Everett shook his head. "The containers aren't airtight, but they are water tight, which means even completely submerged, they'd only leak a little. Besides, we can't do anything now anyway."

Courtney looked out the window to the east. She rested her head on her hand and her elbow on the arm of her chair. "The sky looks threatening. Are we sailing into a storm?"

Everett surveyed the faint glow of daylight

trying to emerge from the east. The horizon was red and orange, like fire. The sky, which should have been lightening up, was still pitch black. "It looks more like a dark haze from smoke than cloud cover."

Sarah stood from her chair and steadied herself by holding onto the back wall of the bridge. "I'm going to attempt to make some coffee and a peanut butter sandwich. Can I interest anyone else in one?"

"Yes, please," Lui said. "But no coffee for me. I'm too nervous already."

"I'll take a sandwich, but I'm not up to the risk of drinking coffee unless you find a sippy cup with a lid." Everett continued to gaze at the ominous sky.

"I believe you're right about it being smoke." Williams studied the sky with the binoculars. The rising sun continued to reveal the heavy haze, which obscured the majority of the daylight.

The vexatious seas persisted throughout the morning and afternoon, calming only slightly with waves around twenty feet. But it was enough that Everett ventured down the stairs to his cabin and took a long nap.

He awoke later that evening and took over the watch on the bridge, allowing Courtney and Sarah to retire. The evening's meal consisted of MREs. Everett had no desire to attempt cooking with the ship still bobbing so much.

CHAPTER 12

And there came out of the smoke locusts upon the earth: and unto them was given power, as the scorpions of the earth have power. And it was commanded them that they should not hurt the grass of the earth, neither any green thing, neither any tree; but only those men which have not the seal of God in their foreheads. And to them it was given that they should not kill them, but that they should be tormented five months: and their torment was as the torment of a scorpion, when he striketh a man. And in those days shall men seek death, and shall not find it; and shall desire to die, and death shall flee from them. And the shapes of the locusts were like unto horses prepared unto battle; and on their heads were as it were crowns like gold, and their faces were as the faces of men. And they had hair as the hair of women, and their teeth were as the teeth of lions. And they had breastplates, as it were breastplates of iron; and the sound of their wings was as the sound of chariots of many horses running to battle. And they had tails like unto scorpions, and there were stings in their tails: and their power was to hurt men five months. And they had a king over them, which is the angel of the bottomless pit, whose name in the Hebrew tongue is Abaddon, but in the Greek tongue hath his name Apollyon. One woe is past; and, behold, there come two woes more hereafter.

Revelation 9:3-12

Early Sunday morning, Everett again looked out at a muffled sunrise shrouded in dark smoke.

"Good morning." Courtney arrived on the bridge to relieve Everett.

"How'd you sleep?" he asked.

"I probably got about four hours. I guess that's good, considering."

Sarah walked onto the bridge as they were talking "I slept like a log."

"We can walk on the deck now. Can we go check on the people in the containers? They've been cooped up with no word of what's going on since Friday morning."

Everett felt absolutely exhausted. As much as he wanted to go straight to bed, he knew she was right. "Okay. We'll go check on them. Sarah, can you handle the bridge?"

"I'll call if I need you."

"Thanks." Everett led the way down the stairs to the lashing deck. He rotated the turnbuckle to loosen the first lashing on the container where Clark and Juan were. Courtney held the large metal rod while Everett performed his task. The two of them removed the second lashing, then opened the container door.

"Are you guys okay in there?" Everett shined his flashlight.

Clark shielded his eyes from the light. "I bumped my head pretty good. Our mattresses got a little wet, but we're alive. What happened?"

Everett decided to fill him in. "Another large meteor crashed into the Atlantic and generated a tsunami.

"You've got a pretty nice gash on your forehead. Let's get you to the sick bay and get something on that bump. I'm sure you guys want a shower. Then you can get some dry mattresses, fresh water, and clean privy buckets. After that, we'll take care of the folks in the other containers."

Two hours later, Everett checked his watch. "Nine in the morning, and it still looks like dawn."

Courtney looked up at the haze all around. "I

know Lui and Nate have radar and all of that, but it makes me nervous sailing when visibility is this bad."

"At least the seas have calmed." Everett watched Clark and Juan who'd just finished giving fresh water, clean buckets, dry mattresses and first aid supplies to the banged-up crew members in container two. "How are you guys coming along?"

"We're all done." Clark closed the container door and placed the pin in the latch. "Do you want us to put the lashings back on?"

"I don't think that will be necessary. Seas should be fairly even for the remainder of the trip. Let's get food and water to Lars and Maria, then wrap it up."

"Yes, sir." Juan held the rod while Clark spun the turnbuckle to loosen the first lashing on container three.

"Ahhh!" Clark screamed in agony.

Everett stepped back and gripped his rifle, unsure if the deckhand intended on trying something stupid. "What happened?"

Clark dropped to the deck of the ship and convulsed in utter torment. "Something stung me in the neck! It hurts so bad, make it stop!"

With that, Everett knew Clark wasn't joking. "Juan, quick, help Clark back to your container."

Juan scooped his cell mate up off the floor. "Can you walk?"

Everett heard something buzz past his ear. "Hurry, Juan!"

Juan picked up the pace. "Yes, sir. I'm trying."

"There goes another one!" Courtney swatted at something.

Juan dragged Clark in the container and positioned him on the dry mattress. Everett shut the door behind him. Clark's screams pierced the doors of the metal container. Everett felt terrible for the young man, but he could do nothing to help. No one could do anything to alleviate the man's suffering.

Courtney frantically waved her arms. "They're all over the place!"

"Don't panic, they won't hurt us." He held her by the arm and escorted her to the door of the bridge castle.

Once inside, Everett looked her over. "We have to make sure none of them rode in on your hair or clothing. If they sting Lui and Nate, we'll be in a mess."

He saw one on the back of Courtney's pant leg. "Hold still." He removed his shirt and threw it around her leg, pulling the locust off inside the shirt. Everett stomped the shirt and walked to the waste can to dispose of the crushed insect. The shirt buzzed as he prepared to toss the bug out. "I can't believe it. That thing survived me stomping it with all of my weight!"

"There's a hammer in the maintenance room." Courtney started down the hall to get the tool.

Everett held his shirt tightly as he followed, careful not to let the repulsive creature get free.

Courtney came out with the hammer. "Hold it on the floor. I'll smash it."

Everett spun the section of the shirt into a tight knot, restricting the area where the tiny monster could crawl. He held the knot out for Courtney. "Hit it!"

She came down with the hammer. CRACK! She pulled the hammer up and smacked the shirt with the instrument two more times for good measure. "That should do it."

Everett cautiously shook the shirt and loosened the knot to see if the creature may have possibly survived. "I think you killed it."

He opened the shirt to see only a smear of goo, a hard piece of the bug's exoskeleton, and what looked like human hair. "Nasty."

"Yeah, that's gross." Courtney curled her lip in disgust. "Let's take it up to the bridge. I'm sure Sarah will want to see it."

Everett stopped off by his cabin to get a clean shirt, then led the way up the stairwell. He and Courtney walked onto the bridge to find Williams sleeping and Lui at the wheel. Lui turned to Everett. "Visibility almost at zero. Between smoke and bugs, I can't see anything. And very difficult to read radar. Bugs look like thunderstorm on radar. I'm very worried we hit other ship."

"How fast are we going right now?" Everett approached the wheel and looked at the radar screen.

"Fifteen knot."

Everett looked over at Sarah. "How long has Williams been out?"

"He lay down right after you guys left the bridge."

Everett paused for a moment. "I hate to wake him. He was up all night fighting the waves, but I think we really need his opinion on this one."

Everett walked over to the mattress and bent

down. He nudged Williams gently. "Captain, wake up."

Williams rolled over and pulled the shirt off his head that he was using to block the light while he slept. "Yes, sir."

"We've got a problem. I need your advice on something, then you can go back to sleep."

Nate Williams stood up and followed Everett to the wheel. He looked out the window in disbelief. "This can't be. Insects can't fly so far away from shore."

Williams looked at the radar screen. "The bugs are coming from the direction of the impact zone. Swarms and swarms of them. It looks like precipitation. Some of the swarms look like land masses and other ships they're so dense."

Williams stared out the window at the locusts as they swarmed around and around, buzzing, sticking on the window for a moment, then flying away. He turned to Everett. "It's not safe to keep operating at this speed. No visibility, we can't trust the radar. We're blind. We could ram right into the side of another ship." He took the throttle all the way back to idle.

Courtney looked at the confusing mass on the radar. "What about the AIS? If it's another ship, the AIS should tell us their information, right?"

"If the other ship's AIS is operational, yes. But that wave would have capsized smaller vessels. There could be thousands of ships floating around in the Atlantic, dead in the water, with no electronics whatsoever," Williams said.

"How fast do you think we can travel?" Everett

watched several complete sweeps of the radar. The swarms of locusts morphed from one globular green shape to another.

"I think we should kill the engines altogether." Williams crossed his arms.

Sarah asked, "Could we do five knots?"

"Someone would have to watch the radar at all times." Williams looked at Lui.

"Yeah, we watch," Lui answered.

"Staring at a radar screen for hours on end is quite demanding on the eyes." Williams turned back to Everett.

Everett stepped back. "So, you guys work it out. Take four-hour shifts, six-hour shifts, whatever you need to do to give your eyes a break. Your sleep is going to be segmented, but none of us are really resting easy in our current situation. Let's keep her going at five knots. No telling how long this swarm will last, and I'm sure you guys are just as anxious to get to port as we are. I'm positive the rest of your crew is."

Lui patted Williams on the back. "You go back to sleep. I watch radar. I wake you up when my eyes are too tired."

Williams didn't look like he was going to be able to go back to sleep anytime soon, but he accepted Lui's generosity. "If you see anything that remotely looks like it could be a ship, maneuver around it. Don't assume it's just bugs. Always act as if it is another ship. Treating bugs as if they were a ship may slow us down, but treating another ship as if it were a swarm of bugs will send us all to Davy Jones' locker in a hurry."

"Yes, Captain. I be careful." Lui gently pushed the throttle forward.

"Five knots. No more." Williams made his way back to the mattress on the far port side of the bridge.

"Five knots, Captain." Lui studied the ever-sweeping radar screen.

Everett unwrapped the soiled shirt to show the bashed bug to Sarah. "What do you make of this?"

She stuck her tongue out. "Yuck! Looks like what the Bible prophesied."

"Yeah, but do you think they're coming out of the asteroid, or do you think chemicals on the comet triggered something that was already here?" Courtney quizzed.

Sarah nudged the exoskeleton from the front of the creature which was still intact despite three solid strikes with the hammer. "DARPA did tons of research on bioengineering for the battlefield, super blood, super soldiers, all that. I'm sure you've heard about Monsanto's corn that will grow on an asphalt parking lot, and made-to-order CRISPR babies where the parents can select eye color, sex, hair color, and even edit out hereditary disease from the child's DNA, but a lot of darker stuff goes on that no one ever talks about."

"Yeah, I've heard about chimeras, creatures made from humans and pigs to try growing human organs." Everett sat in the chair next to Sarah's.

"That all came to light via mainstream channels like National Geographic, PBS, and the New York Times several years ago, but the experimentation had been going on for twenty years before anyone

LOCUSTS

ever admitted it." Sarah frowned. "Cassie, the lady in our group who was taken in the rapture. . ."

"Yeah, you told us about her. She was turned on to all of this stuff. What did she say?" Courtney listened anxiously.

Sarah looked down at her rifle. "Red pilled, she called it; being turned on to what was happening behind the scenes." She looked back up at Courtney and Everett. "Living Foundries is one of many of DARPA's on-the-books programs for genetic research. But, just as the military had places like Gitmo and offshore black sites where they can hold detainees that wouldn't be subject to US law, DARPA also had multiple off-the-books genetic research facilities that received black-box funding from the Pentagon. These sites weren't restricted by normal genetic research ethics codes, yet they had cut-outs or go-betweens that shared research findings between the on-the-books programs and the more surreptitious programs.

"The genetically modified mosquitoes used to combat Zika are one example of sharing. The research for those came from what scientists call the dark side." Sarah pulled one of the small strands of human hair from the bug mush in Everett's wadded-up shirt. "This looks like a prime example of some of the weaponized insects Cassie told me about."

"Why would it have human hair?" Courtney pulled away from the hair as Sarah held it up.

"It could be a side effect. They could have edited in human DNA in an attempt to make the creatures more intelligent."

Everett looked out at the bugs as they lit on the

window for a moment, then flew away. He shivered as he considered all the horrific testing that would have gone into engineering a creature like the locusts. "The toxin certainly sounds like a weaponized product of military experimentation."

Courtney looked at Sarah. "Maybe they created these things, then couldn't kill them, so they dumped the eggs or whatever into the ocean."

Sarah looked up. "Maybe they thought they did kill them, and they washed them down the drain. Perhaps they washed out to the ocean, and something in the comet brought them out of their dormant state."

Everett added to the growing hypothesis. "Maybe they never tried to kill them, but the research facility was swept out to sea by the Las Palmas Tsunami. A black-site research facility like that could have been anywhere. If it had been along the coast of Portugal or Spain, the debris would have ended up in the Atlantic, right around where the comet struck.

"Then, like you said, Sarah, some chemical agent in the Apollyon comet activated the larvae, or whatever dormant form the locusts were in before."

Courtney crossed her arms. "Whatever they are, and wherever they came from, we'll never get the truth out of the Global Republic."

"Yep. They'll never admit that the bugs were prophesied of, and they'll never admit it if they're a product of genetic engineering, especially if the research facility was still operational when the Global Republic took over." Everett stood and walked toward the door. He glanced at his watch.

"If you ladies will excuse me, I'm gonna hit the rack."

"Get some rest. We've got this." Courtney smiled.

Everett proceeded to his cabin and went to sleep.

CHAPTER 13

For in those days shall be affliction, such as was not from the beginning of the creation which God created unto this time, neither shall be.

Mark 13:19

Three days passed, but the smoke and the locusts did not let up. Wednesday afternoon Everett stared into the void of haze and insects from the bridge of the Madison Maersk. From time to time, he'd glance over at the acting captain.

Courtney walked onto the bridge carrying a large metal hotel pan. "I brought everyone some dinner."

"Great! What do we have?" Everett stood up and stretched his arms.

"Baked ziti!" She placed the pan on the break table by the back wall of the bridge. "But it's way better than regular baked ziti. It's got ground beef, tomato sauce, mozzarella, Swiss, black olives, spinach, onions; almost like lasagna, but I didn't have lasagna noodles."

"Sounds fantastic! Let's eat. Williams, put the throttle on idle and join us." Everett took a seat at the table.

Courtney and Williams joined him.

Courtney dished out the food onto plates that were kept on the bridge. "The good thing about it is, it's easy to pop in the microwave and heat up. That way, when Sarah or Lui wake up, they can have some."

Everett looked at Williams who appeared to be waiting for him and Courtney to start eating before he would commence. Everett pulled his rifle around to the side farthest from Williams. "I'm sure you've figured out that we're conscientious objectors to the Global Republic because of our faith. We pray before we eat. But don't worry, my God still hears me when I pray with my eyes open." Everett patted his rifle and winked at Williams. It was one thing to be cordial and polite, but Everett never let Williams or Lui think for a minute that he'd hesitate to put a bullet in their heads.

Williams looked away from Everett's eyes. "Yes, sir."

Everett looked at the beautiful dish made by his wonderful wife. He thanked God for the many blessings they still had despite the cataclysms the rest of the globe was experiencing.

"We need to get food and water to the people in the containers." Courtney took a bite.

Everett washed down his food with a long drink of water, which was in his coffee cup. "Containers one and two have several more days' worth of food and water. I wasn't sure if the seas would kick up again, so I had the guys overstock both."

"I know, but what about container three?"

Everett finished chewing. "If we open their container, they'll be stung."

"If we don't they may die of dehydration."

"The Bible says people will wish they were dead if they get stung. Maybe it's more merciful to let them die."

"It's not up to you to decide." Courtney took another bite of her food.

"Then we'll let them decide. But it has to be unanimous. If we get one yes vote and one no vote, we leave the door shut. A tie means no, regardless of how much the other person protests."

"Fine." Courtney continued eating.

After dinner, Sarah arrived for her shift.

"Hey sleepy head," Courtney gave her a hug. "You've got baked ziti on the break table. Just stick it in the microwave. We're gonna take food and water to container three before it gets completely dark."

"You're going out there?" Sarah yawned. "Are you positive those things won't sting you?"

"They didn't last time." Courtney held Everett's hand.

Everett lifted his shoulders. "The Book has been right about everything else. I can't imagine it would fail us now."

"Yeah, I suppose you're right." Sarah looked over at Williams who was finishing his shift and briefing Lui about the slow progress of the ship. "Make sure none come back in with you. Otherwise, it'll be bad news for these two."

"We'll be careful." Courtney followed Everett down to the exit door.

Everett lined up the buckets of fresh water and several cases of MREs so he could push everything out the door as quickly as possible. "Ready?"

"Just go. I'm right behind you," she insisted.

Everett hit the release latch and pushed the supplies out. Courtney hurried behind him, securing the door. Locusts swarmed all around them. Everett kept his mouth closed and batted the disgusting creatures away from his face. He grabbed the water and hurried toward the third container.

He knocked on the door. "Is everyone okay in there?"

"No, we're not okay. We're out of water, nearly out of food, and we're practically swimming in our own filth." Lars yelled from inside.

Everett looked at Courtney who had placed the MREs at her feet to swat bugs. He yelled to the container and explained the situation.

"If they don't sting you, they won't sting us. Just give us the supplies," Maria yelled.

"It's five months of agony. You will get stung. It's impossible to open the door and have them not come in. And they're extremely hard to kill."

"Just give us the food and water, please!" Lars yelled. "Let us take our chances with the locusts."

Everett called out again. "Put a lid on your privy buckets and leave them by the door. Then step to the rear of the container. If we open the door, and you are not at the very rear of the container, I promise you will not live long enough to find out how terrible the sting from the locusts are."

Seconds later, Lars called out. "We're at the back of the container."

Everett held the gun and let Courtney place the food and water in the container. Everett confirmed the two were in the rear of the container, then grabbed the privy buckets.

Before the doors were shut, Maria yelped in pain. "Oh! My leg! It stung my leg!"

Lars swatted at several locusts. "My hand. Oh, it hurts!"

Everett slammed the door shut and shook his head. By the time he had the privy buckets thrown overboard, the container was echoing with cries of torture. He walked by the other two containers and explained to each of them the situation. All inside had listened to the cries of Clark for the last three days, and vowed to ration the supplies they had on hand rather than have the doors opened.

Everett and Courtney managed to get back inside the door to the bridge castle with only two locusts following them in. The first was apprehended and dispensed with in short order. The other flew into the vent.

The next several days would be spent making slow progress toward Mersin and being certain the rogue bug didn't find its way to the bridge.

One week later, Everett stood on the bridge at the beginning of his shift. The sun shone through the smoke and cloud more brightly than any day since the comet. "Good morning."

Williams forced a smile. "Good morning, sir."

"Morning, Everett." Sarah stood up from her chair.

Everett looked at the radar. "It's clearing up. Do you think we could pick up the speed today?"

"I'm running at ten knots at this moment. I think we'd be safe at fifteen, at least during the daylight hours."

Everett looked back at the mattress where Lui was sleeping, then up at the section of bed sheet duct-taped over the air vent to prevent the rogue locust from finding its way to the bridge. "How long till we get to Gibraltar if we stay at fifteen knots?"

"If the air continues to clear, and we can get back to twenty-five knots, we could pass through the strait on Saturday."

"I want to go through the strait during daylight hours. Even if it means moving slower. We're a big, slow target that anyone can hit any time of day. I want to be able to see if I have to return fire."

"Yes, sir."

"How long from Gibraltar to Mersin?" Everett asked.

Sarah lowered an eyebrow. "Are we still going to Mersin?"

Everett tapped his finger on the AIS. "According to this thing, that's the only place we're authorized to go. If we change course, every ship in the

Mediterranean will know."

"What if the AIS had been knocked out by the wave?"

"Then we'd probably get boarded before we ever passed Gibraltar."

Sarah called Everett out into the stairwell so they could talk privately, yet still keep an eye on Williams. "Could we go anywhere else?"

Everett watched through the narrow pain of glass. "Jerusalem is a long walk from Mersin. If we don't go through the Med, you're talking about crossing continents."

"Mersin it is, then." Sarah opened the door and turned back to Everett. "But you're joking about walking, right? You do know that's like 600 miles."

"I hope so." Everett followed her back in.

"Still going to Mersin, sir?" Williams asked.

"Yeah, how long from Gibraltar?"

"Roughly three days." Williams glanced at the radar sweep. "If we have near perfect conditions."

Everett scoffed. "That's highly unlikely, but we can always hope."

Fair conditions persisted for the remainder of the trip across the Atlantic. Williams paced the journey to arrive at the Strait of Gibraltar just after sunrise on Sunday morning, March 17th. As they passed through the strait, Courtney remained on the bridge. Everett would monitor the starboard side of the vessel, facing Morocco. Sarah kept watch on the port side, facing Spain. Each had several M72 LAW rockets armed, and ready to deploy at a moment's notice if they were to come under fire.

Everett's radio squelched. "All good on this side. How's starboard looking?"

He pressed the talk key. "Calm. Just like it looked right before the comet hit."

"Why did you have to say it like that?" Sarah's voice came back.

"Guess it's the realist in me." He released the talk key.

Three Global Republic Coast Guard boats zoomed up toward the Madison Maersk from the starboard side of the ship. All three boats were light-weight, semi-inflatables with fifty-caliber machine guns mounted on the bow and stern of each vessel. Peacekeepers manned all six guns. Everett stepped up to the rail of the ship, looking down and making eye contact with the peacekeepers who looked straight up at him. Everett saluted the men as they slowed down by the boat. Then, as quickly as they'd appeared, the three semi-inflatables disappeared around the stern of the Madison.

Everett rushed over to the port side where Sarah was stationed. He knelt down, far enough away from the side to not be seen if the inflatables were to pass by her side. "You might have some goons coming around. Just salute them or give them a wave. No radio contact until we know they're out of range."

"Roger."

Everett heard the inflatables buzzing by and saw Sarah wave as he retreated to the starboard side of the ship. He spoke low to himself. "That's probably the first and last time I'll be thankful to see the

GR."

Everett saw several other GR patrols in the area. No other boats came close to the Madison while they passed through the strait.

An hour later, they were in the wide-open waters of the Alboran Sea, and on their way to the Mediterranean.

Everett called Sarah. "I think we're in the clear for now. I'm going to take water and food to our guests in the containers while we don't have any bugs around. If you want to give me a hand, we can call it a day once we're finished."

"I'll see you at the door."

The two of them went through the process of feeding, watering, and providing clean buckets to the crew members in the containers. Clark was in no condition to help with those chores, and Juan seemed to be having a rough time being pinned up with Clark and his incessant suffering. But, Juan was caring for the deckhand as best he could, so Everett didn't change the sleeping arrangement.

Everett quickly shut the door to container three after placing the food and water inside. The continual moaning of Maria and Lars was more than he could handle.

Sarah walked next to Everett on the way back to the bridge castle. "I feel so sorry for them."

"I do too, but it's God's judgment, not mine. The angel in Revelation 16 says righteous are your judgments. So, I'm not going to argue."

Courtney's voice came over the radio. "Everett, get up here fast!"

Everett flung the door open and rushed up the

stairs. "What's happening?"

"The locust, it chewed through the sheet over the vent. It just stung Williams!"

Everett could hear screaming in the background. He pressed the talk key as he hustled up the stairs. "Tell Lui to lock himself in the bathroom until we've got the bug contained."

"Roger." Courtney's response was brief.

Everett turned to Sarah. "Get me the hammer from the maintenance room."

She turned from following him up the stairs. "Be right there."

Everett removed his shirt while he cleared the last flight of stairs. He charged onto the bridge. "Hold my rifle!" He passed his weapon to Courtney and hurried toward Williams who was face down on the floor with his hands over his head and crying out in torment. Everett saw the locust, which landed on Williams back. Everett watched as the scorpion-like tail arched over the locust's back and stung Williams on his lower back near the spine. Everett threw the shirt over the bug and pulled it off.

Williams yelped in pain as the stinger came out of his back. Everett held the creature, wrapped in the shirt until Sarah arrived on the bridge.

Sarah walked in, winded from running up the stairs. "Here's the hammer."

"Give it to me, I've got a knack for killing these things." Courtney took the tool.

Everett held out the knot of the shirt containing the locust. "Watch my fingers!"

"This ain't my first rodeo." Courtney smacked the knot with the hammer, then took two more solid swings.

Everett loosened the knot and shook it.

"Is it dead?" Sarah watched in abhorrence.

"Yeah." Everett looked over at Williams who was writhing in misery. "We've got to get him off the bridge."

"Where do we take him?" Courtney asked.

"We have to put him in a container. I'll get a mattress and put him with Clark."

Sarah watched the man rolling on the ground. "Lui can't dock the ship."

"We'll bring him back up when we get to Mersin, but we can't listen to that for the next three days."

Courtney huffed. "It'll be more like four days without an acting captain."

Everett knew she was probably right. He turned toward the door. "I'll get a mattress set up and come back up to get him in a while."

CHAPTER 14

Therefore I say unto you, Take no thought for your life, what ye shall eat, or what ye shall drink; nor yet for your body, what ye shall put on. Is not the life more than meat, and the body than raiment? Behold the fowls of the air: for they sow not, neither do they reap, nor gather into barns; yet your heavenly Father feedeth them. Are ye not much better than they? Which of you by taking thought can add one cubit unto his stature? And why take ye thought for raiment? Consider the lilies of the field, how they grow; they toil not, neither do they spin: And yet I say unto you, That even Solomon in all his glory was not arrayed like one of these. Wherefore, if God so clothe the grass of the field, which to day is, and to morrow is cast into the oven, shall he not much more clothe you, O ye of little faith?

Matthew 6:25-30

Three and a half weeks had passed when the Madison Maersk finally arrived at the Port of Mersin at dusk on Thursday. Everett brought Williams back up to the bridge, but his pain persisted. Sarah gave the acting captain a shot of morphine from the sick bay.

"How are you feeling?" Everett patted Williams on the back.

"Awful." He gasped for breath. His face was swollen and red from a sting on his left cheek.

Everett passed him a bottle of vodka scavenged from Petrov's stateroom. "Are you going to be able to get us into the port?"

Williams took a deep drink, winced, then handed the bottle back to Everett. "I will try. I'll need Lui, and I'll need one of you to watch from the far side of the bridge."

"Whatever you need. Another drink?"

Williams chugged the bottle again, then handed it back. "Thank you."

Everett coordinated the team as Lui brought the ship through the giant breakwater and toward the dock. Once they pulled up to dock, Williams took the controls.

Sarah watched from the far wing of the bridge.

"You're too close! You're too close!"

BANG! The ship stopped suddenly as it slammed into the side of the dock.

"That's gonna leave a mark." Everett managed not to lose his balance.

"Okay, you're good, you're good." Sarah watched.

Everett gave the command for Sarah and Courtney to follow him. He ripped the mic from the radio so Williams or Lui wouldn't be able to call out after they'd left the bridge. Everett pointed his rifle at the two men. "Give us ten minutes before you start yelling for help, or I will kill you."

"Yes, sir. Lui don't tell anybody, thank you for let me live. I'm very appreciate." Lui put his hands together and bowed.

Everett knew Lui's gratitude was as shallow as the threat of killing them if the team was caught. Now it was time to move, and they had to go fast. The team hustled down the stairs to the gangway where their packs and duffles were waiting for them. Everett now wore Lieutenant Baard's uniform. No more Second Lieutenant.

Everett stormed off the gangway with a snarling scowl, pointing at the sergeant standing guard. "This captain is drunker than a skunk! Get your men up there and arrest him this minute!"

"Yes, Lieutenant." The sergeant saluted Everett and stormed up the gangway.

"Slow down! I need immediate transport to Ankara, and I'm already two weeks late. Where is the GR commandant for the port?" Everett barked.

The sergeant looked confused about whether he

should obey Everett's orders to arrest the captain or to provide directions. He stuttered, "Th, th, there's a white building to the north of the container yard."

"Carry on." Everett waved the peacekeeper on and led the team.

"Are we going to the commandant?" Courtney stepped fast to keep up with Everett.

"No, but if anyone asks him where we went, that's where he'll send them." As soon as the team was behind the cover of the containers, Everett broke into a sprint. "I saw GR Coast Guard vessels to the north. We need one of those."

"How are *we* going to get a hold of one?" Sarah grunted as she jogged behind Everett. "Never mind. I don't even want to know."

After a 400-yard jog, Everett slowed down and regulated his breath. He dabbed the perspiration from his head as he walked up to the Coast Guard office. He pulled the door open. Courtney and Sarah followed him in.

"I need a boat. My corporal saw someone on that large container ship throw something overboard. That ship is full of military supplies, so we're not talking about heroin or pills."

The robust Arabic man sitting behind the desk seemed to bite his tongue as he looked at Everett's rank patch. "We'll be more than happy to check it out for you. It looks like the lieutenant has somewhere to be anyway."

"Yes, I was supposed to be securing a transport to Ankara, but instead, I'm doing the Coast Guard's job because the Madison Maersk had no escorts into the port." Everett fumed as he pointed to the phone.

"Now get me the commandant. I'm going to see this thing through one way or the other. And he'll know why I'm having to involve myself!"

The fat man in the chair waved his hand to the thinner one who'd been speaking with him. He rattled off some orders in what Everett assumed was Turkish. "Hasan will be happy to take you out on the water. Anywhere you need to go. We are at your service."

Everett angrily followed the thin man to the dock.

Hasan motioned toward a semi-inflatable. "This boat. We take. You leave bag here. We come right back."

"No, we'll take our bags with us. Once we've identified what was thrown overboard, you'll drop us as close to the commandant's office as possible. I have no desire to run back and forth because you people can't do your job."

Hasan frowned. "Yes, Lieutenant."

They were soon in the boat and speeding away from the dock. Everett directed Hasan to go out past the breakwater, into the Mediterranean, then east.

As they buzzed further east, Hassan turned to Everett. "Excuse me for say so, sir, but I don't think so ship could be coming from this direction. Perhaps the corporal doesn't remember."

"Just keep going a little further."

A voice, which sounded much like the chubby man in the office, came over the radio. The only word Everett could make out was "Hasan."

The man turned to look at Everett suspiciously. His eyes grew wider as he looked down to see

Everett's pistol pointed at him. POW!

Hasan dropped to the floor, and Courtney quickly took the wheel. Everett motioned to Sarah. "Help me get Hasan over the side." Splash!

"Where to?" Courtney kept speeding forward.

Everett scanned the coast. "Get closer to the beach. If we see a river or canal, we'll turn off. It's night. We've got a good chance of getting away."

Sarah pulled one of the M72 LAWs out of her duffle. "This might increase our chances if we get a tail."

They continued to stay close to the beach for another mile. Everett pointed. "Right there! Take that canal!"

Courtney cut the boat hard to the port side and sped toward the canal. The canal took them roughly five miles inland before it became too shallow to navigate. "Now what?" Courtney asked.

"Take us back to the last bridge. We'll hide the boat under there so it won't be visible by helicopters. No one will see it 'til morning, and we'll be out of the area by then."

They stashed the semi-inflatable GR Coast Guard boat and began following the road, which ran north alongside the canal.

Navigating by only the slim glow of moonlight, the team continued walking up the dirt road through an agricultural area.

"These bags are getting heavy," Courtney complained. "Maybe we should drop the rockets."

Everett pointed ahead. "See that glow? There's a city or a town up ahead. It's less than half a mile. The rockets weigh about five pounds each, and you've only got three in your bag."

"But I've got bullets, magazines, food, and clothes. It adds up."

"You'll make it, soldier. Just keep putting one foot in front of the other." He walked close to her.

They reached the edge of the city in a matter of minutes.

"We have to find a vehicle. I can't keep packing this junk." Courtney repositioned the heavy duffle over her other shoulder.

Everett walked up to an intersection and waved down a dusty, white flatbed truck, stepping in front of it and blocking the lane. "Do you speak English?"

"Little bit. What did I do? Why are you stopping me?" The middle-eastern man held his hand in the air.

"You didn't do anything. But our vehicle broke down a few miles back, and we need a lift into town. It's for His High and Most Prepotent Majesty, Angelo Luz." Everett softened his stern expression. "What's your name?"

"Ali." The man looked curiously at Everett and the girls. "I drove this road. I didn't see GR vehicle."

"We got turned around, we were coming from the other direction."

Ali's face showed that he wasn't buying Everett's spiel. "I never see only three peacekeepers in Tarsus. Always I see twenty, thirty together. It's very dangerous here for you."

"Tarsus? As in Paul of Tarsus?"

"Tarsus, yes. Have St. Paul's well in the old city.

But I don't know about other Paul here. Do you not know where you are?" Ali looked surprised.

"Why would you say it's dangerous for us here?"

"MOC."

"Mock, who is Mock?" Everett quizzed.

Ali grew visibly impatient with the imposters. "MOC. Martyrs of the Caliphate. They have many skirmish with the GR in Tarsus and Mersin."

Instantly, Everett understood how vulnerable his team was. He stuck his hand in his pocket and pulled out the small velvet sack given to him by Tommy. He reached inside and took out a one-carat stone. He held it up so Ali could see it. "Take me to the person who can convert this into a local underground currency, gold, silver, whatever, and ten percent of it is yours."

Ali protested. "Are you kidding me? You just ambush me like you are GR peacekeeper, and now you want me to take you to someone who operates in black market? GR punishment for this is death. You are not peacekeeper. How do I know this is not set up?"

"Who'd set you up, Ali? The GR? I thought you just said we're not GR?"

Ali shook his head and waved his hands feverishly. "No, no. I don't get involved with this."

Everett lowered the stone, putting it back in his pocket. "We might not be real peacekeepers, but the guns are real."

Ali looked at Courtney and Sarah who were standing back with weapons at low ready in case he tried something foolish. Ali turned back to Everett. "Twenty percent."

Everett motioned for the girls to get onto the flatbed, then walked around to the passenger's side. "Twenty percent."

Ali swallowed hard and put the truck in gear. "I take you to Sadat. But if the diamond is not real, he will kill you."

Everett watched cautiously out the window as Ali drove through town, and down a boulevard lined with three and four-story apartment buildings, stacked one against the other. Most of the buildings were in poor condition. Some were cracked, some were missing the front wall, or upper floors, and some were merely piles of rubble. Everett guessed most of the serious damage had occurred in the great quake. However, the majority of the buildings didn't look like they'd been painted since the 1970s. Ali parked in front of a row of buildings, which were still standing.

"You must hurry. Don't let anyone see you." Ali got out of the truck and directed Everett and the girls to a run-down café.

The shabby eatery sat at the ground level of a four-story, faded-green apartment building. The man behind the counter looked as if he were counting the minutes. When he looked up and saw Everett and the girls, his mouth dropped open, and his eyes widened.

Ali spoke to the man in Turkish, and he calmed down. The man pointed to the store on the left.

"I'll be right back." Ali headed for the front door.

Everett watched as Ali exited. "Keep your heads on a swivel. I hope he's not about to pull a fast one."

"I don't like it." Sarah glanced at the man behind the counter, then at the front door.

Everett pressed his finger on the trigger guard of his rifle. "Me either, but we have to see how it plays out. We're in a country where we don't speak the language or know a soul. It's not the best situation."

Ten minutes later, Ali returned. "Follow me."

Everett and the girls followed Ali out the back door, into the alley, and through another door, which came in the back of another shop, on the same strip of buildings. They climbed a flight of stairs, and Ali knocked on a door.

A thick, towering man with a black suit and a bald head opened the door. The smell of hashish wafted in Everett's face. The man said, "Come in. Give me rifles."

"No way," Everett protested.

"Then get out!" The giant of a man drew his own large-frame, semi-automatic pistol and stepped forward, keeping Everett from entering.

Ali put his hand on Everett's back. "It's okay. Nothing will happen to you. Sadat is business man. But you must go by house rules."

Everett looked back at Courtney and Sarah.

"We really don't have much of a choice." Courtney pursed her lips.

Everett reluctantly handed his rifle to the man at the door, who then let him pass. Everett and the girls held their duffles close to their bodies as they walked down the narrow, smoke-filled hallway. They passed some doors where music was playing very loudly, and finally came to a door at the end of the hall.

Ali knocked. A voice from inside spoke in English. "Come in."

Ali led the way, and the team followed. Inside, was a large room that looked like it used to be an apartment but had been converted into something that looked like a VIP area from a night club. A giant, plush sectional couch wrapped around a coffee table. Speakers surrounded the room as well as video screens. What looked like stage lighting was mounted to the walls, and a disco ball hung in the center of the room. Two more bald giants wearing black suits with Uzis hanging from slings over their shoulders stood on either side of the door.

"Studio 54," Courtney whispered.

Sarah replied softly, "More like Area 51."

Ali led the way to a huge mahogany desk. Behind it sat yet another bald man. This one was less muscular than the others Everett had encountered but appeared to weigh about the same.

"This is Sadat," Ali said.

"Nice to meet you. I'm Everett, thanks for seeing us." Everett offered his hand.

Sadat looked at Everett's hand but did not shake it. "I was having party. I need to get back to my guests. What is it you want? And please tell me this will be more interesting than one little diamond. I'm not small-time broker. For that, you go to guys on street."

Everett felt uncomfortable. Sadat was higher up on the food chain than who he'd hoped to meet. "I need local currency. Whatever you're using to get around the Mark."

Sadat looked at the uniforms, then glanced at the back of Everett and the girls' hands. "Most people using silver coins, gold coins, or just barter for goods. So, it depends, what do you need currency for?"

"For now, we need a secure place to sleep for the night, and we need transportation. But, I'm still going to need currency."

"Why you don't go to GR outpost at port in Mersin? It's like 25 kilometer."

Everett looked Sadat in the eye. He knew Ali had informed the man that the team wasn't really GR peacekeepers, but obviously, the gangster was going to make him say it. "These are just uniforms."

Sadat smiled and nodded his head slowly. "GR is looking for you?"

"Does it matter?"

"I want to know, in case somebody ask."

"If anyone asks, you haven't seen us." Everett smiled.

"I can get for you car. All of this building, and building next door are mine. So, I'm sure we can work out some deal. How far do you need to go?"

"About 600 miles."

"So about 1,000 kilometer." Sadat crossed his hands and leaned back in his office chair. "1,000 kilometer. You're going to Istanbul?" He stared silently into Everett's eyes. "No. Jerusalem. Why are you going to Jerusalem? Particularly if you don't want to be near GR?"

"What will you charge us for a car?" Everett ignored the interrogation.

"You need something fast, four-wheel drive, and

something tough. The earthquake made the roads very bad. And on top of that, you have to go through Syria and Lebanon. Thanks to your old government, Martyrs of the Caliphate control that entire region. When you get to Syria, don't stop until you cross over into Jerusalem." Sadat laughed. "And don't wear this silly uniform. You won't even make it out of Turkey."

Everett neither confirmed nor denied Sadat's speculation about their intended journey. "How much?"

"Six carats for the car. Nothing smaller than quarter carat, and at least two one-carat stones in the mix."

"What makes you think I have five carats?"

Sadat lost his congenial demeanor. "Don't play around. I don't have time. Peacekeepers come from America all the time with bags of diamonds. You don't walk in here and try to buy car with one-carat diamond."

Everett didn't want to give up the smaller stones. He needed them for smaller transactions. And he knew the larger stones were worth much more. He stuck his hand in his pocket and felt around for a big one. He pulled it out and glanced at it in the palm of his hand before showing it to Sadat. *Two and a half*, he thought. He held it up to the light for Sadat to see. "Will you take this for a good vehicle? Land Rover, Humvee, something hardy like that with clean tags?"

Sadat snapped his fingers and held out his hand. "Let's see."

Everett gave him the rock.

Sadat pulled out his loupe and inspected the diamond. He looked at one of the guards by the door and spoke in Turkish. The man nodded and left the room. Sadat pulled out a small cloth and wiped the stone down, inspecting it yet again, holding it to the light.

The man returned a few minutes later and handed Sadat a vehicle key, speaking to him in Turkish.

Sadat nodded and looked at Everett. "I give you 2016 Volkswagen Tiguan White. All-wheel-drive. Many of these vehicles on the roads."

"And fuel?"

"No." Sadat held up the stone. "This is for car only. One carat for full tank and extra thirty liters."

"You'll take four quarter-carat stones?"

"I'll take two half-carat stones and give you place to sleep tonight."

"Can we see the car?"

"Be my guest. Ali will show to you. But let's settle up now. I need to get back to my guests."

Everett looked at the stone in Sadat's hand. "You've got my rifles, and roughly a two-and-a-half-carat stone. I've got nothing. If you don't mind, I'd like to see the vehicle and get the keys before I give up anything else."

Sadat spoke to Ali in Turkish and gave him a key. He opened his drawer and handed him another key. Ali took the keys and replied in Turkish.

Sadat stood up from his desk. "Ali will bring you to my party after you have seen Tiguan." Sadat pointed to his bathroom. "If you have other clothes, I suggest you put them on before walking out in the street. And by no means come to my party dressed like this. You will ruin the ambiance." He walked out of the room, but the guards stayed.

Ali held out his hand. "You promised me twenty percent. So, I should get at least half-carat stone for all of this."

"You wanted twenty percent of the converted currency from a one-carat stone!" Everett protested.

"Oh no. I wanted to be left alone. But you insisted, and I agreed to twenty percent of whatever you did with Sadat!"

Everett pulled out a quarter-carat diamond and gave it to Ali.

Ali inspected it. "Too small. Give me one bigger. At least twice this size."

"Will you get us something to eat tonight and tomorrow morning so we don't have to go back out?" Everett took out another quarter-carat diamond.

"Okay. Dinner and breakfast. But give it now." He snapped his fingers two times and held out his palm.

Everett handed him the second stone. "Girls, get changed."

Courtney and Sarah went into the bathroom. They came out wearing jeans and flannel tops over tee shirts. They still wore their combat boots, but the legs of their jeans were pulled over the top.

Everett changed into cargo pants and a light jacket. The evening temperatures would get in the low fifties. He used an inside the waist holster to tuck his Sig in the back of his pants. His Glock 43 backup gun went in his front pocket. He hoisted his duffle over his shoulder.

Ali pointed at the floor. “You can leave bags here. No one will take them.”

Everett might have taken him up on the offer if the duffles had only contained a change of clothes and a clean pair of socks, but he had a feeling the M72 rockets might be useful crossing the territory held by MOC. “They’re no trouble. We’ll carry them.”

They made their way down the stairs, out of the alley, and to a parking lot where the Tiguan was parked. Everett quickly confirmed the vehicle was in good working order, then the team followed Ali to the top floor of the building. It was much more quiet and didn’t smell like hashish.

Ali opened the first door by the stairs and flipped on a light. “This is your room. Electricity might not stay on all night. So, if you need it for something, use it while it’s on.”

Everett walked in. The furnishings were old, like items that had been tossed out by a thrift store, but it was clean. The paint on the walls looked like it was the same ugly green that was on the outside of the building, and probably applied in the same year. “How does Sadat have parties when the electricity goes out?”

“Sadat have generator.” Ali walked back out the door. “I bring guns when I bring food.”

“Okay.” Everett closed the door behind him. He looked at the girls. “I’m going downstairs to settle up with Sadat. Keep the door locked.”

“Don’t get lost.” Courtney winked.

He chuckled. “I won’t.”

Everett took only the two stones he needed to pay his bill with Sadat.

CHAPTER 15

And he shall confirm the covenant with many for one week: and in the midst of the week he shall cause the sacrifice and the oblation to cease, and for the overspreading of abominations he shall make it desolate, even until the consummation, and that determined shall be poured upon the desolate.

Daniel 9:27

Everett awoke to the sound of a television in the other room Friday morning. He sat up. Dim light shone through the sullied bedroom window. Everett stuck his feet in his boots and walked out into the living area of the small rented apartment to see the girls watching TV.

"How did you sleep?" Courtney took another bite of the pastry she was eating.

"Not bad. After living in a cave for so long, I have rather humble standards when it comes to accommodations. What are you guys eating?"

"Baklava and some kind of sugary apricot rolled in pistachios. Have some." Sarah passed the white bakery box to Everett.

"I see the electricity is back on. What are we watching?"

"Global Republic Broadcasting Network, what else?" Courtney said sarcastically.

Sarah passed a Styrofoam cup with a lid to Everett. "Luz has a big announcement in a little while."

Everett sipped his coffee and nearly choked. He coughed and cleared his throat.

"You okay?" Courtney fought a smile.

"That's like espresso! Why is it so big?" Everett looked at the cup as if it were intended for an entire family.

Sarah giggled. "You don't have to drink the whole thing."

A knock at the door startled Everett, and he grabbed his rifle. He checked the peephole. "It's Ali." He removed the chain and flipped the latch to the deadbolt.

"It's good. No?" Ali pointed at the bakery box.

"Fantastic!" Courtney picked up another baklava.

"And how did you sleep, Everett?" Ali stepped past the doorway so Everett could close the door.

Everett replaced the chain. “Very good. The room was just what we needed.”

“What time will you be leaving?”

“Luz is supposed to be speaking soon, so it must be an important announcement. We were going to hang around for a little while to hear it and head out after that. Unless Sadat wants us gone right away. He didn’t specify a time for checkout.”

Ali waved his hands. “No, no. Sadat don’t care. I am asking because he said he would exchange some silver coins for more diamonds if you want. If you are not in a hurry, that is. He has some meeting on other side of town, but will be back around lunch.”

“Another chance to milk us dry, I’m sure.” Everett picked up his coffee.

“Why you say that? Sadat like you. He is a business man, but he give the best exchange rate. Many people in this city would have killed you and robbed you.”

Everett looked at Ali. “You’re right. He didn’t rob us. And we are grateful. Although, I’m not so sure about him liking us. He wouldn’t even shake hands.”

“This is Turkey. People keep distance until they know you. But trust me, Sadat like you. He like anyone who is not GR. But, you are crazy American, traveling through dangerous part of world, and with two beautiful women.” Ali glanced at the girls and blushed as if he’d experienced a momentary lapse in discretion.

Everett chuckled. “Yeah, well, America ain’t what she used to be. Believe it or not, this place is paradise compared to what we left. And you can tell

Sadat that we'll stick around until lunch time."

"I tell him." Ali let himself out. "Bye-bye."

Everett waved, then locked the door.

"It's starting!" Courtney pointed at the television.

Everett sat beside her and popped one of the sugar soaked apricots into his mouth.

The television focused on an elaborate marble podium which was positioned on the Temple Mount in Jerusalem. An elevated stage was erected between the Dome of the Rock and the new Jewish temple. Wide panels of white linen with bright red dragons facing each other flanked the stage.

Harrison Yates and Heather Smith provided the commentary from an on-site news booth situated above an ocean of people who filled the Temple Mount.

"From what we've been told, today's announcement is going to be huge." Yates turned to Smith.

"Yes, Harrison. His High and Most Prepotent Majesty hasn't made a public appearance in a while. And neither has Pope Peter, so to have them both here, it's a significant address."

"I noticed the Dome of the Rock got a little makeover. It's had Arabic calligraphy inscribed on the outside of the golden dome. In keeping with the tradition of the building, the calligraphy has been done in mosaic. You've researched what it says, would you like to share with us?"

"Thanks for asking Harrison. It echoes the inscription which used to be on the inner dome. It says, In the name of Angelo Luz, the Merciful, the Compassionate. There is no god but Angelo Luz. He is One. He has no associate. Pope Peter is the Messenger of Angelo Luz, the blessing of Angelo Luz be on him.

"Mosaic artisans were also commissioned to change the inscription inside the dome. Where it used to read Allah, it now reads Angelo Luz. And, Muhammad's name has been replaced with Pope Peter. It's all in the spirit of unity. For decades, religion has been the most divisive element on the planet. And perhaps nowhere more so than here, in Jerusalem. His Majesty has brought us into the light and revealed that all religions were actually pointing in the same direction all along."

"Heather, here comes the Global Republic Minister of Religion, Jacob Ralston to the stage."

The commentators fell silent as Ralston walked to the white stone podium which had a red dragon engraved on the front. "Citizens of the Global Republic, whether you are with us in person today, or whether you are joining us via television, we are all together in spirit, and I welcome you to the holy city of Jerusalem. As many of you know, *Jerusalem* is Hebrew for *city of peace*. And after centuries of conflict over this small parcel of land, it was His Most Beloved Majesty, Angelo Luz who finally brought peace to this city. It has been prophesied that such a savior would come, ushering in an age of peace, not only for the city of peace, but for the entire world.

"It has not been without bloodshed, and it has not come without cost, but in the end, we can say that it has been worth it all.

"But enough of my rambling, please offer a warm welcome to His Holiness, Pope Peter of Rome."

The crowds cheered as the pontiff made his way to the podium. The pope shook hands with Ralston and kissed him on both cheeks. The pope spoke reverently. "My little children. It was from this mount that Muhammed journeyed into heaven, and it was upon this mount that King Solomon built the first Temple of God. Many traditions also say this mount was the location where King David made the sacrifice and stopped the destroying angel. Most scholars believe this is also Mount Moriah where Abraham offered up his son Isaac. So, it is most fitting that this should be the place where the greatest revelation in the history of mankind is made.

"Please, fall to your knees and worship the great and mighty king, the savior, the messiah, the highest Imam, our Most Precious, Great and Glorious, Angelo Luz."

The pope prostrated himself on the stage as Luz walked out, wearing a long white robe with gold embroidery around the collar, cuffs, and down the front.

"Thank you, my most loyal servant. Please rise." Luz offered his hand and helped the pope to his feet.

Luz gazed out at the crowds who were still bowing. "Please, children. Rise up."

He paused while he drank in the worship. He offered a big smile and a steady nod to communicate that their worship was pleasing to him. "Thank you, you are blessed."

Luz put one hand on the marble podium and with the other, he motioned to the buildings on either side of him. "These buildings have always represented man's attempt to seek me. Places like the Dome of the Rock, the Temple, the Church of the Holy Sepulchre, St Peter's in Rome, the Kaaba in Mecca, the Mahabodhi Temple in Bodh Gaya, India, and the heavens themselves have been where mortals with veiled understanding have reached to me. Now, I am come. And these things are no longer necessary, for I walk among you.

"However, we will not do away with these places so rich in heritage, but we will hold them in even higher honor. For these are the places on the Earth that have been dedicated to me. I am your god, so are they not mine to do with as I please?

"As we walk together into the new age of enlightenment, an age where technology merges with the spiritual." Luz held up a tablet computer, snapped the fingers of his other hand, and the tablet became a white dove which flew away.

The crowd awed in wonder.

"Please. Some guy did that same trick on America's Got Talent. I expected more out of the Anti-Christ." Courtney rolled her eyes.

Luz continued his speech. "We must understand how the two work hand in hand to bring us to ever higher states of evolution. As you all know, Dragon was attacked and brought down by criminals in the

Americas. Today, we are releasing Dragon Version 2.0. Unlike the previous Dragon, it is decentralized, like the internet itself. Dragon is now omnipresent. Six quantum computers have been placed in the holy sites I just mentioned to you. Each will have a hologram Image of myself where religious clerics may go and inquire of me for spiritual guidance. Dragon and myself are now one."

Luz motioned to the Temple of God. "In the Temple, my Image will be projected in the very Holy of Holies where the priests presently go to beseech what they have imagined to be God. But gone are the days of imaginary gods. I am here. I am with you.

"The seventh quantum computer has been placed above in the very heavens where you would expect an omnipresent god to make his home. The seventh computer is on a space station as we speak, looking down from above. This station is very similar to the former ISS in size, but as a home for the primary computer for Dragon, it is ideal. Solar panels produce all the energy needed by the new energy efficient system, and the cooling system uses the frigid temperatures of space itself."

"Too long have many of you worshiped only technology and forsaken the way of the ancients. And for too long have others clung to bygone superstitions and rejected the gifts of knowledge. It was this fear of knowledge that held back Adam and Eve in the garden. Only when they embraced the forbidden fruit of understanding was the human race able to advance to where we are today." Out of nowhere, Luz was suddenly holding an apple.

"Having the components of Dragon housed in these sacred spaces will serve as a constant reminder of how technology and spirituality are not opposites but parts of the same puzzle."

Everett heard screaming outside the window in the street below. Instinctively, he grabbed his rifle and made his way over to look out.

"What's going on?" Sarah asked.

"A man is walking around in the street screaming in Turkish with his hands in the air. And there's another one. He's ripping his shirt."

Rifle fire rang out.

"What's that?" Courtney shouted.

Everett stood back far enough from the window to not be seen. "Some guy, popping off rounds in the air. He looks angry as well. People are pouring out of their houses."

"It's about the Kaaba in Mecca, and about the Dome of the Rock." Sarah stood up and walked toward the window. "I bet these are all Sunni. They're mad about the computer stacks being erected in their most holy sites."

"Let's hope they settle down quickly, or we won't be going anywhere." Everett watched as more and more people poured out into the street below, yelling, chanting and firing AK-47s into the air.

"Settling down quickly isn't a common trait for Sunnis." Sarah sighed.

Everett turned back to the television. "I doubt the Jews are going to be too happy about this either. Well, I'd say this qualifies as Luz setting himself up over everything that is called god, breaking the treaty, and the abomination of desolation being set up in the Holy Place."

Courtney looked at him from the couch. "So, what does that mean for us?"

"It means this is the midpoint of the tribulation. We've got exactly three and a half years from today."

Sarah pointed at the television. "You guys have got to see this."

Everett looked back at the screen.

The crowd sighed in amazement.

"Lift up your hands with me." Luz held his apple high.

The people in the crowd held up their hands. Each of them held an apple. They all examined their apples as if they had no idea where they came from.

Courtney pointed toward the screen. "Did he just make apples appear in everybody's hands?"

Everett studied the TV. "I wasn't paying attention. But if he did, that's not a trick you see on AGT."

"What's that verse about the Anti-Christ performing counterfeit miracles?" Sarah stared at the television.

"Second Thessalonians, 2." Everett continued watching the broadcast. "Verse nine, I think."

Luz waited for the crowd to get quiet before speaking again. "With Dragon, we have overcome the curse of death. We are now able to upload your consciousness into a specially designed realm within Dragon. It is a realm where technology meets the supernatural. A domain not constricted by time, or space, or matter. It is an interdimensional place that we call the Nirvananet.

"Release your hold on mortality and become, like me, immortal, liberated."

Luz took a bite of his apple. "Join me. Eat the fruit of knowledge, embrace your emancipation."

The cameras panned over the crowd as everyone bit into their apples as well. Rhythmic music began to play. Luz left the podium, and Pope Peter took the stage once more.

"Ladies and gentlemen. Today will be a great celebration. We have wine, beer, cocktails, as well as other various substances to help you get into a more relaxed state so you can properly worship His Majesty through music, dance, and sexuality.

"Bars and booths are set up all around the Temple Mount. Please help yourselves, but do keep your attention focused on the video screen above the stage over the next few moments. We'll be televising His Majesty's first visit into the Holy of Holies where he will commune with the hologram projected from the mind of Dragon in the perfect Image of Our Precious Leader, Angelo Luz."

The music played and the video screen showed Luz walking between the pillars, up on the porch, and through the Temple doors. Scantily clad women danced and offered him drinks as he strolled through the first section of the Temple known as the Holy Place or Sanctuary. He pulled back the curtain which had been replaced with a blood-red tapestry embroidered with white dragons facing each other.

The cameras followed Luz into the Holy of Holies. Smoke poured out of the room, slowly revealing what was inside. In the spot designated for the Ark of the Covenant sat a golden throne. On either side, where the cherubim would have stood, were finely-sculpted golden dragons. Each one stood ten feet tall, with their wings arched over the golden throne and touching at the tips. Luz sat down on the throne. Suddenly, a hologram of Luz appeared between him and the camera.

The life-sized hologram spoke. "This is the house of god, and this is the throne of god. Hear o Israel. I am your god, and I am one. Whether you see me or you see my image, we are the same, and all honor, and power, and glory, and wealth, and riches, and worship belong to me. Bow your knees and bow your head and worship me, and me alone."

Luz stood up in the midst of the hologram and became one with the image.

The camera panned over the Temple Mount. Everyone bowed low. The camera went back to Luz who walked out of the Holy of Holies as the hologram took the throne. He took a glass of wine from one of the exotic dancers in the Sanctuary. He took a long, deep drink, then looked at the camera. "Now stand up! Drink, dance, enjoy one another's bodies, for we have overcome the grave!"

The television cut back to Harrison Yates who held a glass of champagne in his hand. "Wow, how was that for an announcement? His High and Most Prepotent Majesty has defeated the grave! He's offering eternal life, Heather. What do you say?"

She sipped her champagne. "Sign me up!"

Yates scooted closer to his co-anchor. "And you heard that last little bit he said about enjoying each other. Can I invite you back to my room after we've wrapped up here?"

"Harrison, I'm married!" She giggled and sipped from her glass.

Yates topped off her champagne. "Don't be so old-fashioned. How about we finish this bottle and decide later?"

She flipped her hair and toasted Yate's glass. "I suppose it's a special occasion."

The camera cut back to the crowd that seemed to be quickly embracing the spirit of absolute debauchery.

"I can't watch this. It's disgusting." Courtney picked up the remote.

"Wait!" Everett pleaded. "Look back by the Dome of the Rock. What are those people doing?"

Sarah looked closely. "Break dancing? Forming a mosh pit maybe?"

"To this music? It's slow, hypnotic, like new age jazz." Everett turned to her.

Courtney lowered her brow and curled her upper lip. "They're swatting at something."

Everett observed the broadcast a little longer. "Locusts. Look, there's more!"

Soon, a haze of insects appeared over the Temple Mount. The music and sounds of merriment were quickly drowned out by screams of torment. Those who could run fled from the assault of the locusts. Many seemed to be demobilized from the pain and rolled around on the ground, waving their hands or covering their faces. The feed cut, and the screen went black.

"Wait." Courtney looked on in amazement. "Isn't Apollyon the king over the locusts?"

"Yeah, why?" Everett asked.

"Apollyon is another name for Satan, right? I mean, why would this guy spoil his own coming-out party?" She stood up and placed her hands on her hips.

Everett shook his head. "Are you kidding me? That's how he rolls. Like Lucy pulling the football away from Charlie Brown. He's been offering total satisfaction, then jerking the chair out from under people when they go to sit in it, since the beginning.

"Think about all the heroin addicts chasing the ultimate high. They end up with a bad case of dope sickness instead. The husbands that want a little something on the side, but end up throwing a fragmentation grenade and blowing up their whole family. If they'd have counted the cost, you think they'd still have had that affair?"

Everett held his hands out. "This is exactly what I would expect for his coming-out party. He promises pleasure and life but delivers hell and death."

Sarah turned off the television and set the remote on the coffee table. "Finish what you were saying about us having three and a half years left. What happens at the end of that?"

Everett dug out his Bible and his calendars from his duffle. He flipped through the pages of the Bible until he came to Daniel 12. "Listen to this. And from the time that the daily sacrifice shall be taken away, and the abomination that maketh desolate set up, there shall be a thousand two hundred and ninety days. Blessed is he that waiteth, and cometh to the thousand three hundred and five and thirty days."

"Okay, I guess this qualifies as an abomination. But it doesn't say anything about it being in the Temple." Sarah looked on at his Bible.

"Okay." Everett flipped over to Matthew 24. "When ye therefore shall see the abomination of desolation, spoken of by Daniel the prophet, stand in the holy place, whoso readeth, let him understand. Then let them which be in Judaea flee into the mountains."

Everett looked up. "Another name for the Holy of Holies is the Most Holy Place."

"And we're running in the opposite direction of where Jesus told us to go. Great." Courtney plopped back down on the couch.

"We'll be with Elijah. We'll be protected," Sarah said.

"I hope you're right about that." Courtney crossed her arms. "Anyway, back to what you were saying about the three and a half years."

"Today is March twenty-second." Everett silently wrote down a series of numbers and made calculations. Then he counted out the dates on his Jewish calendar as well as his Georgian one. Minutes later, he looked up. "1290 days ends on October second. Yom Teruah."

"Isn't that like Rosh Hashanah? Jewish New

Year's?" Courtney asked.

"That's when the Jews celebrate New Year's, but Yom Teruah is on the first day of Tishri, the seventh month. By definition, New Year's pretty much has to come on the first day of the first month. They got that stuff about it being New Year's during their time in Satan's original kingdom, Babylon. As a matter of fact, the months never even had names. Tishri was simply called the seventh month. They carried the stench of Babylon with them when they left captivity."

Courtney pursed her lips. "Sorta like Protestants keeping Christmas trees and Easter eggs when they left the Catholic Church."

"Exactly." Everett nodded.

"So, what is it?" Sarah tilted her head. "Yom Teruah?"

"The Feast of Trumpets."

"What's that about? And why does Daniel say blessed are the people that wait until the 1335 days? That's like another forty-five days. What happens then?"

Everett shook his head. "I don't know. I think Messiah comes back at the Feast of Trumpets, then fights the final battle. It could be a forty-five-day battle. Once that's over, on day 1335, maybe the new millennium starts."

"But He's God!" Sarah threw her hands in the air. "Why would it take Him forty-five days to defeat Satan?"

"Oh, it wouldn't take Him that long unless He wanted it to."

Courtney puckered her forehead. "And why,

pray tell, would He want it to?"

Everett lifted his shoulders. "Six thousand years of history. It'd be kind of anti-climactic to end it all in a thirty-minute fight to the death with Satan. And in case you've never seen a beautiful sunset, God kinda has a flare for the dramatic."

"Yeah, okay." Courtney stood by the window. "I can see that, I guess."

Suddenly, the building shook, with a loud boom. The glass in the windows rattled. Everett pulled Courtney back and shielded her from the window. He turned to see a giant mushroom cloud in the distance, billowing toward the sky.

Courtney looked around him. "Where was that?"

"Looks like it was about a mile away. If I had to guess, I'd say it was a car bomb at the nearest GR outpost."

Sarah looked out at the cloud, then down at the rioters in the street. "Doesn't look like we'll be going anywhere today."

CHAPTER 16

And the sixth angel sounded, and I heard a voice from the four horns of the golden altar which is before God, Saying to the sixth angel which had the trumpet, Loose the four angels which are bound in the great river Euphrates. And the four angels were loosed, which were prepared for an hour, and a day, and a month, and a year, for to slay the third part of men. And the number of the army of the horsemen were two hundred thousand thousand: and I heard the number of them. And thus I saw the horses in the vision, and them that sat on them, having breastplates of fire, and of jacinth, and brimstone: and the heads of the horses were as the heads of lions; and out of their mouths issued fire and smoke and brimstone. By these three was the third part of men killed, by the fire, and by the smoke, and by the brimstone, which issued out of their mouths.

Revelation 9:13-18

At first light on Saturday, Everett woke Courtney. "The street is pretty calm outside. I think this is our window to get out."

"I just went to sleep." Her eyes were swollen.

"I know, I didn't get much rest either with all the gunfire and yelling."

Everett wrapped a shemagh around his neck and handed one to Courtney. "You should cover your head with this."

"No word from Ali about getting us some hijabs?" Courtney folded the middle eastern cloth into a triangle and placed it over her head like a giant handkerchief.

"No. Sadat owns the clothing store next to the café, but evidently he only sells westernized clothing."

"Westernized. Ha!" Courtney tucked her backup pistol in her waistband. "That's a stretch. I saw the mannequins in the window. It's all like hooker clothing from the late nineties."

Everett nudged Sarah and handed her a shemagh. "We've gotta go."

She sat up on the couch. "Did the natives finally calm down?"

"They're probably trying to get some sleep." Everett laced up his boots and checked the magazine well of his rifle to double check that it was loaded. He watched the street below while he waited for the girls to get ready. Burned out vehicles, smoldering heaps of tar and ash that had been burning tires only hours earlier, littered the roadway and left soot marks on the surrounding buildings.

"Do you have the silver you got from Sadat?" Courtney pulled the shemagh up around her face.

Everett patted the pockets of his cargo pants. "Got it."

"I'm ready to go." Courtney slung her duffle over one shoulder, and her rifle over the other.

Sarah adjusted the straps of her duffle bag and her backpack. She pulled her shemagh down to cover her eyebrows and picked up her rifle. "Me, too."

"Let's move as quietly as possible." Everett opened the door and led the way down the hall and to the stairwell.

Ali met them on the third floor carrying a small shoulder bag. "Mr. Everett."

"Ali, what's going on?"

"My truck. The Martyrs of the Caliphate took it to make a car bomb. They are attacking the port at Mersin. But it could have been worse."

"MOC stole your vehicle to make a bomb. How could it have been worse, Ali?" Courtney followed Everett as he continued to the first floor.

"They wanted me to volunteer to drive it."

"That would have been worse." Sarah stayed

close behind Courtney.

"Anyway, can you give me ride to my cousin in Antakya? It is Shia territory. Morc safe."

Everett's eyes widened. "Ali, that's a big favor to ask. We're not a taxi service."

"It is on your way to Jerusalem. I help you get out of Tarsus. I know the best road."

"Can't Sadat help you get to your cousins?"

"Sadat leave last night. He go to his villa on the Black Sea. He invite me to come, but I don't go because I think I will go to my cousin in Antakya." Ali pulled out one of the diamonds Everett had given him for the introduction to Sadat. "I pay you."

Everett opened the back door to the alley. He saw two young men with AK-47s enter a door at the end of the alley. He slowly closed the door and looked at Ali. In a low voice, Everett said, "Keep your diamond. Just get us to Antakya safely."

"Yes, I will do it."

"And when we get there you've got to get us food, lodging, and find out as much information as you can about the best route for us to take to Jerusalem."

"I do all these things." Ali nodded.

"Do you have a weapon?"

Ali lifted his shirt, revealing the handle of what looked like an antique1911.

"Does it work?"

"Oh, yes. Very good gun. I buy from Sadat."

Everett pressed his lips together. "I guess those are still around for a reason. Be ready to use it if we get in trouble."

Ali walked past Everett. "I lead the way to the

vehicle. I look around the corner. If someone is there, I tell you. Maybe I don't stand out so much as crazy Americans."

Courtney pulled her shemagh down so she could talk. "You can still tell?"

Ali smiled revealing his big teeth. "Everybody can still tell."

Everett gave Ali a five-yard lead, then led the girls out quietly. He waited for Ali to clear the corner of the alley. Ali waved for them to follow him quickly. The team sprinted to the Tiguan.

"Thank you, Jesus!" Courtney tossed her duffle and her pack into the rear of the Volkswagen.

Sarah placed her bag in the rear with Courtney's, but took her duffle bag to the back seat with her and closed the door. Everett stowed his belongings, gently closed the rear hatch, and took the driver's seat. Ali rode shotgun, placing his small bag in the floorboard of the passenger's seat.

"Where to?" Everett started the engine and put the vehicle in gear.

"That way!" Ali pointed to the street on the left side of the parking lot.

Everett remained in a hyper-aware state all the way through town. He followed Ali's directions, and they quickly escaped Tarsus.

Everett began to breathe a little easier. "Good job, Ali."

Ali still looked tense. "Don't count the chicken when he is in the eggs."

Perplexed by the statement, Everett glanced over at Ali curiously.

From the back seat, Sarah translated. "You mean,

don't count your chickens before they hatch."

"Forget about the chicken." Ali waved his hand. "I mean we still must go through Adana. It is big city with many MOC fighters. Do not celebrate now."

The chicken is still in the eggs, Everett thought. "How far?"

"Fifty kilometer."

"No way around it?"

Ali shook his head adamantly. "No. This best way."

Thirty minutes later, Everett began to notice more buildings lining the highway. Soon afterward, they were in a densely-built metropolitan area.

Ali pointed. "Roadblock!"

"Technicals," Sarah said from the back.

Ali seemed not to understand. He turned to the back. "Technical?"

"That's what the US military called civilian vehicles which had been modified for the battlefield." She pointed ahead. "Both of those Toyota pickups have fifty calibers mounted in the back. If we have to engage, those will be our biggest problem. I'll get two rockets ready to fire."

"They're flying black flags. Looks like ISIS," Courtney said as they slowed down.

"It is the black flag of MOC," Ali clarified. "But don't shoot. I can get us past the checkpoint."

"Any chance we can just turn around and make a run for it?" Everett asked.

"No. I will talk to them. We will get through."

"Don't sell us out, Ali. I'll kill you first." Everett gave Ali a serious look to let him know he wasn't kidding.

"Don't worry."

Everett's heart thumped in his chest. He pulled up slowly to the checkpoint.

Ali rolled down the window. "Allahu akbar."

"Allahu akbar," the MOC fighter replied. The two conversed shortly and Ali held out his right hand, turning it from side to side.

Ali turned to Everett. "Flip your wrist."

Everett held out his hand and flicked his wrist, in the way he'd seen so many people do to activate their Mark. Ali instructed the girls to do the same.

The fighter addressed Everett directly in Arabic.

"What did he say?"

Ali translated, "He said my enemy's enemy is my friend."

Everett wasn't so sure about all of that, but he smiled just the same.

The man waved the first Toyota out of the way, and Everett pulled through slowly.

"Good job, Ali!" Courtney said.

Sarah leaned forward. "What did you tell him?"

"I tell him you are bring weapons from America to Aleppo for the Caliphate. I say you work for Sheik Tariq. The Sheik is big arms dealer. He supply much weapons to Caliph Marwan Bakr."

"And how did you know this story would check out?" Courtney asked.

"Sadat friends with Sheik."

"Of course he is," Sarah stated matter-of-factly.

"Dragon went back online last night." Everett glanced at Ali. "How did you know our Marks wouldn't activate when we flicked our wrists?"

"You have bad counterfeit." Ali pointed to Everett's hand. "Also, I know you are Christian. We have some in Tarsus, but they all go in the disappearance."

"All of them?" Everett knew that wasn't the case in America.

Ali simply nodded. "All."

Everett figured it was much more difficult to identify as a Christian in this part of the world. Most of the fakes were likely winnowed out by some form of persecution. "Why didn't your Mark activate?"

"The Sunni in Tarsus say don't take it. They don't believe Luz is from Allah."

Everett kept his eyes on the highway. "I thought you said you were Shia? Isn't that why you're going to Antakya?"

"No. I say Antakya is Shia. I am not really like Sunni or Shia. I am survivor."

"But you're Muslim, right?" Everett quizzed.

"I believe Islam, but I think Sadat have a good life. He don't care about these things at all."

"What do you know about Jesus?"

"He is prophet, like Mohamed. It is the same for me."

Everett smiled. "Not quite. Mohamed's youngest wife, Aisha, was six when he married her. If Jesus would have been a child molester, I promise you, I would not be a Christian."

Ali listened but said nothing.

"Another big difference, Muhammad died, without naming a successor, I might add. Which is the reason the Shia and Sunni can't seem to get along."

"So what? Jesus die also."

"Yes, but he came back to life."

"Anybody can say this thing. I can say Muhammad come back to life. You weren't there. You don't know."

"I wasn't there, but we've got plenty of historical documents about how the apostles died. All of them were executed because they would not cease and desist telling people that Jesus was the Messiah and that he rose from the dead. I mentioned Paul of Tarsus when we first met. He was a religious leader of the Jews. He persecuted the Christians until he met the risen Jesus. Then, he gave up his power and position to be persecuted and ultimately beheaded for his faith."

"Yeah, so? The suicide bombers of MOC give up their life for religion."

"But that's because they are deceived. If the resurrection of Jesus was a charade, Paul and the apostles would have been the ones perpetrating the lie. Would you sacrifice your life for something you knew to be a falsehood, or would you just admit it wasn't true so you could live another day?"

Ali looked at Everett without answering, then turned away to the passenger's window, staring silently for the next several miles.

Everett said, "You used the name Caliph Marwan Bakr. Any relation to Abu Bakr al-Baghdadi, the former leader of ISIS?"

"Yes. Marwan is the nephew. MOC is basically same thing like ISIS. Is all about have Islamic caliphate."

Everett turned on the radio and scanned the stations, looking for an English GRBN station. He finally found one.

The female reporter spoke with a British accent. "Details continue to come in about additional suicide bombings. The total count for today currently stands at 148. Multiple bombings have occurred in the major cities of Europe, including London, Rome, Paris, Brussels, Prague, Munich, Sarajevo, Zurich, Athens, as well as many, many other cities. Never have so many suicide attacks been reported in a single day. It is a sad day. His Majesty has worked so hard to bring about peace on this tormented planet. And we've had so much suffering to endure from earthquakes, tsunamis, poisoned water, comets, food shortages, and financial calamities, it is simply unconscionable how human beings can still find reason to hurt each other in such a crude and barbaric manner.

"It is days like today that I find it so difficult to do my duty as a journalist.

"For those of you just tuning in, the massive wave of bombings appears to be made up primarily of single individuals wearing explosive suicide vests targeted at markets, Global Republic Peacekeeping stations, and other government facilities. A few have been larger explosions caused by car bombs in densely populated areas.

"Preliminary scans are showing extremely high levels of radiation near detonation sites in Paris, London, and Munich. Authorities are urging people who do not live in those cities to stay away, as the threat of radiation poisoning is serious.

"Furthermore, the Global Republic is recommending that all citizens shelter in place. Do not leave your homes unless it is absolutely necessary. A dusk-to-dawn curfew will be going into effect this evening across all territories of the Global Republic. Violators will be subject to being detained."

Everett glanced over at Ali. "A lieutenant colonel I spoke with in America said he estimates about half of the Sunni Muslims were wiped out in the plagues or disasters. Does that sound right to you?"

Ali raised his shoulders. "If you counting the children who disappeared, half is probably about right for Tarsus, Mersin, and Adana. But I don't know about other area."

Everett kept his eyes focused on the road ahead, but his mind was spinning. "Prior to the disappearances, the global Sunni population was one and a half billion, so roughly 750 million remain. Half of them are men, so 375 million, and most are capable of wearing a suicide vest if they so choose. What percentage of Sunni do you think are radicalized?"

Ali looked at Everett. "Before, or are you talk about now that the Kaaba in Mecca and the Dome of the Rock have been desecrated?"

"Current estimate."

"Everybody, man. Maybe many Sunni are like me. Don't really care. But they don't say this. Now that Luz desecrate the writing on the Dome of the Rock, make himself to be Allah, and make Pope more high than Muhammad, everybody must say they are for jihad. And don't think about woman or man. Woman carry AK, drive car bomb, wear suicide vest, everything man do. Already many Martyrs of the Caliphate are woman, or are wives of Martyr who want to be in jihad. Why you ask this?"

Everett glanced up at the rearview. "Courtney, can you dig my Bible out of my duffle?"

"I've already got it. Thought I might read a little on the way."

"Can you flip to Revelation 9 and let Ali read it?"

Seconds later, she passed the small book up to Ali.

Ali slowly read the chapter. "Ah, okay the comet, the locust. Somebody wrote this book last week, after already happened these things."

"Keep reading."

Ali continued. "I don't know what I am reading."

"The 200-million-man army."

"What about it?"

"What are their breastplates made of?"

Ali studied the chapter. Finally, he read, "breastplates of fire, and of jacinth, and brimstone: and the heads of the horses were as the heads of lions; and out of their mouths issued fire and smoke and brimstone. By these three was the third part of men killed, by the fire, and by the smoke, and by the brimstone." Ali looked up. "What is this? It sounds like bad dreams."

Everett glanced over. "Breastplates of fire and brimstone? That sounds like a suicide vest to me. And 200 million, that sounds like a fairly accurate number of radicalized MOC martyrs."

Ali carefully examined the passage. He murmured, "Third part of men killed, by the fire, and by the smoke."

Everett nodded. "That would be pretty easy to do, especially if a significant amount of the attacks are dirty bombs. The radiation is mixed in with the smoke. Otherwise, smoke is pretty harmless unless you die of inhalation. It'd be pretty hard for a third of mankind to die of smoke inhalation."

"Why would he say the power is in their mouth and their tails?" Ali continued looking at the Bible.

Sarah spoke from the back. "The horses spit fire out of their mouths. A technical with a fifty cal or an anti-aircraft gun would look like it's spitting fire to someone 2,000 years ago. An AK-47 might look like a tail."

Courtney added. "And what does every MOC fighter yell when he detonates his vest?"

"Allahu Akbar." Ali looked up.

"John, the guy writing this, might have thought that they were giving a command for the vest, or in his words, the breastplate to explode. To him, it'd seem like their power was in their mouths to trigger the bombs."

Ali flipped to the front of the Bible. "1611. No way this book was written more than 400 years ago."

"That's when this edition was translated. The section you're reading was written around 96 AD." Everett smiled.

CHAPTER 17

We are troubled on every side, yet not distressed; we are perplexed, but not in despair; Persecuted, but not forsaken; cast down, but not destroyed.

2 Corinthians 4:8-9

The trip was uneventful until they reached the Turkish coastal city of Iskenderun. Shortly after the highway crossed into the city limits, plumes of smoke could be seen rising up from various spots in the west. The road followed the edge of the mountains to the east and offered an elevated vantage point of the buildings below.

“Looks like this city has seen their share of suicide bombers.” Courtney’s voice was glum.

Sarah exclaimed, “We’ve got three technicals on our tail flying black flags! Any chance you can talk to these guys, Ali?”

Ali checked his side view mirror. He sounded unnerved. “No. This isn’t checkpoint. These guys are look and destroy.”

Everett figured he meant *search and destroy*, but the message was clear enough. “What are we going to do?”

“We must fight.” Ali lowered his window and pulled out his pistol.

Everett glanced in the rearview. “Think you can do a little better than a peashooter, Sarah?”

“Roger that. I’m gonna have a rough time hanging out the window with you doing eighty, though.”

Everett checked the distance between the Tiguan and the pickups on his tail. “If I slow down, they’ll close the gap quick. You might not get a shot off.”

“I’ll open the rear hatch. Sarah can shoot straight out the back!” Courtney exclaimed.

“Watch out for the back blast!” Everett passed his rifle to Ali. “This might work better for what you’re trying to do. Give the girls some cover fire when they throw open the hatch.”

Ali took the rifle and stuck it out the window.

Everett could hear the wind from outside the vehicle when the rear hatch popped up. Automatic gunfire rang out from the pickup behind him. A series of bullets flew through the cabin of the vehicle and shattered the front windshield. “You need to take this guy out, Sarah!”

“Deploying now!”

Everett ducked low in his seat and shielded his face with his arm from the violent back blast of the rocket being fired inside the vehicle. The sound of the M72 LAW launching from the back seat drowned out the noise of Ali shooting as well as the gunfire from the truck behind them.

BOOM! Everett couldn't look up to see what had happened. He had to stay focused on the small section of unshattered windshield in the lower left corner so he could see where they were going. The cheers and yelps from the back seat told him that at least one of the vehicles had been taken out. Ali continued to fire the rifle, which told Everett at least one vehicle was still on their tail. "What's happening?"

"Take cover! Deploying rocket two!" Sarah's voice preceded a second loud blast from the back seat.

BOOM! Everett quickly checked the side view, which was right beside his small driving porthole in the windshield. It only took a second for him to see one of the vehicles explode into a ball of flames. A second vehicle emerged from the fireball, careened into the guard rail between the road and the cliff, then took flight. Everett put his eyes back on the road but could hear the smash as the second vehicle landed fifty feet below the edge of the road on his right.

"Good work team. Is everybody okay?" Everett kept driving.

"We're fine," Courtney said.

"I am alright, too." Ali lowered the rifle.

Sarah added, "I'm good, but it's a little breezy

back here. You might want to pull over so we can close the hatch.

Everett confirmed that they weren't being followed and pulled onto the shoulder. He'd make use of the pit stop to kick out the windshield. The rest of the trip would be windy, but he couldn't drive much further without being able to see out the front.

The team arrived at the outskirts of Antakya two hours later. The trip should have taken only one hour, but the roads through the mountains were heavily damaged from the quake. Towers of smoke rose up all around the city, accented by distant rifle report. Everett slowed down. "Let me know where to turn."

Ali's expression revealed his displeasure. "This is not good."

"Sounds like fighting." Sarah leaned forward from the back seat.

"Probably MOC and Hezbollah."

"This is a little far north for Hezbollah, isn't it?" Courtney asked.

"Hezbollah send up some militia to stop MOC from advance into Antakya. Antakya have last big Alawite population after Syria fall to ISIS and later take over by MOC."

"Regretfully, I was involved in that conflict," Sarah said. "I thought I was helping to spread democracy and liberate the Syrian people when we took down Assad. As it turned out, he was a saint compared to the radical Sunni cleric who ultimately ended up with all the power in the region."

Ali looked like he had a comment to add to Sarah's confession, but said nothing.

"Is Hezbollah made up of Alawites?" Courtney inquired.

"Most, no." Ali turned around to face the back seat. "But have some. Lebanese Shia, Hezbollah, Alawite, all are Twelver."

"Twelvers. Those are the Shia that believe in the Twelfth Imam, the ones who are backing Luz, right?" Everett glanced over.

"Correct." Ali pointed ahead. "This is road to my cousin."

Everett slowed down to turn off the main road. A loud blast erupted a quarter mile down the street, and a plume of smoke mushroomed toward the sky.

Ali began speaking in Turkish as if to Allah, but more likely to himself.

Everett heard the exchange of small arms fire at the end of the street and stopped the vehicle. "Ali, buddy. That's a hot zone down there. I can't drive through. I don't know who's who, and neither MOC nor Hezbollah is going to be very excited to see a vehicle full of Americans."

"They'll take a break from killing each other long enough to wipe us out," Sarah said. "I've already had the pleasure of being shot at by both teams the last time I was in the neighborhood."

"Can we drop you off here?" Everett let the engine idle.

"I don't know." Ali stared at the fighting only a few blocks away. "I come here to get away from all this."

"We've got an MRAP flying a MOC flag coming

up behind us! Everett, we've got to get out of here!" Sarah yelled.

Everett looked up at the rearview to see the huge armored vehicle headed right for him. He floored the gas pedal and sped straight for the fighting. "Ali, you've got to get us out of here!"

"Left, turn left now!" Ali pointed and shook his hand.

Everett swung the vehicle down the dirt road where Ali pointed. "Now what?"

"The next left! Take it. We must get to the highway that go around Antakya."

Everett turned hard again and gunned the engine, speeding down another road, blowing past stop signs.

"Another left, then first right!" Ali yelled as he looked backward.

"Are they still behind us?" Everett asked.

"I think so, no." Ali turned around and watched the road in front of them.

Everett quickly made the maneuver and sped up a narrow, paved road, which led through some olive groves.

"We lost them," Courtney confirmed.

Feeling relieved at escaping the latest peril, Everett took a deep breath. "I can't go back through there, Ali. If you want me to drop you off somewhere else, let me know."

"I don't even know if my cousin will still be there. Maybe he leave. Or maybe he killed."

"You're welcome to go to Jerusalem with us," Courtney offered.

Ali looked down at the floorboard and then up at

Everett. "What do you say about that?"

Everett turned to Ali. "If you want to come, we'd be glad to have you. You know the region better than any of us. Plus, you speak Arabic and Turkish."

"And English," he added.

"That's stretching it," Everett quipped.

"What? You don't understand my English?" Ali sounded insulted.

"It's a joke, Ali." Everett chuckled. "I understand you just fine."

Ali's face softened. He nodded. "I go to Jerusalem with you guys."

"Great. Just tell us how to get there."

"I never go before. But probably better you go by coast."

Everett lowered his brow. "Isn't the coast more populated?"

Ali replied confidently, "Yes, but Latakia, Tartus, Tripoli, Beirut, all have port. All port have Global Republic military base now."

Courtney reminded him, "I would think we want to stay as far away as possible from port cities. You said MOC took your truck to make a car bomb to attack the port in Mersin."

"Exactly." Ali showed his big white teeth as he nodded. "If MOC is busy to attack GR in port, they don't have time for us. If Everett drive inland, to the east, all territory is held by MOC. They don't have more to do than kill American driving through.

"Especially Tripoli and Beirut. MOC have to fight Hezbollah and GR. Other choice is go through Homs and Damascus. I don't pointing finger, but

Sarah do very good job there. All Assad regime gone. MOC control everything. Between there and coast, is only desert and mountain."

Sarah made a tisking sound. "Thanks for the compliment."

Everett stretched his arms and loosened his neck. "The coast it is, then."

The team continued south, navigating toward the sea. Each city they passed showed evidence of attacks. Small arms fire could be heard in some. Smoke plumes from fires and bombs were visible in all. Everett maintained the highest speed that road conditions would allow. He encountered very few other vehicles, but the conditions of the highways were pitiful.

CHAPTER 18

O Jerusalem, Jerusalem, thou that killest the prophets, and stonest them which are sent unto thee, how often would I have gathered thy children together, even as a hen gathereth her chickens under her wings, and ye would not!

Matthew 23:37

The team eventually crossed the imaginary line that had once been the Israeli border. The trip which should have taken only fourteen hours had taken more than a day. GRBN radio played continuously in the cabin of the Tiguan. Most of the information was the same report played in a twenty-minute loop, which was updated every two hours. Everett noticed the sound of the reporter's voice to be different and guessed it was an updated news release.

While still female and British, it was a different GRBN news anchor who said, "The Global Republic's official list of suicide bombings has broken through 1,000 with more confirmed attacks being added every minute. Estimates say as many as 10,000 personal ordinances have been detonated worldwide, but in many instances, the occurrences have yet to be added to the official list because no communications are in working order to report the incidents, or no survivors are available.

"Global Republic peacekeepers have been deployed to set up hard perimeters around the capital city of Jerusalem. The cities of Tel Aviv, Haifa, and Ashdod have also been cordoned off by Global Republic security forces. Tel Aviv has the only international airport to service the new capital, while Haifa and Ashdod provide major seaports for cargo ships."

Ali held a paper map and motioned for Everett to turn. "Quickly. Turn left!"

Everett complied. "What's up?"

"Haifa is just ahead. Probably you don't want question from GR checkpoint."

"Good call. Can we get to Jerusalem this way?"

"Yes, but I don't know what we do when we get there. Nobody have Mark."

"We'll come up with a plan." Everett tried to project confidence in his voice, but he had no idea how they'd get through the checkpoint.

"You better make fast. We be there in one hour and a half."

"We've still got seven rockets," Sarah said.

Ali buried his head in his hands. "Crazy American going to get me killed for sure."

Courtney reached up from the back and placed her hand on Ali's shoulder. "We'll come up with something more subtle."

The team arrived at the Jerusalem checkpoint just before sunrise, Sunday morning.

"Okay, what is the plan?" Ali asked confidently.

Everett pulled into a parking lot across the street from the guard gate, cutting the lights and the engine. "I'm still thinking."

Ali's smile faded. "Still thinking? What do you mean? We need plan now."

"I count four vehicles and twelve peacekeepers. Four rockets will clear them right out," Sarah's voice revealed that she wasn't serious, but Ali didn't pick up on the intonations.

"No, no, no. They will have peacekeeper all around city looking for us! We never get away!" Ali's hands flapped in the air violently.

Everett fought back a grin. "Relax, Ali. We're not going in with rockets."

Ali shook his finger toward the back seat. "This is not time to play."

Tink! Everett heard what sounded like a rock hitting the hood of the Tiguan.

"What was that noise?" Courtney asked.

Everett turned to Ali with a look of urgency in his eyes. "I could tell you were thinking about what

I said regarding Jesus. I'm guessing you've been mulling it over in your mind for the past few hours. If you trust what I said about him being God, about him being the Messiah, the Savior of the world, now is the time for you to tell him you believe."

"Everett, you are scaring me. Are we going to die?" Ali's eyes opened wide.

"No, but if you hesitate on making that confession of faith, you'll wish you were dead."

Ali swatted a bug that flew in the hole left by the missing windshield. "Locusts!"

"What do you say, Ali?" Everett pleaded.

"I . . I . . I can't say. I don't know. What you say, maybe is true. I don't know." Ali looked at Everett with an expression of sincerity.

Everett pressed his lips together with a nod. "I understand." Everett quickly thought up a plan. "Courtney, Sarah, fast! Change places with me and Ali."

The girls rushed out of the back doors.

"Cover your face and get in the back floorboard, Ali!" Everett yelled as he jumped out of the driver's seat.

Ali swatted another bug, then complied with Everett's instruction. Everett lay on top of Ali in the floorboard, shielding Ali's body with his own. Everett called out to Courtney who'd taken the driver's seat. "As soon as the locusts hit the peacekeepers, crash through the gate, and keep driving!"

The sound of buzzing grew louder inside the cabin of the Tiguan. Courtney called out, "Okay, the peacekeepers are getting stung all over. I'm going to go for it. Hang on!"

The engine raced. Everett heard the crash of the vehicle barreling through the gate. Courtney continued speeding through town, away from the checkpoint.

"Are we being followed?" Everett asked.

"All clear. Those guys have enough problems. They don't have time to worry about us," Sarah said.

Everett could still hear the locusts buzzing around the cabin. "What's the bug situation outside?"

"Still pretty thick," Courtney said.

"Okay, let me know if they thin out. For now, let's head for the old city."

Courtney slowed down but continued driving for several miles. Sarah gave directions from a paper map of Jerusalem.

Minutes later, Courtney said, "The bugs are gone."

Everett sat up to see that they were traveling on a narrow road that weaved between old stone walls and through tunnels that passed beneath ancient towers. The sun was rising.

Finally, the street opened up, with the wall of the city on the right, and several small shops on the left. Everett glanced at his watch. "Six o'clock. Maybe the shops will be opening soon."

He helped Ali get up from the floor board. "Are you okay?"

Ali straightened his shirt and combed his hair with his fingers. "Why the locusts don't sting you?"

"You read the book. They can't hurt the people

with the mark of God."

Sarah pointed ahead. "There's a parking spot. You better take it. I doubt we'll get closer to the Temple than this."

Courtney parked behind another vehicle, which had pulled up on the curb between a stone building and the outer wall of the city. "I guess if it gets towed, we'll figure something out."

Everett got out of the vehicle, folded the stock of his rifle and stowed it in his duffle bag. He put on his pack, and let the duffle hang in front so he could get to the rifle in a hurry if need be. The team elected to wear civilian clothing given the recent popularity of peacekeepers with the Martyrs of the Caliphate. He waited for the girls to gear up as well. "Ready?"

Sarah put on her sunglasses to block the bright light coming from the east. "Let's roll."

Everett led the way with Courtney at his side, Ali in the middle, and Sarah taking the rear. They passed beneath a small pedestrian tunnel that passed through a building from the street. Once on the other side, Everett stared at the walls on either side of the narrow passageway. Off-white, roughly hewn stones made up the walls, staircases, and buildings.

The signs were in Hebrew. He quickly identified the area as being the Jewish Quarter. The path beneath his feet was also made of the large stones. They finally came to a row of tables covered with umbrellas. Everett looked around. "That's the Temple Institute. I'm going in this café and see if I can get us something to eat."

"How are you going to do that?" Courtney

flipped her wrist as if trying to activate her fake Mark.

"A lot of these folks have fakes. I've got silver. Just watch my stuff." Everett dropped his pack and duffle by one of the tables.

He walked up to the deli-style counter. An Orthodox Jewish man was opening the store.

"Excuse me, do you speak English?"

"Yes." The man turned to him.

"Could you accept silver as payment?" Everett flipped his wrist for the man. "When Dragon came back online, my Mark never reactivated. Some kind of glitch, I guess."

The man's face tightened as he looked out the door, through the window, and all around the inside of the café. "You should be careful, my friend," he said just above a whisper. "How do you know I won't report you?"

Everett understood that his lame explanation fell flat. "From what I hear, if you reported everyone with my problem, you wouldn't have many customers left." He reached into his pocket and pulled out a silver one-ounce coin he'd bought from Sadat. He slid it towards the man. "I just want four coffees and some breakfast."

The man looked around once more before scooping the coin off the counter. "I have lox, cream cheese, and bagels. It's okay?"

"And coffee?"

"Yes, and coffee."

"That'll be fine." Everett smiled and waited as the man prepared his order. "I don't suppose you've seen a couple of old Jewish men, very eccentric, long gray beards."

"You've just described twenty percent of the population in this part of the city."

Everett added one more descriptor. "Messianic."

The man stopped what he was doing for a moment. "I don't have a very good memory." He turned and handed a white bag to Everett. He placed the four coffees in a cardboard carrier. "I'm sure you'd appreciate my forgetfulness if someone were asking about you."

Everett took his order. "Yes. I suppose I would."

"Good day, sir." The man returned to setting up his shop for the day.

Everett took the food outside and sat at the table.

Courtney dug in. "Smoked salmon! No way! I haven't had this in years."

"These are fresh bagels." Sarah smelled them.

Ali found the cream cheese. "No fish for me. But coffee smells good."

"Hopefully it's not as strong as what you brought us." Everett took the lid off his coffee. "Let's thank God for bringing us here safely and ask him to bless the food." Everett bowed his head and said a quick prayer, then they began eating.

"I cannot deny, the bug don't sting you. Your God, He must be real." Ali bit into his bagel.

"Oh, He is." Everett began to describe how God had reached out to him over and over before the rapture, but how he'd avoided thinking about it. Starting with the fall of man in Genesis, Everett explained how everyone on Earth had sinned against God one way or another. He told how the blood of Christ provided the perfect sacrifice, which purified the believer, granting him access to heaven."

"What must you do to be believer?"

"Tell God you believe that Jesus is the Messiah, that He was crucified and raised from the dead. Then repent of your sin. That just means that you'll study the Bible to see how God expects you to live, then ask Him for the power to live that way."

"What if you don't get it right? Misunderstand, or maybe sin again." Ali crossed his arms.

Everett chuckled. "Ali, we all mess up. I sin, Sarah sins, Courtney still sins . . ."

"Not as much as Everett." Courtney covered a mouth full of bagel with her hand as she interrupted.

Everett let the joke go without a retaliation. "But there's grace. Grace, grace, and more grace. God knows we won't be perfect, he just wants us to be in relationship with him. John 15 says *I'm the vine and you're the branches. If a man remains in Me, and I remain in him, he'll bear much fruit.*

"All I have to do is stay connected to the vine by worshiping Him through song, by speaking to Him through prayer, and by letting Him speak to me by reading the Bible. According to that, I'll naturally start living a life that is more pleasing to God."

Ali took a sip of coffee, then crossed his arms tightly again. "Sounds too easy."

"Well, God expects me to be involved, and it's my responsibility to stay connected to the Vine, but you're right. Jesus has done the heavy lifting."

"So, Jesus forgive me, then I can live any way I want, kill people, rob people, and still go to heaven?"

Everett chuckled. "Not at all. Hebrews 10 says if we sin willfully after we have received the knowledge of the truth, there no longer remains a sacrifice for sins, but a certain fearful expectation of judgment, and fiery indignation which will devour the adversaries.

"Unfortunately, tons of American so-called Christians skipped over that section of scripture. That's why so many of them were left behind in the disappearances. The Book of First John says that if we walk in darkness, we aren't really Christians, but if we walk in the light, even though we fall short, and we all fall short, we can ask for forgiveness and receive it. We could never earn our salvation by being good enough, but as long as we stay in the light of Jesus, we can know that we're going to heaven."

"Nobody else say this. In Islam, you never know for sure you go to heaven. Only if you die as a martyr." Ali finished his bagel. "Sounds too good to be real. But I will think about it."

"I hope you will," Everett said.

Courtney spoke softly. "Don't look, but I know this guy that just sat down at the table on the end."

"Where?" Everett looked down the row of café tables.

Courtney closed her eyes and sighed. "I said, don't look!"

"Sorry. One of the two middle-aged men at the last table?" Everett turned away from the person she referred to.

"Yeah, the one facing the building."

"Where could you possibly know him from?"

Sarah inquired curiously.

"I had his file when I was at NSA. Operation Guardian. We kept an eye on the activities of all our allies' intelligence agents."

Sarah sounded sarcastic. "That was nice of us. Let me guess, Mossad?"

Courtney pressed her lips together and nodded. "Yeah. Tobias, I think."

"So, go say hi," Sarah joked.

"I think I will." Courtney stood up.

"Nope." Everett shook his head adamantly.

"He's here for a reason. I think this is a God thing." Courtney walked off before Everett could stop her.

"This is faith?" Ali asked.

"Or stupidity." Everett sipped his coffee and kept his hand close to his pistol.

Courtney spoke loud enough to be heard by the team. "Tobias, hi! Courtney, we met years ago. How have you been?"

The man shook his head, looking around suspiciously. He waved his hands and spoke much lower than Courtney who continued to attempt to strike up a conversation. She failed to win his confidence and returned to the table.

"How was your date?" Everett quipped.

She rolled her eyes and took her seat. "He didn't ask me to cook for him, if that's what you mean. So, I guess I've had worse first dates."

Everett huffed as he watched the two men get up and leave. "You spooked them. They were up to something." He collected the empty cups and placed them in the empty bakery bag. "Let's get to the

Western Wall. If we're going to find Elijah anywhere, it'll be there."

The team loaded up the bags and proceeded toward the Temple Mount. They made their way down yet another narrow passageway. When they emerged into the light of the other side, a man with a pistol drawn jumped out. "Don't move!"

It was Courtney's friend, Tobias. "Who are you? What do you want? Why are you here on this day?"

Everett calculated his odds of drawing a weapon before a highly trained Mossad operative could gun them all down. He concluded his chances weren't favorable.

"I thought I went to school with you in America. George Washington University. It was only a mistake. I'm sorry!" Courtney pleaded. "Please don't kill us."

Tobias looked the team over. He shook his finger at Courtney as he thought. Then he stared at Everett. "I know who you are. But I don't know why you would come here. Your government, your agency, does not exist anymore. You should go back to America. Or at least what's left of it."

Everett gritted his teeth wishing he could take back what his wife said next as he heard Courtney push the envelope.

"Your agency doesn't exist either." Courtney kept her hands up.

"Oh yeah? And what agency is that, my American college friend?"

Everett shook his head. "She says crazy stuff like that. We don't want any trouble. I'm sure you don't either."

"No. No trouble. I just want to know what non-existent agency my friend thinks I work for. Come on. You can tell me. After all, we're old friends."

"Mossad."

As badly as Everett wanted to will her not to say it, she did. The genie was out of the bottle.

Tobias laughed. "Ah, that's good. Listen. I don't know why you are here, *especially today*, but you need to leave. Leave the city now. Consider it professional courtesy, from one non-existent intelligence agent to another."

Everett nodded politely. "Okay, thank you. You won't see us again." He ushered Courtney past Tobias when he stepped out of the way to let them pass.

"Not cool. We are not here to make waves. We want to blend in, find Elijah and fly under the radar. That was the polar opposite of what you just pulled," Everett lectured.

"Something big is about to go down today. I was just looking for a clue," she rebutted.

Everett kept the team moving quickly until they reached the Western Wall. He looked up at the famous landmark in awe. Recalling his mission, Everett scanned the people standing around the wall to see if he could identify Elijah or Moses. No one looked familiar. He looked up. The sun shone over top of the Western Wall. He shielded his eyes. "I wonder if we can get up to the Temple."

Sarah pointed at a group of peacekeepers at the top of an iron spiral staircase on the adjacent wall. "We'd have to go through them."

"Maybe the bugs will come around," Courtney

said.

"Let's hope not!" Ali replied.

Everett stared at the wall for a while, thinking of what the next move should be.

A man walked up to him from behind and passed him a folded piece of paper. "This is where you will find the prophets."

Everett opened the note to reveal a map. The street names were clearly marked with a building identified as the destination. "Second floor. Room three."

"What's that?" Courtney looked on.

"A map."

"I can see that. Where to?"

"The place where Elijah is staying."

"Where did you get it?"

"That guy gave it to me." Everett studied the map.

"What guy?"

He looked up and behind him, but the man was gone. "I don't know."

"Could have been Mossad." Sarah scanned the area for anyone walking away from them. "It might be a trap."

"I don't think so." Everett kept looking for the man. "He said the prophets. Tobias didn't have any idea why we were here. I said something to the guy at the deli. It could have been him."

"Maybe Elijah had someone out here looking for us," Courtney said.

"Yeah, could be." Everett led the way to the building on the map.

CHAPTER 19

And I beheld another beast coming up out of the earth; and he had two horns like a lamb, and he spake as a dragon. And he exerciseth all the power of the first beast before him, and causeth the earth and them which dwell therein to worship the first beast, whose deadly wound was healed. And he doeth great wonders, so that he maketh fire come down from heaven on the earth in the sight of men, And deceiveth them that dwell on the earth by the means of those miracles which he had power to do in the sight of the beast; saying to them that dwell on the earth, that they should make an image to the beast, which had the wound by a sword, and did live. And he had power to give life unto the image of the beast, that the image of the beast should both speak, and cause that as many as would not worship the image of the beast should be killed.

Revelation 13:11-15

Everett stood atop an ancient stone staircase and knocked on the old wooden door. He looked down to the narrow alleyway to see if the team had been followed.

"Everett! Come in, come in." Elijah held the door open for the team.

Moses didn't get up from the couch but offered a polite nod.

"This is Ali. Ali, this is Elijah and Moses." Everett closed the door behind Courtney and Sarah.

"Pleasure to meet you." Ali shook Elijah's hand. Moses looked less hospitable, so Ali merely waved and gave the uneasy smile that an uninvited guest might give.

"Please, put your bags here. Might I offer you something to eat?" Elijah placed his hands together.

"We just ate, thank you." Courtney embraced the old prophet with a warm hug.

Sarah unzipped her duffle and retrieved the wooden staff. "We brought this for you." She handed it to Moses.

His surly expression melted into one that bordered on being cordial. "Thank you. But I left it for you. I hope you didn't come all this way over this."

Elijah's forehead frowned. "You know why they are here. You shouldn't tease them."

A betraying look of mischief preceded a slight grin beneath Moses' heavy beard.

Everett couldn't help feeling that he'd missed the joke.

Elijah ushered the team into the salon and brought out two chairs from the dining area. "Tell me, how did you find us?"

"A man handed me a note with directions. We thought you probably had him waiting for us." Everett took a seat on the couch adjacent to the one where Moses sat.

Elijah shook his head and turned to Moses. "We didn't send anyone."

"Maybe it was the man at the deli near the Temple Institute. I asked if he'd seen a couple of Messianic men who might fit your description."

Moses shook his head. "No one knows we're here."

"Well, somebody gave me this note." Everett stuck his hand in his pocket to retrieve the directions. The paper wasn't there. His hair stood on end as he realized his encounter had most likely been with a being from another realm.

Courtney looked at him curiously, then turned to Moses. "Someone must know. How did you get this apartment?"

Moses crossed his arms. "Airbnb. We used fake names and online check in. No one saw us."

Questions began piling up in Everett's head. The bizarreness of the entire situation was giving him a peculiar feeling in the pit of his stomach. He decided no further inquisition would explain the unexplainable and made a conscious effort to let his questions go.

Elijah held out his arms for Sarah. "I see Kevin is not with you."

She opened her mouth as if she were about to explain why, but her face shifted into a look of unfathomable sorrow, and she began to weep.

Elijah pulled her close and let her cry into his shoulder. He looked at Everett. "Tell me about your trip."

Everett provided the details of the ship, the comet, meeting Ali, and the locusts. Even Moses seemed to enjoy the lengthy telling of the great adventure.

All of a sudden, a loud pop echoed in the distance.

"Was that a gun?" Sarah asked.

"Could be. There's been a lot of that in this city over the decades." Moses' answer held a hint of sarcasm.

Elijah stood up from his chair. "Moses, we must be going." He turned to Everett. "We must be on our way, but please, make yourselves at home. We are going to the Temple Institute to reason with the rabbis. We have spent the last several days explaining why Yeshua is indeed the Messiah who was prophesied of in the Hebrew Scriptures."

Moses stood. "And that Luz is the anti-messiah who was prophesied of in the Greek Scriptures."

"How's that going, anyway?" Courtney asked.

"Could be better, could be worse." Elijah placed

a Hebrew Bible as well as a King James Bible in his shoulder bag.

"Do they . . . know who you are?" Sarah asked cautiously.

"Not a clue." Moses fought back a grin.

"Who is this Yeshua that Elijah spoke of?" Ali whispered to Everett.

"It's the way the Jews pronounce Joshua. It means God saves. Jesus is Greek for Joshua."

Ali nodded. "Ah, okay. I know there is Father, Son, and Spirit, but all are One. I thought maybe I am missing somebody."

Elijah opened the door and stopped short of walking out.

Everett heard the sound of GR peacekeeper sirens. He stood up from the couch.

Moses put his hand on Elijah's shoulder. With the other hand, he pointed to the sky. "Helicopters."

Everett heard the noise to which the prophet referred. "Sounds like it's coming from above the Temple Mount."

Moses pointed to Ali. "Get the remote. Turn on the idiot box."

"Sorry?" Ali looked confused as if he were not familiar with the moniker.

Moses explained gruffly, "The television. It is a box which consists of idiots, talking about idiots, directed by idiots, and consumed by idiots."

Ali fumbled with the remote and found the power button.

Elijah closed the door and returned to his seat, as did Moses.

GRBN reporter Heather Smith was speaking between sobs, with heavy mascara running down her cheeks, making her look like some vile female version of the Joker. "I repeat, His High and Most Prepotent Majesty has been shot. Our beloved leader was here, on the Temple Mount before the altar of the new Temple. Animal sacrifices by the Jewish rabbis had been postponed until today."

She paused to take a cloth from someone off camera. She wiped her face with the damp towel and handed it back to the person off screen. She sniffed, nodded, and said to that person, "Just give me a minute."

Smith took a bottle from the mystery person, had a drink, then passed the bottle back. She sniffed again, then turned her attention back to the camera. She composed herself. "I apologize, but this is the most devastating event I've experienced not only in my career as a news anchor but in my entire life.

"As I was saying, animal sacrifice had been suspended until today. This morning, animal sacrifices were to resume at the altar with the understanding that all such sacrifices and worship were to be directed at His Majesty, naming him by his full name rather than in the manner he'd previously accepted them with compassion toward those who ignorantly referred to him as God, The Almighty, or Hashem.

"At this morning's rededication ceremony . . ." She broke down in tears again. The person out of view handed her the towel again, and Smith dried her eyes.

"Oh, I just can't believe this is happening. It's

such a nightmare. His High and Most Prepotent Majesty was shot in the head with a high-powered, large caliber weapon. All I can say is there was a massive amount of damage."

"Especially today. That's what Tobias was referring to!" Courtney snapped her fingers.

"He may have been the shooter," Sarah added.

"Yeah, him or the guy he was having breakfast with," Courtney tapped her finger on her lip.

Waves of helicopters circled overhead. Everett could hear the same sirens screaming out on the television and outside the apartment window. He continued to listen to the mournful, mentally-enslaved, servant of Satan as she expounded on what had happened to Luz.

"We have footage, but I'm not sure if we are going to roll it." Smith pressed her earpiece. "Yes, I've just been informed by the director that we will provide the clip of the moment our precious savior was brutally murdered."

The scene cut to the ceremony going on outside the Temple. Luz bathed bare-chested, as if in a jacuzzi, in a large bronze basin to the left of the Temple. The basin sat atop twelve bronze bulls, three facing east, three west, three north, and three south. Thirteen men in black hooded robes, who looked more like a coven of witches than Jewish priests, ascended the stairs of the altar, across from the bronze basin, on the right of the television screen. The priests, or witches, carried a screaming animal to the top of the altar.

"What is that thing?" Sarah pointed to the creature, bound with ropes, being carried up the stairs.

Courtney turned away in disgust. "I don't know. I can't look."

Everett shivered as he looked at the horror before him. The thing had short fur, with stripes like a zebra, the head looked like a badger or a raccoon. It was low to the ground on its feet and plump like a pig, with a long, fat tail like a kangaroo. Its eyes were red, like an albino lab rat.

Sarah peeked through the fingers of her hands, which covered her face. "It's genetically modified. Man-made. They've used gene editing to put together some amalgamation of every possible unclean thing in the Old Testament. It's the ultimate unclean beast."

Everett forced himself to watch as the thirteen men fell upon the wretched creature, stabbing it over and over with sacrificial knives, rather than humanely slitting the cursed being's throat. Then he heard the gunshot.

The screen highlighted and zoomed in on the area of the footage where Luz sat, soaking in the basin like it was his personal hot tub. His head snapped hard to the left toward the Temple. A massive hole appeared in his forehead while flesh and blood rode the wake of the bullet. Luz slumped forward, face down in his wicked wash. Peacekeepers rushed out and surrounded the area while the unholy priests rushed down from the altar to the basin and pulled Luz's naked body from the water.

"Ha ha!" Moses laughed out loud and pointed at the television. "Now that's some good footage. They played that Zapruder film over and over for weeks. I hope they'll at least let us see this one a few more times."

Heather Smith seemed to need to recompose herself again. She sniffed and wiped her eyes. "His Holiness, Pope Peter will be making a statement any moment." Completely abandoning any similitude of professionalism, Smith pressed her earpiece again and nodded to someone off camera. "It is expected that His Holiness will make a statement about the continuity of government. The Global Republic charter, which named His High and Most Prepotent Majesty as supreme sovereign of the Earth and the heavens, made no provision for succession of the throne.

"Certainly, none of us thought this day would ever come. And indeed, I took him at his word when he said that he had overcome death . . ." She broke down weeping yet again.

The camera cut to the porch of the temple. Pope Peter stood behind Luz's white marble lectern with the red dragon etched on the face. With his deep Italian accent, he said, "My little children, do not suppose that your savior Angelo Luz has left you. Only hours ago, he, himself told you that he has overcome the grave. Faith is not faith if we have it only in the easy times. It is when we are faced with the greatest challenges that we must choose to believe.

"Our blessed savior, the son of the gods, Angelo Luz will always be among us. Come with me, follow me as I bring you to the throne of power, the hidden mysteries, and place of knowledge!"

Pope Peter turned and the cameraman followed him. Two witches in black robes opened the Temple doors for the pope and the cameraman. They passed through the sanctuary. Two more witches pulled back the curtains with the red dragons, allowing the pope and the cameraman to walk into the Holy of Holies.

The pope lifted his hands. "Sovereign Master. Tell us, are you still among us?"

The hologram of Luz appeared between the wings of the two golden dragons. "Behold, I am with you always, even unto the end of the world." The hologram's arms opened wide. "Fear not, worship me and believe!"

Pope Peter bowed before the image. "Precious savior, can you tell us who it was that shot you?"

"The one who pulled the trigger is insignificant. And when the sun sets, you will see just how insignificant this action truly was. But ultimately, my assassin was all those who do not worship me. It is all those who do not believe. Either you are for me or you are against me. There is no middle ground. And with great wrath and terrible fury will the servants of my kingdom hunt down all of those responsible for this act of cowardice, hate, and wickedness.

"But let us not focus on such negativity at this

time. Join me here at sunset for a grand celebration of life when I will prove to the world that I have truly overcome the grave. It will be my final attempt to reach the lost. After the world has seen what I reveal to you tonight, unbelievers will be without excuse."

Elijah grabbed the remote and turned off the television. He looked at Moses. "The Messiah arose at sunrise; a symbol of the light He would bring to the world."

Moses nodded grimly. "And Luz will arise at sunset, a symbol of his darkness coming over the Earth."

Elijah stood up and placed his bag over his shoulder. "Come, Moses. We must hurry. Our time to convince the leaders of Shas, the Temple Institute, and the Chief Rabbinate Council is short. The great persecution will begin tomorrow."

Moses stood to join Elijah.

Elijah turned to Everett. "You know the reason you came to Jerusalem was not to bring a wooden stick to a crazy old man, don't you?"

"They brought the staff to me, not you." Moses scowled.

Elijah lifted his index finger. "I know who it is they brought the stick to."

Everett had a sense of what Elijah was saying deep within his heart. "No one has articulated the details to me."

"That will be revealed in time. For now, rest and eat. You will need your strength." Elijah closed the door as he walked out.

CHAPTER 20

And I saw one of his heads as it were wounded to death; and his deadly wound was healed: and all the world wondered after the beast. And they worshipped the dragon which gave power unto the beast: and they worshipped the beast, saying, Who is like unto the beast? who is able to make war with him? And there was given unto him a mouth speaking great things and blasphemies; and power was given unto him to continue forty and two months. And he opened his mouth in blasphemy against God, to blaspheme his name, and his tabernacle, and them that dwell in heaven. And it was given unto him to make war with the saints, and to overcome them: and power was given him over all kindreds, and tongues, and nations. And all that dwell upon the earth shall worship him, whose names are not written in the book of life of the Lamb slain from the foundation of the world.

Revelation 13:3-8

Everett awoke to Ali shaking him. "The sun is setting. You told me to wake you."

"Yeah, thanks." Everett felt stiff from sleeping on the floor. Courtney had one couch, and Sarah the other. "Are the prophets back?"

"Who?"

"Elijah and Moses."

"No. They didn't come back. It is curious that you call these men prophets. Quran speak about the Hebrew prophets with these names."

"Yeah, that's them." Everett got up to get some water and start a pot of tea in the kitchen. Elijah always had tea.

Ali followed him. "No, I talk about the men who live many centuries ago."

"I know. That's these two."

Ali's brows twisted together. "Everett, just when I think possibly you are right, possibly it is Jehovah and not Allah who is the one true God, you say something so crazy."

Everett walked back to the living room with his water and sat by his duffle. He pulled out his Bible and handed it to Ali. "Read the last book, Revelation. The whole thing; it's only a few pages. It's all in there. The great quake, the famine, the plagues, the comet, the locusts, blood, and fire falling from the sky. It talks about God's witnesses who will prophesy for three and a half years. That's Elijah and Moses." Everett sat on the floor next to the couch where Courtney was sleeping and picked up the remote. "And it talks about Luz getting shot in the head and coming back to life. You saw part one this morning. Part two is coming up in a few minutes."

The television sprang to life. Luz was wrapped in a linen shroud and lay in state upon a white marble pillar on the porch of the Temple. Like the podium, the altar was engraved. Only the altar had two dragons, each bowing to the other, with the tips of their wings touching, like those in the Holy of Holies. Rhythmic music played in the background.

Harrison Yates was on the Temple Mount reporting. "Droves of devotees are here to pay their respects this evening. The global citizens are also somewhat intrigued. Only three days ago, His Majesty told us that he had overcome the grave. In light of this morning's tragedy, most of us assume that his statement was in reference to the technology which allowed him to upload his consciousness into the Dragon quantum computing network. Everyone that heard the holographic Image of His Majesty speak today can testify that it certainly encapsulated the essence of our precious savior.

"However, there are rumors. Some think that the

event to which the Image referred could actually be the resurrection of His High and Most Prepotent Majesty. I hate to speculate on such matters. And I want to be responsible and say that for me personally, when I look upon the image, it's just as if I'm looking upon His Majesty. I feel that we are in strong and capable hands if we have the Image and Pope Peter to lead us."

Everett nudged Courtney's foot with the tip of the remote. "You're gonna want to see this."

Her eyes were swollen. She peeked at the TV and put her head back down. "Definitely not. Can't he at least stay dead until tomorrow?"

Sarah yawned and opened her eyes. She looked at Ali who was reading Everett's Bible. "Does it say we can't put another bullet in his head as soon as he gets up?"

A look of surprise covered Ali's face. "All of you. You are all convinced this is going to happen. People just don't come back to life. I don't care what this book says."

"You still have some diamonds?" Sarah sat up. "I'll give you two-to-one odds that Luz is walking around before we go back to bed tonight."

"You are Christian." Ali scolded her. "It is not right to gamble."

"You're right." Sarah stretched her arms and legs and got up to go to the kitchen. "Five-to-one?"

"Sarah!" Courtney sat up to give her an accusatory look.

"Kidding!" She disappeared through the kitchen doorway.

"What are the witches doing?" Courtney asked.

"It looks like they're making a pentagram around Luz's body with blood."

"Real blood?" she asked.

"I can't imagine they'd cut corners if they're trying to reanimate the Anti-Christ."

The teapot whistled. "I've got it," Sarah called.

"You better get in here quick. The last glimmer of sunset is fading over the horizon." Courtney watched the television anxiously.

Everett had to remind himself to keep breathing. He watched the corpse like a hawk, waiting for the least indication of movement. Giant fire pits all around the Temple porch illuminated the white marble altar where Luz lay.

Scantily clad young women danced on the porch to the rhythmic music. The girls wore red masks, white veils, red heels, and very little else. They twisted and twirled around the witches who wore the black robes, touching and rubbing their bodies on them as if to seduce them. The witches went to their knees, encircling the altar and chanting in a language Everett had never heard. The dancers slowed and bowed toward the altar, kneeling in the spaces between the witches.

The pope came out carrying his staff and wearing a tall black miter and a long black robe. He lifted his hands and chanted with the witches.

Courtney gasped and covered her mouth. Everett felt the hair on his neck, arms, and legs stick straight up toward the ceiling. The linen wrapped corpse began to move.

The witches and the pope continued to chant while the dancers pulled the linen cloth away from Angelo Luz who stood up, completely naked, and opened his eyes. An enormous scar remained on his forehead, but the massive cavity from the large caliber bullet was gone.

The pope removed his robe and wrapped it around Angelo Luz, then he and everyone else in attendance bowed down, and prostrated themselves on the ground.

Elijah and Moses came through the door with two other men and quickly shut the door.

Courtney looked at the men who'd followed the prophets into the house. "Tobias?"

"Do you two know each other?" Elijah puckered his forehead in confusion.

Tobias stared at the reanimated Luz on television as he answered. "We went to college together. In America. Or so I'm told."

Everett recognized the other man who'd been with Tobias at breakfast. He figured the chances were pretty good that one of these men had shot Luz. "Sorry it didn't take."

Tobias nodded as if he could not believe what he was seeing.

Moses held up two large white bags. "We have falafel, hummus, pita, olives, and cheese. Let us bless the food so we can eat. Everything that must be said can be covered while we nourish ourselves. The next few hours are critical, so not a minute can be wasted." Moses bowed his head and said a prayer in Hebrew.

Afterward, Elijah made introductions while getting plates from the kitchen.

Everett shook hands with Tobias and the other man whom Elijah introduced as Gideon.

As they ate, Elijah told the team about his progress convincing the Jewish religious leadership that Jesus was, in fact, the Messiah.

"So, they believe?" Courtney dipped her pita into the common bowl of hummus.

Elijah covered his mouth until he'd finished chewing. "Some do, some are not yet sure. We led those who were willing to accept Yeshua in a prayer of commitment, then served communion to the new believers."

"Even though many did not pray to receive Messiah, all we spoke with are in agreement that Luz is *not* Messiah. This is a major shift from where we were a week ago," Moses added.

"But enough about this." Elijah put his plate down and looked Everett in the eyes. "Tomorrow, the great persecution will begin. Luz is alive, and he will begin to hunt down all those who will not take the Mark and worship the image."

Elijah turned his attention to Everett. "Tonight, we will commence Operation Eagle. Tobias and Gideon worked for Mossad prior to the rise of the Global Republic. Since its decommission, they have been acting under the direction of Rabbi Weizman and Rabbi Herzog, the Chief Rabbinate Council of Israel.

"They have maintained a tight-knit cell of former Israeli Defense Force and Israeli Air Force soldiers.

They had to keep it small because Luz would have infiltrated it otherwise. Tonight, they will be following the direction of Messiah. They will be leading massive amounts of Jews out of Jerusalem and to the mountains, to a place prepared by God where they might be nourished for forty-two months, from the face of the serpent. You and the girls will be going with them."

"Why are we going with them?" Sarah spooned some olives and cheese onto her plate.

"Because it is why you are here. You are to be their escorts to Tel Aviv." Moses put his hand on her shoulder.

"Why would the IDF and IAF need us?" Courtney broke a pita in half, giving part of it to Everett.

Elijah laughed. "It is not the entire army. We are talking about a hundred troops."

"That's counting me and Tobias." Gideon appeared from the kitchen with two glasses of water. "Not to mention, thirty of them are pilots and co-pilots who will be flying the planes. That leaves us with only seventy combatants. We had to keep it small.

"Elijah tells us you are battle hardened. You've all seen combat. He said you were responsible for taking down Dragon. That's quite a feat. If the four of you will join us, you'll increase the security force by a significant percentage."

Everett looked at the girls. "What do you think?"

"That's why we're here, right?" Courtney looked at Elijah.

He smiled warmly and gave her a gentle nod.

"I'm in." Sarah took Moses' hand and held it for a moment.

Everett turned to Ali. "What about you?"

Ali finished chewing. "I go where you go."

"Where are we going?" Everett asked Gideon.

"The Lesser Caucasus Mountains. In Georgia, the former Soviet Republic. We'll be landing in Batumi, then going into the mountains via the roadways that run along the Acharistskali and the Chorokhi rivers." Gideon dipped his pita into the hummus.

"Do you think the natives will take kindly to us being there? From what I've heard, Georgia is mainly Armenian Orthodox. They're not all that tolerant of other faiths, and I doubt many of them went up in the disappearances." Everett stuffed a falafel ball into a pita to make a sandwich.

Tobias answered. "We still had HUMINT sources on the ground in Georgia when the plague broke out. Ninety-nine percent of the population in Batumi and the surrounding mountain areas were wiped out. But the landscape, the buildings, even the fauna and flora, they haven't been touched by any of the other disasters."

"How many people are we talking about moving?" Everett looked at Elijah.

"Eventually, 144,000 at least." Elijah bit into his pita. "But we guess about 5,000 will be leaving with you tonight."

Sarah seemed to be doing the math in her head. "Thirty pilots and co-pilots, so fifteen planes. You better hope most of your planes are Airbus A380s. Because you'll need to cram over 300 people on each flight to move 5,000 passengers."

Tobias replied, "We have a few big planes, but we'll have to work with some smaller ones also. It's only a two-hour flight each way. We can fly two sorties if need be, but we have to move fast."

Everett rubbed his temples as he tried to get his head around this cockamamie scheme. "How do you expect to take over the Tel Aviv airport with seventy troops?"

"Seventy-four." Tobias smiled. "We haven't told you everything yet. MOC is attacking Tel Aviv as we speak, and one of our outposts spotted a large number of MOC vehicles headed towards Jerusalem from Hebron. They could be attacking the city at any moment."

"You say that like it's a good thing." Everett clinched his jaw.

"It is precisely the diversion that we need," Gideon said.

"It's also another layer of risk for us, and for the people we're trying to help," Everett countered.

"Many of the people who will be fleeing the city served in the IDF. We'll be able to arm them. Mossad had various off-the-books programs. We've got about 200 Tavors, the standard IDF bullpup battle rifle chambered in 5.56. Then we have over 1,000 AK-47s."

"AKs, huh? The standard battle rifle for all of Israel's enemies." Courtney crossed her arms.

Tobias smiled. "It's also the standard battle rifle of our enemies' enemies."

"I guess we're blessed that they never found their way over to the radical jihadists they were intended for." Courtney returned the forced smile.

Tobias looked at Everett. "Yes, the CIA black-box program, which sourced and purchased the AK-47s, was late on delivering them." He turned to Courtney. "Then the NSA lost contact with the opposition leaders, so we were stuck with the weapons until they found someone else to give them to. The world fell apart before that happened.

"Mossad rarely acted alone in these types of operations. Typically, we were little more than messenger boys or a delivery service. But I'm sure the two of you know nothing about that."

Everett wondered whether Tobias may have seen a dossier on him and Courtney, or if it were only coincidence that he'd looked at Everett when mentioning the CIA, then Courtney when allocating blame to the NSA.

Courtney looked away from Tobias. "Well, that world is gone anyway. No sense in beating a dead horse."

"I agree. We should be going." Gideon took his plate to the kitchen.

Everett did likewise, then began gearing up to fight it out with the Global Republic and the Martyrs of the Caliphate, all at the same time.

CHAPTER 21

And the woman fled into the wilderness, where she hath a place prepared of God, that they should feed her there a thousand two hundred and threescore days.

Revelation 12:6

Everett led his team as he followed Tobias and Gideon down the narrow footpath of Hayei Olam Street. Old robes given to them by Elijah and Moses concealed tactical vests stuffed with loaded magazines. If anyone happened to give them a second look, it would be obvious that they were outfitted for battle, but the robes served to obscure their true state of readiness. They arrived at the Istanbuli Synagogue.

Tobias opened the door for the team. "Come in."

Everett led his team inside.

Gideon waved and continued up the street rather than going inside the synagogue. "I'll see you soon."

"Where's he going?" Sarah asked.

"Hurva Synagogue. The same thing that is happening here is going on there."

Everett looked around. The main room was filled with people sitting in wooden pews and loading magazines from green metal ammunition boxes.

"We're planning to shoot our way out?" Everett dropped his duffle on the floor.

"I'd rather not. But if we must, yes." Tobias led them to a side room with a table where they all took a seat.

On the table was a map of the Jewish Quarter. Tobias pointed to the south side of the map. "This is the Zion Gate. Just beyond the Zion Gate is a parking lot where we'll have buses to shuttle people to Tel Aviv."

"Doesn't the GR have peacekeepers at the Zion Gate?" Courtney asked.

"Only four. It's primarily a pedestrian gate. The Zion Gate tower was built into the wall in the sixteenth century. From outside the city, the entrance is perpendicular to the wall, but it takes a ninety-degree turn and you come out parallel to the wall. Definitely not designed to accommodate modern vehicles.

"Our plan is to take out the four guards simultaneously so they don't have a chance to radio for help. Then, we'll plant our people at the gate to look like peacekeepers. This will minimize suspicion."

"Who will pose as the peacekeeper?" Ali asked.

Tobias looked at Everett. "I was hoping your team would volunteer."

"What do you have in mind?" Everett inquired.

"You'll stay at the Zion Gate until 2:00 AM, or until we're discovered. If we're discovered, you'll be the rear guard. It will be up to you to hold off the peacekeepers until we can get as many buses as possible out of range."

"Sounds like a suicide mission," Sarah said.

"We usually like those, but couldn't some of your other guys do it?" Courtney quizzed.

"I mentioned that many of the people fleeing are former IDF. My team will be coordinating the former military personnel into units. My people will be acting as the squad leaders for the impromptu security force."

Everett looked at the rest of his team to see if they were all on board. Ali and the girls nodded. Everett turned back to Tobias. "It's the reason we're here. We'll do it."

"Just so happens that we have GR uniforms," Courtney said.

Tobias' eyes lit up. "Really?"

Everett nodded. "We have three. We'd still need one for Ali."

"You can take one from a peacekeeper at the checkpoint after you've dispatched them," Tobias said.

"Please, someone take a good clean head shot. I hate blood." Ali waved his hands in the air.

"And be ready to change out of the uniforms quickly once we leave Jerusalem." Tobias stood up to give them the room. "Peacekeepers will be targeted by MOC more than civilians once we get to Tel Aviv."

"I can't wait." Everett's response dripped with sarcasm.

"Good." Tobias looked at his watch and headed for the door. "We'll roll out to take the Zion Gate in fifteen minutes."

"It was a joke," Everett said, but Tobias was already gone.

Minutes later, Everett, Courtney, and Sarah were dressed in their peacekeeper uniforms and following Tobias toward the Zion Gate. As they passed through the Jewish Quarter, the sound of celebration over Luz's resurrection could be heard from inside windows and roof-top patios above. Unfortunately, everyone in the quarter had not yet been convinced that Jesus was the true Messiah.

When they arrived at the wall, Tobias peeked around the corner at the guards by the gate. "Two of them are visible. The other two are probably on the other side of the wall. We need a way to get them all together."

"I have idea. Wait one minute." Ali walked back down the narrow pathway they'd come from. He opened a door directly below one of the roof-top parties and went inside the apartment.

"What is he doing?" Courtney whispered strongly.

Everett shook his head as he waited. Seconds later, Ali returned, carrying a bottle of Jack

Daniel's. He passed it to Everett. "Offer this to the peacekeepers. Tell them it is from Luz who wants everyone on duty to join in the celebration."

Everett stared at the bottle in his hand. He looked up at Tobias. "What do you think?"

"I don't have a better plan."

"I'll go with you," Courtney said.

Everett kissed her on the cheek. "Sarah has a higher rank. It will look better if she goes with me. You help Tobias and Ali cover us. As soon as you can see all four guards, start taking them out."

Courtney pressed her lips together as if she didn't believe Everett was being honest about why he was taking Sarah instead of her.

Everett sauntered up to the guards inside the Zion Gate.

Both men saluted him as he approached.

Everett saluted them back. "At ease. The office of His High and Most Prepotent Majesty wants everyone to join in the celebration this evening." Everett held out the bottle.

The peacekeepers began to smile. One held out his hand. "Thank you very much, sir."

Everett held back the bottle. "Not so fast. MOC fighters are in Tel Aviv. We have to be ready for anything tonight, so I need you to promise me you'll be responsible. A few sips, then finish it after your post."

"Oh absolutely, sir." The second peacekeeper nodded.

"And call the other men over here. I need to be sure they understand."

"Guys, can you come over here for a second?"

The first guard called.

Two more peacekeepers emerged from inside the covered stone corridor, below the Zion Gate tower. The first looked suspiciously at Everett and the bottle in his hand. "What is . . ."

POP! CRACK! CRACK! POP!

Everett jerked, dropping the bottle on the stone pavement. The four peacekeepers fell to the ground, their blood mingling with the broken glass and spilt whiskey.

"Mazel tov," Sarah said.

Everett bent down. "Help me drag the smaller one into the cover of the gate before his uniform gets covered with blood and whiskey."

Sarah did so.

Tobias and the team began dragging the other three out the gate while Everett and Sarah removed the uniform for Ali. Everett heard a loud pop, then Tobias, Courtney, and Ali returned through the stone gate.

"Where did you put the bodies?" Everett asked.

"Grab an arm. I'll show you." Tobias grabbed one arm of the dead peacekeeper while Everett took the other. They dragged him out the gate and into the parking lot on the other side. Tobias lifted the trunk of a car and helped Everett load the man inside.

Tobias closed the trunk. "We'll be gone by the time they start stinking."

"I hope so." Everett followed him back to the cover of the gate where Ali was dressed as a peacekeeper.

"The first wave of refugees will be coming

through in a matter of minutes." Tobias lifted his small radio. "Don't break radio silence unless it is an emergency. But if you really need me, don't hesitate to call."

"Got it." Everett directed Sarah and Ali to stand guard outside the gate while he and Courtney waited inside.

Soon, a steady flow of Jews proceeded quietly and orderly through the Zion Gate. Some wore more orthodox clothing, black hats, black jackets, white shirts, and black pants for the men while the women wore long black skirts with white shirts or long black dresses. Others looked more secular in their dress. Still some wore old uniforms from their days with the Israeli Defense Force. The latter carried either their own personal weapons, which they'd managed to keep hidden from the GR, or they carried one of the AK-47s or a Tavor given to them by Tobias' underground organization.

The procession continued for several hours. Thousands of feet trod across the place where the peacekeepers and the whiskey bottle fell. The blood and the smell of sour mash faded with each passing step.

"The first planes must be landing in Batumi by now." Courtney stood vigilantly, guarding the passageway.

"Yeah, I hope everything is going this smoothly in Tel Aviv." Everett tried to smile at as many people as possible who passed through the gate. He knew how hard it was to walk away from one's home.

No sooner had he commented on the excellent progression of the plan than a series of three loud blasts rocked the city walls. Bright flashes lit up the sky from the direction of the Temple Mount. Shortly thereafter, the sound of rifle report rang out from the same bearing.

The peacekeeper's radio came to life. "All gates, all gates, this is Command. Lockdown, I repeat, lock down the city! We are under attack! Suicide bombers have detonated three devices on the Temple Mount and multiple gunmen are firing into the crowd!

"All gates, report back to confirm that you are locked down. No one in or out."

A different voice said, "New Gate, confirmed locked down. No activity on our side."

"Harrod's Gate, locked down. No activity," called out yet another voice over the radio.

Everett pushed the talk key. "Zion Gate. Locked down. No activity."

"Zion Gate, who is this?" Command came back.

Everett gritted his teeth. He came back with the name and rank that was on the uniform which Ali was wearing. "Corporal Brockwell."

"Where is Sergeant Dean?"

Everett thought up a quick cover story. "He's dealing with a drunk and disorderly, sir. We've had quite a bit of that at our post tonight."

Command came back, "Tell him to cut the drunks loose and man that gate. We'll send reinforcements when we can, but it could be a while. I've got to call in all off-duty personnel and get this situation contained."

"Yes, sir." Everett let go of the talk key, hoping that would do it.

"Think he bought it?" Courtney looked worried.

"I hope so." Everett replied.

Gideon rushed toward the gate. "Start pulling all the armed Jews out of the line. We need them to be ready in case the Zion Gate is hit by MOC." Gideon pointed at the narrow stairs that ascended to a walkway along the top of the wall. "Send twenty or thirty up the stairs so they can watch out over a distance."

"GR Command is sending reinforcements to lock down all entrances into the city. We should have them watching in both directions," said Everett.

Gideon looked up at the wall. "The parapet only provides cover for an attack coming from outside the city. If we get hit from inside, they'll be totally exposed."

"Then maybe we should only send up five or six. That way, if we're attacked from the inside, they can get down quickly. If MOC hits us from outside, we can send up reinforcements."

"Good thinking." Gideon nodded.

More explosions rang out from inside the city wall. "Those sounded close!" Courtney tensed up, pushing the stock of her rifle into her armpit.

Everett pulled the former IDF soldiers out of the line as they passed by him. He sent the first five up the stairs as lookouts. The others, he directed to start forming squads on each side of the gate tower.

One of the watchmen yelled out from above. "Four white pickup trucks are charging toward the parking lot!"

"MOC!" Everett looked at Courtney. "Keep pulling the soldiers from the line. Send some of them out front to fight with Sarah and Ali." Everett grabbed his duffle and raced up the stone staircase. He pointed at all the men on the right side of the gate. "Follow me!"

Everett dropped his duffle bag when he reached the top. He bent down and pulled out an M72 LAW rocket and armed it. Machine gunfire peppered the top of the wall.

"Fifty-caliber! Second vehicle!" The former IDF fighter on Everett's left took aim and began firing.

"Got him!" Everett took aim and deployed the rocket. BOOM! The second pickup rode a puff of flame ten feet into the air. The third vehicle lost control and flipped over on its side. The fourth maneuvered around the explosion and joined the first truck in continuing the assault.

MOC fighters fired indiscriminately into the crowd of Jews heading out of the Zion Gate toward the buses. The people below screamed in terror as several of them were shot down.

Everett popped back up and unleashed a barrage of rifle fire at the two pickups.

"RPG!" The IDF fighter on Everett's right grabbed him by the shoulder and pulled him to the ground.

Everett covered his head with his hands and closed his eyes. The rocket-propelled grenade exploded on the outside of the wall, only a few feet from where Everett sat curled up in a fetal position. As soon as the shaking ceased, Everett pulled out a second M72 rocket. He armed it, jumped up, and found his target. He squeezed the trigger, and the rocket flew like a bolt of lightning into the front MOC vehicle. BOOM! Only one pickup truck remained, but it was driving straight for the Zion Gate. Everett tossed the spent tube of the rocket aside and joined the other IDF soldiers in shooting at the charging vehicle. The truck careened into the pedestrians below, mowing down more than twenty before detonating into a massive fireball. BOOOOM!

The shock wave knocked Everett from his feet, tossing him against the metal guard rail behind him. He stood up and looked over the wall to take stock of the casualties. Bodies lay everywhere, littering the street below. "Sarah!" He grabbed his bag and rushed down the stairs.

When he got outside of the gate, Courtney was already kneeling by Sarah's side. He put his finger on her neck to check for a pulse.

Courtney held her hand. "She's gone, Everett. She's with Jesus, and Kevin, and all the people from her group back in Tennessee that she always talked about."

Everett fought back the tears. A time for grieving would come, but he had to see the mission through. Everett tore his eyes away from his fallen friend. He stood up and directed the uninjured people to keep moving toward the buses. "Let's keep going, folks. Get on the buses. Don't let the deaths of these people be in vain."

Family members of the fallen lingered by the bodies of their loved ones. A few others helped the injured to the buses.

Ali rushed over. "Oh, Everett, Courtney, I'm so sorry. Sarah was a wonderful person."

Everett turned to look at Ali. "You're bleeding. Your arms, your face. Are you okay?"

"It's only a few scratches. The wall of the gate shielded me from most of the blast and shrapnel."

The peacekeeper's radio sounded off. "Zion Gate. What's your situation? We saw a big explosion coming from your direction."

Everett growled and pressed the talk button. "We had a suicide car bomb. It detonated outside the gate, but we don't have any other threats."

"Was anyone hurt?"

Everett was sure Command would want to talk to the sergeant, so he fed them the best answer he could think of. "The sergeant is down. He's unresponsive. We need a medical team."

"I'm dispatching medical and a twenty-man backup team. They'll be at your location in ten minutes. Just hold tight."

Everett just wanted to cry, to mourn the loss of his friend, but he couldn't. And neither could he allow his wife time to process her loss. "Courtney, come on. We've gotta get up. Peacekeepers are heading this way. We've gotta be ready for them."

Courtney nodded. She bent down and kissed Sarah on the head, then stood up and steeled herself for the next battle.

Gideon met Everett and the rest of his team inside the gate. Everett walked passed him. "We've got twenty peacekeepers heading this way. We can engage them, but as soon as we do, Command will dispatch hundreds more right behind them. I'd say we can hold this position for fifteen, maybe twenty minutes. No more."

Gideon nodded. "I'll get the people moving as fast as I can."

Everett began positioning the available IDF fighters to defend the avenues of approach to the Zion Gate.

CHAPTER 22

And the dragon was wroth with the woman, and went to make war with the remnant of her seed, which keep the commandments of God, and have the testimony of Jesus Christ.

Revelation 12:17

Everett crouched between the city wall and the front bumper of an old Mitsubishi parked on the side of the road. He placed Courtney behind the engine block, which was the only part of the vehicle guaranteed to stop a rifle bullet. Gideon stood with his rifle leveled on top of the car, and Ali positioned his weapon on the trunk. Former Israeli soldiers lined the street using the other parked vehicles for cover, waiting for the GR peacekeepers to arrive.

Everett called out to the soldiers. “Keep yourselves hidden. Don’t fire until all twenty of them are exposed. They’re not expecting to get hit.”

Everett ducked down as he heard the sound of boots against the stone pavement. He held his fist up where Gideon, Courtney, and Ali could see it. He waited anxiously for the platoon to finish rounding the corner to the east. Everett could barely make out the last peacekeeper. He dropped his fist and stood up to commence firing. The Israelis followed his cue and half of the peacekeepers were dead before they knew what hit them. The other ten retreated behind a corner of a building at the end of the street and began returning fire from a distance.

Everett and the others continued firing, holding them back until the remaining Jews could get through the gate.

“Courtney, I want you to go. The buses will need armed escorts to get to Tel Aviv.”

She continued shooting at any peacekeeper who showed his head. “I’m not leaving you, Everett. I’ll submit to anything you say, except that.” She changed magazines and sent another volley of bullets down range.

Gideon paused and turned around to look at the gate. “I think we can all get out of here. That looks like the last of our people leaving now. Any others that wanted to leave have probably been cut off. Hopefully, they’ll have the wisdom to hunker down until they get another opportunity to escape.”

Everett nodded. “Okay. Ali, Courtney, start backing up. Lead the other soldiers to the gate. Send them to the buses, then lay down cover fire for me and Gideon."

Everett and Gideon continued shooting to give the others time to back out. The peacekeepers advanced as Everett and Gideon moved back to the gate tower.

Ali popped around the side and fired several rounds, allowing Everett and Gideon to reload. "The buses are loaded and moving out."

Courtney joined with them in firing at the peacekeepers. "Looks like another platoon just showed up."

"Yeah, we've got to get out of here." Gideon pulled out his keys. "Can you drive a stick?"

"Sure." Courtney changed magazines.

Gideon passed her the keys. "There's a Golan, a beige armored vehicle, in the parking lot where the buses were. Pull around to the gate. Blow the horn when you're at the gate."

"Roger." She exited through the gate tower.

"Ali, go with her. And grab our duffles." Everett fired three more rounds toward the peacekeepers. "Once Gideon and I pull out, they'll be on us like a swarm of hornets."

"Okay." Ali grabbed the bags and followed Courtney.

"Watch that team to the east!" Gideon lay prone and began firing under the vehicles. "They're trying to flank us!"

"If I turn my back on the ones coming from the west for a second, they'll be on top of us." Everett tried to place his rounds, but he wasn't getting any kill shots. His rifle bolt locked open, and he quickly switched to the pistol on the front of his vest. "I'm almost out of ammo!"

Everett heard Gideon's bolt lock open. "Me, too."

BEEEEP!

"That's our ride! Let's go!" Gideon tapped Everett as he spun around to run out the gate.

"Right behind you!" Everett emptied his pistol as he backed out of the gate and jumped into the Golan.

"Go! Go! Go!" Gideon shouted his directive to Courtney who smashed the gas pedal while quickly pulling her foot off the clutch, causing the vehicle to jerk forward. Ali held on to the door handle for dear life as the team sped away. Bullets peppered the rear of the vehicle for a few seconds, then ceased.

"Everybody good?" Courtney's voice sounded distressed.

"I'm okay." Everett took a few breaths before changing the magazines in his rifle and pistol.

"Yeah, good." Ali shook the door of the Golan to ensure that it was closed securely.

Gideon also changed his magazine. "No leaks here."

"Great. Can you tell me how to get to the airport?"

Gideon made his way up to the passenger's seat. "Follow this road until you get to 60, then head north to 1. Westbound 1 goes directly to Tel Aviv."

Forty minutes after leaving the parking lot, Gideon directed Courtney to exit the highway.

Pillars of smoke illuminated by the fires burning below rose to the sky on both sides of the highway.

“This doesn’t look good,” Courtney said.

Everett peered out the front windshield to see a bus stopped at the front gate of the airport. Three GR Humvees blocked the entrance. “That’s the bus that left right before we did.”

“The GR must have just now taken control of the gate,” Gideon said.

Everett looked down at his civilian clothes, which he’d changed into on the road. “Should have waited to change.”

“I still look official.” Since Courtney was driving and couldn’t change, she still wore her peacekeeper uniform.

“We can’t talk our way out of this one.” Gideon picked up his rifle from beside his seat. “Besides, that bus is filled with the former IDF soldiers who were fighting with us. No amount of discussion is going to get them through the gate.”

Courtney slowed the vehicle. “I could ram the GR Hummer. It would create a diversion. Maybe give the IDF guys a chance to get the jump on the peacekeepers.”

“Don’t hit it too fast. We still need the Golan to get us to the tarmac.” Gideon braced himself.

“You know this vehicle better than I do, tell me how fast of an impact you think it can take.”

Gideon shook his head. “The Golan is a much bigger vehicle, but still, it would have to be at least twenty-five kilometers an hour to knock the Humvee clear of our path.”

“Twenty-five it is, then. Everybody hang on tight!”

Everett buckled his seat belt and pulled another

M72 rocket from one of the duffles.

SMASH! The vehicle slowed dramatically but kept rolling.

"We made it!" Courtney shouted.

Everett released his seat belt, jumped up to open the top hatch of the Golan and stuck the rocket tube out the roof. He took aim at one of the other Humvees and fired.

BOOOM! The sphere of flame sent the Hummer flipping side over side, crushing five peacekeepers as it rolled.

Everett tossed the spent tube and raised his rifle at the other peacekeepers. In a matter of seconds, the IDF soldiers were pouring out the front and back of the bus and eliminating the rest of the GR troops.

Courtney waited for the IDF troops to get back on the bus and catch up. Courtney led the way to the tarmac. "Looks like some heavy fighting going on at the other end of the airport."

Everett heard rifle fire and could clearly make out a convoy of MOC technicals engaging with a shrinking number of GR peacekeepers. "As long as they're keeping each other occupied, we're okay."

Tobias's voice came over Gideon's radio. "Gideon, is that you in the Golan?"

"Yes. And that is the last bus behind us."

Tobias came back over the radio. "I'm in the gray C-130. I'll have the back ramp down. Get in here fast. The Martyrs of the Caliphate are all around the airport."

Gideon pointed in the direction of the skirmish. "His plane is over there, by the fighting."

"That's not great." Courtney slowed down to let the bus catch up.

Gideon stuck his head out of the top hatch when the bus pulled alongside. "There's your ride. We'll create a diversion so you can get boarded."

Gideon dropped back down and closed the hatch. "I hope that's okay with everyone."

"Great," Ali replied. "I've been getting volunteered for stuff since the moment I met these guys."

"How many more of those rockets do you have?" Gideon looked at Everett.

Everett scratched through the duffle bags. "Four. But maybe MOC and the GR won't notice us."

"Too late for that." Courtney pointed at a tan Maxx Pro flying the black flag of MOC from the whip antenna, flanked by two Toyota technicals, each with a fifty-caliber machine gun mounted in the bed. The three vehicles were racing toward the bus.

"We have to help these guys, Everett. If we don't do something, those fifties will eat them alive while they're trying to board the plane." Courtney turned and looked at him with imploring eyes.

He knew she was right. He'd have no trouble doing it himself, but once again, he found himself in the situation of having to approve a suicide mission for his beautiful wife. "Okay. Let us get a couple rockets armed, then start heading right for them."

Courtney put the Golan in gear. Everett handed a rocket to Gideon, one to Ali, and armed the third for himself. The vehicle raced headlong into the path of the three MOC vehicles. Instantly, the Golan began taking fire from the fifty-cal. Everett popped out of the hatch and aimed toward the grill of the Maxx Pro.

BOOOM! The Maxx Pro teetered and finally fell on its side. Rifle fire struck the metal hatch and whizzed by Everett's ear. He dropped down into the vehicle, and Gideon replaced him, sticking his missile tube out the hatch.

BOOM! Everett saw one of the Toyota pickup trucks explode into a blazing ball of heat and metal. He took the third rocket from Ali and prepared to pop up in Gideon's place.

Gideon dropped back into the cabin.

"Good shot!" Everett slapped him on the back as he jumped up to stick his head out of the hatch. Jihadi fighters were coming out of the Maxx Pro, which lay on its side. The vehicle had been incapacitated, but the heavy armor protected the people inside. Every one of them took aim and fired their AK-47s at Everett, forcing him back inside the hatch.

"It's too hot. I can't stay out there long enough to take aim." Everett held the rocket in his hand.

Gideon shouted out instructions. "Courtney, cut left. Ali, you and I will shoot from the gun ports in the side windows. We've got to thin these guys out so Everett can take a shot."

Everett watched as Ali and Gideon exchanged gunfire with the jihadis. Slowly, Gideon and Ali picked them off, but the second technical was circling around the Golan, peppering it with the large gun. The windshield shattered when several fifty-caliber rounds cracked, then penetrated it.

"Courtney, are you okay?" Everett peered around her seat, his heart pounding from the fear of what he might see.

"I'm fine, but it just got harder to drive. You've got to take that thing out!"

Everett readied his rocket tube, flung the hatch open, and said a quick prayer. "God, direct this rocket." He jumped up. Bullets from the AK-47s and the fifty-cal whizzed by his ears. Everett pointed the tube in the general direction of the technical and fired the weapon. He dropped back into the cabin. BOOM!

"Did I hit it?"

"Yes!" Courtney turned the vehicle around and hurtled toward the military cargo plane.

"Don't count the chicken!" Ali warned.

"Did anyone ever tell you that you're a pessimist, Ali?" Courtney said.

Everett wanted to celebrate as well, but he knew there was wisdom in Ali's caveat.

Tobias' voice came over the radio. "We have to take off now. Six MOC vehicles just breached the northwest runway. And four more are coming from the private jet tarmac to our right."

Everett saw the plane taxi to the runway.

"I told you . . ." Ali started.

Courtney cut him off. "I know, I know, don't count the chicken when he's in the eggs."

"We've got one rocket left," Everett said.

"And no planes," Gideon added. "Courtney, follow the C-130." Gideon pressed his talk key. "Tobias, leave the back ramp down. We'll drive right in. We've still got one rocket to knock out the technicals coming out of the private tarmac."

"If I slow down, we'll never get past the MRAPs coming out of the northwest."

"Hopefully, you won't have to." Gideon looked at Everett. "Make that rocket count. Courtney, push the skinny pedal on the right."

The Golan sped toward the runway. Everett armed his last rocket, took a deep breath, and lunged out of the hatch. A military Humvee, most likely stolen from US forces in Syria or Iraq, flew a black flag and had a fifty-cal mounted in the rear. It was the lead vehicle coming from the private jet tarmac. Bullets flew by Everett's head in one direction, and heavy wind from the high speed of the Golan breezed by from the other. He leveled the launch tube and deployed the rocket. It struck just in front of the Humvee and exploded on the runway. But the Hummer lost control, swerving back and forth, and eventually flipping over and landing upside down. The small pickup truck directly behind the Hummer hit the blast of the rocket and flipped on its side. The third vehicle crashed into the pickup, and the forth smashed into the side of the upside-down Humvee.

Everett flung the tube out onto the runway and fell back into the cabin, closing the hatch behind him. From the side window, he could see the cargo bay of the C-130 only a few feet away.

"Hang on. I've never done this before." Courtney called out as she gunned the engine.

The Golan jumped up onto the fast-moving ramp of the C-130, then Courtney slammed on the brakes. The vehicle skidded to a halt inside the cargo bay of the C-130.

Gideon's face was white as he hit the talk key of his radio. "We're in."

Everett could see out the rear opening of the cargo bay as the runway began to fall away beneath them. Gunfire rang out from below.

Tobias' voice called out over the radio. "We're still taking fire. Keep your seat belts on."

Tink. Tink. TINK, TINK, TINK. Everett heard bullets hitting the belly and wings of the aircraft. A large explosion detonated and the plane pitched hard to the right. Everett's life flashed before his eyes. The distinctive sounds of a stalling plane and failing engines filled the bay of the giant aircraft.

Tobias' voice was distorted by static over the radio. "RPG just took out one of the left engines. Hang on, people."

Everett closed his eyes and began to pray, to beg God, to plead that He would not let them die like this. Of all the ways there was to leave this world, a plane crash had always ranked among the lowest on Everett's list.

Finally, the plane leveled out. But only for a second. A second blast just like the first rocked the cargo bay of the plane as it yawed and rolled to the right. Everett felt sure it was a second RPG.

Gideon called Tobias on the radio. "What's the situation?"

The radio was silent. The plane shook and rocked for what seemed like several minutes to Everett. But finally, it leveled back out.

Tobias eventually responded, the radio still staticky. "We lost two engines, but we've still got two. We're already up, so we should be good. What's better is that we're over the Mediterranean and out of range of GR and MOC fighters on shore. We'll have to fly over Turkey to get to the Black Sea, but aside from the coasts, most of the areas we'll be over are fairly remote."

Ali unbuckled his seat belt and stood up in the rear of the Golan. "I believe it, Everett."

"You believe what?"

"Everything. Jesus is Son of God. He die for my sin. All these things, I believe."

"Oh!" Everett was still catching his breath from multiple near-death experiences, so the topic caught him off guard. "Good. You just decided this now?"

"No. Before, but I don't want God to think I only pray to him to get me out of the trouble."

"That was pretty risky. We could have died back there; about eight different times. God is not Allah. You don't have to win his favor. Jesus paid a high price for you to be able to come to him, so he's not too picky about what motivates you to do so."

"Yes, but what is done is done. I want to be in the Vine now. To be forgiven. To go to the heaven of Jehovah when I die."

"Great. Why don't you tell God what you just told me?"

"I do not know how I should speak to Him."

"Speak to Him like a friend. The same way you speak to me. Like I said, He paid a big price and I'm sure He doesn't want any of His precious blood to go to waste. He doesn't care how you come to Him, as long as you come."

Ali bowed his head and began to pour out his

heart to God. He asked for forgiveness, asked for guidance, and asked that God would give him the strength to stay connected to the Vine.

Everett and Courtney hugged Ali and welcomed him to the family.

Gideon smiled and shook Ali's hand. "Congratulations. I just accepted the Messiah myself, earlier today."

The team exited the vehicle into the cargo bay where the rear ramp had finally been closed. Everett shook hands with several of the IDF soldiers who fought alongside him at the Zion Gate and with refugees who'd been on the bus.

Afterward, he and Courtney went back in the Golan by themselves so they could spend the rest of the flight mourning the loss of their dear friend, Sarah. They'd been unable to retrieve her body from the blast site as it would have cost them their lives to do so. But, even in their grief, they knew she was not lying on the asphalt back in Jerusalem, but that she was enjoying the rewards of heaven, reunited with her husband, Kevin, and praising her King, Jesus.

CHAPTER 23

And to the woman were given two wings of a great eagle, that she might fly into the wilderness, into her place, where she is nourished for a time, and times, and half a time, from the face of the serpent.

Revelation 12:14

The first two weeks in Batumi were spent allocating housing to the refugees. Salvaging food, which still sat on grocery store shelves, helped provide for basic nutrition in the initial days. Just beyond the city were vineyards, orchards, corn, and wheat fields, as well as cattle, goats, and sheep, which had managed to survive on their own for the past three years.

Batumi had been home to more than 160,000 people prior to the plague that wiped them all out. Plenty of housing existed to accommodate not only the initial wave of refugees but all that were anticipated to arrive in the coming weeks and months. However, the massive and sudden die-off had left the city like a ghost town. No municipal services existed such as water or electricity. Therefore, refugees were forced to select homes with a hand pump on a well, near the Chorokhi River, or by one of the tributaries which fed into it.

Most homes had shallow graves in the front or backyards, where the initial victims of the plague had been buried. Many houses still had heavily decayed corpses lying in the beds where they'd died, the last of the fatalities with no one left to bury them.

Everett and Courtney settled in a simple two-bedroom home with a red tile roof approximately eight miles outside of the city. The quaint dwelling sat on the bank of the Acharistskali River, just above the place where it flowed into and became part of the Chorokhi River.

From their front porch, they had picturesque views of the two rivers and the mountains, which surrounded the valley on all sides like an impenetrable fortress. Fig trees grew along the back fence. Tomatoes, cucumbers, and potatoes, which sprung up voluntarily from crops planted three years earlier, grew in a large garden plot in their backyard.

Ali shared a four-bedroom house across the road with Tobias and Gideon. Ali's home was right on the bank of the river, so it was from his backyard that Everett did most of his fishing. Many other refugee families lived along the same road. The closer one went toward Batumi, the more densely populated it became. The further one traveled up the road, the fewer people were to be found.

Four weeks after their arrival, Everett sat at the small kitchen table studying his Bible late one Monday morning. He sipped a cup of tea. Since tea had been a major crop in the district during the Soviet era, it was more available than coffee. So, Everett learned to drink tea instead of coffee.

Courtney kneaded dough to bake bread in the outdoor cook stove. “Do you know what you’re going to speak on?”

“It’s Passover. I’m going to talk about the symbolism of the lamb and the blood, how it all pointed to Yeshua. This will be these people’s first Passover as believers.”

Courtney smiled at him and continued kneading. “I can’t believe you’re a preacher now.”

“I’m not a preacher. That tiny church up the road fits like twenty people. It barely qualifies as an official Bible study group. And most of those people know the Old Testament inside and out. I’m just sharing the little bit I know about the New.”

“But it’s so romantic. You standing behind the pulpit in that chapel built with the rounded stones from the river, the orange brick portico, and the red tile roof.” She paused from her work. “It’s really like something from a fairy tale. Nothing like what I expected the apocalypse to be.”

Everett looked down at his Bible. He didn't remember turning there, but it was opened to Second Peter 2:9. Because of its uncanny relevance to the subject of their conversation, he read it aloud. "The Lord knoweth how to deliver the godly out of temptations, and to reserve the unjust unto the day of judgment to be punished."

Someone knocked on the door. Everett's instinct to put his hand on his pistol at every noise was fading, but he still unsnapped the strap on his holster as he got up to answer the door. Courtney followed him to the door with her hands covered in flour.

Everett's eyes lit up with joy as he opened the door. "Elijah! Moses! What are you two doing here?"

Courtney threw her white-powdered hands around Elijah, getting flour all over his back. "I'm so glad to see you."

"Come in, please!" Everett took their bags.

Elijah looked around. "We led another wave of refugees here. Nearly 10,000 this time."

"Seems I'm letting that become a habit." Moses strolled in and took a seat. "I will say, this bunch moved a lot faster. Of course, we didn't have forty years to kill either."

Courtney noticed what she'd done. "Elijah, I'm so sorry. I've made a mess all over your back. Let me get you a towel."

"It is fine, child. Don't fret." Elijah took a seat on the couch next to the other prophet.

Moses shook his finger at the fireplace. "You've put my staff over the mantle, there. I can't say that I ever thought of it as a decorative item."

Courtney retrieved a hand towel from the kitchen. "We like it there. It reminds us of you, and Elijah, and Sarah, of course."

"Yes, well, maybe I'll have to find you a nice picture of the river or the mountains."

"How long are you staying?" Everett asked.

"We'll leave after Passover. We must get back to the city right away," said Elijah.

Courtney brushed the flour off Elijah's back. "Only two days? You'll stay here, won't you? In our home with us? The guest room has two twin beds."

"Yes, child. Thank you for the invitation." Elijah smiled.

"Everett is teaching a Passover Bible study at a little chapel up the road this evening. The few people who live right around here come every Saturday to our study. You'll be so proud to hear him." Courtney took a seat on the arm of the lounge chair where Everett sat.

"That is wonderful, but I will be speaking at the big gathering on the bank of the river in the village of Khelvachuri. It is half way between here and Batumi. It is not far. Six kilometers perhaps. You may bring your friends from the area. It will be the largest gathering since the Jews came to Georgia."

"We'll be there. It sounds exciting." Everett loved the location where they lived, especially compared to living in a cave. But, he also liked going to the larger communities and meeting the interesting people who'd come to the place many were starting to call Goshen.

Everett helped the prophets get settled in for their visit. Courtney finished baking her bread. Then, the two of them took their bicycles around to let everyone know of the change of plans for the evening.

They returned home at 4:00 in the afternoon. Elijah and Moses were waiting for them.

"We should go. The gathering begins at sunset." Elijah stood.

"It's going to be dark on the way home." Courtney packed the bread she'd made to take to the gathering.

"Well, the sky is clear, and Passover always begins on a full moon, so we'll be able to see just fine. It's a good even road." Elijah led the way out the door.

"I'm sure Ali and Gideon would lend you their bikes if you'd rather ride." Everett locked the door on the way out.

"The short walk will take little over an hour. We'll need the exercise; especially after a big meal." Moses walked next to Elijah. "It helps one sleep better."

The four of them did some catching up on the long leisurely stroll to the gathering. Elijah and Moses told of the on-going conflict between the Martyrs of the Caliphate and the Global Republic in and around Jerusalem. They also told of the multiple attempts by Angelo Luz to have them arrested. Even with Courtney's persistence at trying to pry it out of them, neither offered any details about how they'd escaped incarceration, time after time.

The sun sank low in the sky and the four of them arrived at the gathering. Mismatch tables were lined up end-to-end in an open field. Every imaginable style of chair was included in the seating accommodations. Tiki torches would provide additional light to that of the full moon.

Moses spoke with Rabbi Weismann and Rabbi Herzog who made up the Chief Rabbinate Council, arranging to get seats for Everett and Courtney by his, near the head of the table.

Elijah took the seat at the very head of the table.

"Hmpf," Moses grumped as he sat. "You'd think that since I was at the first Passover, if anyone were going to have a seat saved, it would be the person who actually led the Jews through the desert."

Everett saw his point but made no comment.

Rabbi Weismann put his hand on Elijah's shoulder. "Friend, I am sorry. But, I must ask you to move over. Even though we now believe that Yeshua is the Messiah, we still have our traditions. This seat has always customarily been reserved for the Old Testament Hebrew Prophet, Elijah."

Courtney's forehead puckered. "Wait, do you still not know who he is?"

Elijah smiled and pulled out his Bible and opened it to the book of Malachi. "Behold, I will send you Elijah the prophet before the coming of the great and dreadful day of the Lord." He took the rabbi's hand. "I know who the chair is reserved for."

Rabbi Weismann's face paled. He turned to Rabbi Herzog and nodded.

Whatever had caused their slowness in

understanding who Elijah actually was, disappeared when Elijah took the rabbi's hand.

At sunset, Elijah prayed to bless the meal. Afterward, he read from the Hebrew Scriptures, opening the eyes of all in attendance to how Passover pointed to the sacrifice of Jesus. He explained how the blood of the Passover lamb smeared over the doorposts to protect against the judgment in Egypt symbolized the blood of Christ, which is spread over the doorposts of the believers' heart to keep them from the ultimate day of judgment. He expounded on the fact that the Passover lamb had to be pure, without blemish, just as Christ had to be perfect and without sin. He explained how Christ was actually crucified on Passover, and how his blood ran down the wooden cross on the very day that the Jews commemorated the blood running down the wooden doorposts in Egypt.

Afterward, he explained the period in which they were now living, the Time of Jacob's Trouble. "God has prepared this place to keep you. But be aware, the Anti-Christ, Angelo Luz, will not quit harassing you. Therefore, you must stay vigilant. You must continue to train for battle.

"He will continue to persecute your brothers and sisters. Many have come to this place already, but many more are coming still. Please always welcome them with open arms when they arrive in this sanctuary.

"You are being provided for by Adonai Himself, but terrible plagues are still coming against this planet. You have witnessed many adversities, earthquakes, plagues, famines, wars, and much tribulation." Elijah held his Bible in the air. "But the worst is yet to come. When writing about these last days, John the Revelator said *And I saw another sign in heaven, great and marvelous, seven angels having the seven last plagues; for in them is filled up the wrath of God.*"

Everett held Courtney's hand tightly as he listened to the prophet. He was far too familiar with the final plagues known as the Seven Vials of God's Wrath. Everything the Earth had experienced so far was only a warmup compared to the torment and unabated destruction that was coming next.

DON'T PANIC!

Inevitably, books like this will wake folks up to the need to be prepared, or cause those of us who are already prepared to take inventory of our preparations. New preppers can find the task of getting prepared for an economic collapse, EMP, or societal breakdown to be a source of great anxiety. It shouldn't be. By following an organized plan and setting a goal of getting a little more prepared each day, you can do it.

I always try to include a few prepper tips in my novels, but they're fiction and not a comprehensive plan to get prepared. Now that you're motivated to start prepping, the last thing I want to do is leave you frustrated, not knowing what to do next. So I'd like to offer you a free PDF copy of *The Seven Step Survival Plan.*

For the new prepper, *The Seven Step Survival Plan* provides a blueprint that prioritizes the different aspects of preparedness and breaks them down into achievable goals. For seasoned preppers who often get overweight in one particular area of preparedness, *The Seven Step Survival Plan* provides basic guidelines to help keep their plan in balance, and ensures they're not missing any critical segments of a well-adjusted survival strategy.

To get your **FREE** copy of ***The Seven Step Survival Plan***, go to **PrepperRecon.com** and click the FREE PDF banner, just below the menu bar, at the top of the home page.

Thank you for reading
The Days of Elijah: Book Three
Angel of the Abyss

Reviews are the best way to help get the book noticed. If you liked the book, please take a moment to leave a five-star review on Amazon and Goodreads.

I love hearing from readers! So whether it's to say you enjoyed the book, to point out a typo that we missed, or asked to be notified when new books are released, drop me a line.

prepperrecon@gmail.com

Stay tuned to **PrepperRecon.com** for the latest news about my upcoming books, and great interviews on the **Prepper Recon Podcast**.

Keep watch for
The Days of Elijah: Book Four
The Seventh Vial

If you liked ***The Days of Elijah***, you'll love the prequel series,

The Days of Noah

In ***The Days of Noah, Book One: Conspiracy***, You'll see the challenges and events that Everett and Courtney have endured to reach the point in the story that you've just read. You'll read what it was like for the Christians in Kevin and Sarah's group in their final days before the rapture, and how the once-great United States of America lost its sovereignty. You'll have a better understanding of how the old political and monetary system were cleared away, like pieces on a chess board, to make way for the one-world kingdom of the Antichrist.

If you have an affinity for the prophetic don't miss my EMP survival series, ***Seven Cows, Ugly and Gaunt***

In ***Book One: Behold Darkness and Sorrow***, Daniel Walker begins having prophetic dreams about the judgment coming upon America for rejecting God. Through one of his dreams, Daniel learns of an imminent threat of an EMP attack which will wipe out America's electric grid and most all computerized devices, sending the country into a technological dark age.

Living in a nation where all life-sustaining systems of support are completely dependent on electricity and computers, the odds for survival are dismal. Municipal water services, retail food distribution, police, fire, EMS and all emergency services will come to a screeching halt.

If they want to live, Daniel and his friends must focus on faith, wits and preparation to be ready . . . before the lights go out.

You'll also enjoy my first series, *The Economic Collapse Chronicles*

The series begins with ***Book One: American Exit Strategy***. Matt and Karen Bair thought they were prepared for anything, but can they survive a total collapse of the economic system? If they want to live through the crisis, they'll have to think fast and move quickly. In a world where all the rules have changed, and savagery is law, those who hesitate pay with their very lives.

When funds are no longer available for government programs, widespread civil unrest erupts across the country. Matt and Karen are forced to move to a more remote location and their level of preparedness is revealed as being much less adequate than they believed prior to the crisis. Civil instability erupts into civil war and Americans are forced to choose a side. Don't miss this action-packed, post-apocalyptic tale about survival after the total collapse of America.

78917236R00187

Made in the USA
Columbia, SC
15 October 2017